ELIZABETH'S HEART RACED...

HAD HE SEEN THEM? Simon's arms pulled her close. He pressed them both into the base of the tree and covered her quickly with his cloak.

The hoof beats grew louder, closer, until it sounded like he was right on top of them. Suddenly, the horse whinnied and shied. He tried to urge the animal on, but it refused, and reared and pranced around nervously. From under the edge of the cloak, all Elizabeth could see were the horse's legs and the man's boots in the stirrups as he dug his heels into the horse's flank. But still, the animal refused to move. It snorted and cried.

Elizabeth wrapped her fingers around one of the oak tree's roots and tried to slow her heart. If he just looked down, he would see them. For a moment, she felt just like a little hobbit hiding from the Nazgul. Except, luckily for her, this rider appeared to be flesh and blood. She hoped...

Out Of Time Series: Monique Martin

"Featuring charismatic characters, vividly portrayed time periods, and historically accurate details, Monique Martin's Out Of Time romantic time travel mystery series displays literary acumen, dedication, and sophistication."

From *Toplist:Bestfictionbooks.com*

ALSO BY MONIQUE MARTIN

Out of Time: A Time Travel Mystery (Out of Time #1)

When the Walls Fell (Out of Time #2)

Fragments (Out of Time #3)

The Devil's Due (Out of Time #4)

Thursday's Child (Out of Time #5)

MONIQUE MARTIN

Thursday's Child

Out of Time Series
Book #5

Cover Photo: Karen Wunderman
Cover Layout & Interior Formatting: TERyvisions

ISBN 10: 0984660712
ISBN 13: 978-0-9846607-1-1

For more information, please contact
writtenbymonique@gmail.com
Or visit: www.moniquemartin.weebly.com

Acknowledgements

This book would not have been possible without the help and support of many people: Robin, who I truly would not be able to do this without; Mom and George; Dad and Anne; Eddie and Carole; Gerald and Yara; Michael; JM; Melissa; Cindy; the lead inventor of doxycycline, Keith Blackwood, and all the wonderful people who sent notes of encouragement along the way.

I'd also like to thank the thousands of people who help preserve the past through books, websites, museums and sheer will.

Thursday's Child

(Out of Time Book #5)

Monique Martin

CHAPTER ONE

IT SMELLED LIKE PIGS. Pigs and horses and mud.

It took Elizabeth a few moments to clear her head. Through the cobwebs that time travel always spun inside her brain, she heard Simon ask if she was all right.

He gave her arm a gentle shake and squeeze. "Elizabeth?"

She blinked up at him, the fog lifting. "I'm fine."

His eyes searched hers quickly as if to make sure she wasn't holding anything back. Satisfied, he slipped the watch and key into his pocket and turned his attention to their surroundings.

As planned, they'd arrived unseen behind a warehouse. Not part of the plan though was the two inches of mud they were standing in. Elizabeth lifted the hem of her beautiful white and pale green cotton dress and wrinkled her nose. That had to be a record. They'd been there less than a minute and her clothes were already dirty.

She let out a sigh, or at least tried to. The darn corset Simon had cinched her into that morning was already squeezing the life out of her. She tugged uselessly on the edge of it to try to shift it into a more comfortable constriction.

"Wait here a moment," Simon said. He straightened his black wool plantation-style hat and took a few steps forward before carefully peering around the corner of the warehouse.

Never being one to wait, even for a moment, Elizabeth dutifully ignored his request, picked up her skirts and followed him. Leaning against his back for balance, she poked her head out just enough to see.

The wharf at Natchez, Mississippi was a well-orchestrated chaos. Men yelled, horses whinnied and wooden carts thumped as they all slogged through the muddy, rutted street. An enormous paddle wheeler, straight out of a Mark Twain novel, disgorged passengers and freight across rickety planks almost as quickly as it took on the same. A large man with an even larger voice barked orders at a flatboat on a nearby landing where huge bales of cotton were being loaded and crates of supplies were unloaded. Some goods were taken into nearby ramshackle warehouses and others were stacked precariously onto horse-drawn dray carts, the pickup truck of their day, and hauled up the long, sloping road that cut into the side of the bluff to the town above.

It was thrilling and unsettling at the same time, familiar in some ways and so very foreign in others. That was the way with time travel. Life was the same everywhere, and everywhen, and yet somehow completely different. Elizabeth felt a tingle of anticipation inch up her back. Another adventure awaited.

Simon stood straight again and frowned over at the two large trunks they'd crammed full with everything they thought they might need. Both were already sinking into the mire.

"Will you please wait here?" Simon asked with his *I mean it this time* look.

Elizabeth glanced at the traffic, carts spraying mud, horses trotting in every direction and decided waiting might not be such a bad idea. She offered him a coy smile and batted her eyelashes.

Simon narrowed his eyes, but she could see the smile in them. He grunted and took a step out into the chaos. He called out to a man with a buckboard who appeared to be waiting for passengers from the boat. Traffic whizzed along the sloppy road in front of him. Simon called out again and even tried whistling, but it wasn't nearly loud enough.

Elizabeth gave a quick look around and then tugged off her kid gloves. She lifted two fingers to her mouth and let out a piercing whistle. The man with the cart and several others, including Simon, turned to stare. Instantly demure, she fiddled with the bow on her bonnet and pretended to be as surprised as the rest.

Simon caught her eye and she gave him a little shrug before nodding toward the man with the cart. Simon made arrangements and the man pulled his cart over to the edge of the warehouse. He tipped his hat to Elizabeth before hauling their trunks into the back of his buckboard. Leaping up into the seat, he took hold of the reins. "Where to?"

"The Mansion House," Simon said.

There was precious little information about the hotels in Natchez in 1852, but the Mansion House had come up several times and seemed as good a choice as any. Not that it mattered to her. She'd spent a week staying at Cousin Jimmy's Motor Lodge and Bingo Emporium just outside of Waco with her father once; anything would be a step-up.

Simon stood at the side of the cart and held his hand out and tried to hide his smile. Elizabeth was having a tough time adjusting to the clothing of the period. As if the darn corset weren't bad enough, a lady had to wear an obscene amount of clothing. Despite her arguments to the contrary, Simon had insisted she was, in fact, a lady, and so here she was buried under layer after uncomfortable layer. It was the petticoats that made the whole arrangement so unwieldy. Crinolines, a sort of wire cage that replaced multiple petticoats hadn't been popularized yet. That meant she had to wear at least three pet-ticoats under her dress so she'd have the desired bell shape of the period. Dumbbell was more like it. Who in their right mind would wear six layers of clothing on a beautiful spring day in Mississippi? Simon was looking at her, that's who.

Elizabeth hefted up her skirts and tiptoed through the mud to Simon's side. He was definitely enjoying this too much. She should miss the foot-rail and fall and break her neck. That'd show him. Unfortunately, Simon wasn't about to let her fall. His strong hands held her as she lifted herself and her voluminous skirts up and onto the bench-like seat. Once he'd slid in beside her, the driver urged the horse on and they started the long, slow climb up Silver Street to the bluffs above, where Natchez and Mary Stewart waited.

The short drive to the hotel was bone-jarring. As far as Elizabeth could see, none of the roads in town were paved, although some sidewalks appeared to be. Even though the road smoothed out con-siderably after they'd made the muddy trek up Silver Street to the town proper, the suspension on the buckboard wasn't exactly cloud-like. They'd hit one pothole and if Simon hadn't had his arm around her, she probably would have bounced right out of the thing.

She watched the town with growing wonder. They'd been given a precious gift with Simon's watch and she was going to savor every moment. That first hour in a new time period was a waking dream. Intellectually, she knew she was here, but it was hard to accept at the same time. History books, no matter how well written, were flat and distanced. This was living and breathing and *right here*. The sights and sounds were odd and unfamiliar. And she loved every minute of it.

At the top of the hill, she gawked at the men on horseback and the fanciful dress both sexes wore. The horses' hooves clopped loudly against the hard-packed earth and the wooden wheels rattled as they trundled along. It was amazing, invigorating, until a large wooden cart pulled over ahead of them and parked along the side of the road. Two men jumped out of the seat and called out to three black men in the back. Two of them carefully inched their way to the back of the cart and jumped down. The loud clatter of chains followed. Their hands and feet were bound by shackles with heavy links of iron between the rings. Large iron collars hung around their necks. Slaves.

Elizabeth went cold and gripped Simon's forearm.

"I see them," he said in a coarse whisper.

They'd read the history books, tried to prepare themselves. She knew the truth of slavery. Seeing it happen before her eyes, though, was almost too much to process. It didn't seem real. She half expected to see a movie crew over her shoulder. And yet, she was here and it was happening. It had happened.

And she was powerless.

The men shuffled toward a brick building, the jail, Elizabeth belatedly realized. The third man didn't move and the white driver climbed into the cart and dragged him out of it. His once white shirt was brown with dirt and dried blood, the back of it in tatters where the whips had ripped through cloth and flesh.

It wasn't the first time she'd seen slaves, she realized. No doubt the black men working on the landing were slaves. There were very few free blacks in Natchez at the time. It just hadn't registered. She was used to seeing people of all colors doing all sorts of things, but that would not be the case here.

Their wagon passed and the men were left behind, but Elizabeth knew that was an image she would never forget.

Simon glanced over at her, his disgust and anger apparent. "Probably runaway slaves."

Bounty hunters were handsomely rewarded for returning runaways to their masters. Elizabeth started to say something, but there just weren't any words. Simon took her hand in his and it was a comfort, but she also realized this mission was going to be far more difficult than she'd imagined.

IT WAS ANOTHER TEN minutes before they arrived at the hotel. The driver pulled the cart over in front of the hotel and then Simon and the driver bounded out of their seats with showy agility. Elizabeth eyed the near three-foot drop to the ground with uncertainty. Getting into the dang thing had been hard enough, she wasn't sure how she was going to get out. The corset kept her from being able to bend at the waist, so she couldn't crouch down and grab onto anything for support. She had to sort of bunny-dip at the knees and hope for the best. Not to mention that her skirts were sure to catch on the large wooden wheel. She thought about lifting up her petticoats, but flashing the citizens of Natchez probably wasn't her best move just yet. A big old belly flop onto the sidewalk might be her only option. It was going to be a long trip if she couldn't manage to get in or out of things without someone's help. Heck, she couldn't even dress herself.

Simon saw her consternation and smiled. People wearing pants could afford to smile, Elizabeth thought. Simon reached up and gripped her waist and before she could ask what he was doing he hoisted her out of the buckboard and gently deposited her onto the ground.

"Thanks," she grumbled.

"You'll get the hang of it," he said as he took her arm and wrapped it into his.

The interior of the hotel was dark, lit only by a few oil lamps. "Your best suite, please," Simon said as they reached the front desk.

The man behind the counter nodded primly. "Of course, sir." He fiddled with some index cards then and opened an enormous leather-bound ledger. "Thirty dollars a week. Will you be needing livery service as well?"

"Yes," Simon said as he signed the register. "Where is the stable? We'll be needing a buggy this afternoon."

The hotel clerk gave Simon directions and then placed a large brass key on the desk. As he took the cash Simon held out, he frowned. "Oh, I'm sorry, sir. I'm afraid we don't accept notes from these banks."

Simon frowned, but took the notes back and dug into his wallet for replacements. He cast Elizabeth a quick arched eyebrow.

Even though she thought it was nearly impossible for *anyone* to make sense of the wackiness that was the antebellum money system, Elizabeth waited for the squinty-eyed, don't try those shenanigans here look from the clerk, but none came. Apparently, they weren't the only ones who had trouble navigating the ins and outs of this multiple currency insanity and trying to give the wrong bills for payment wasn't cause for alarm.

It was a wonder anyone ever knew what to use. Before the Civil War, the United States government issued no paper money. Every state chartered banks and issued its own unique bank notes. In just eight year's time, over 8,000 different banks were printing their own money. To make matters worse, everyone, including large merchants and railroads, and even druggists and grocers, also issued their own currency. The notes came in all shapes and sizes, and various colors and denominations, even tiny amounts called "shinplasters" for twenty-five, ten and even six cents. Banks and merchants would honor some notes and not others. If a bank or a business went under, the notes they'd issued were worthless.

The madness ended after the Civil War when a national banking system was developed. Luckily for Simon and Elizabeth, a great many of these obsolete notes survived and they were able to amass a small fortune without paying one for it.

Their room arranged, Simon took the key and put a hand on the small of Elizabeth's back. "Shall we?"

After they'd climbed the stairs to their rooms, Simon oversaw the bellhops and their trunks as Elizabeth explored. The rooms were spacious and comfortable by 1850's standards. In the sitting room there was a large mahogany sofa and side chairs resting on a beautiful ornamental rug that made Elizabeth feel guilty for tracking in mud. The bedroom had a decent-sized double bed and lounge chair. The one glaring omission, and it was a big one, was the bathroom. There wouldn't be one down the hall either. Indoor plumbing wouldn't become common until after the Civil War. For now, a small table with a porcelain ewer and wash basin would serve as a sink while an odd-looking wooden chair with a boxed-in seat in the corner was probably the commode. Elizabeth carefully lifted up the upholstered seat of the chair to reveal a toilet-like wooden seat with a hole under which a chamber pot was discreetly hidden.

"Everything all right?" Simon asked as he joined her in the bedroom.

Startled, Elizabeth dropped the lid to the commode.

Simon chuckled. "You said you wanted adventure."

Elizabeth walked over to him and slipped her arms around his waist. "It will be that."

Simon pulled her closer and kissed her. "Are you ready for a little reconnaissance? Or do you want to rest first?" His brow drew together as one long finger traced the edge of her cheek. "You're flushed."

Simon arched an eyebrow and Elizabeth shook her head and laid a hand on his chest. "If we unlace me, there's no going back."

"I meant actual rest, but now that you mention it…" The gleam in his eye and the rumble in his chest did very little to help cool things down.

Elizabeth sighed. As tempting as it was to loosen her corset and shed a few dozen layers of clothing with Simon, they came here with a purpose. "I'm gonna regret this, but recon first. Then dinner. Then…" she added with a smile.

"Until then," Simon said and leaned down and kissed her once more.

THE LIVERY STABLE WASN'T far from the hotel, but even with paved sidewalks, it was a dusty affair. Men on horseback, carriages and carts kicked up the dirt from the street and it swirled around between the buildings, an inordinate amount of it landing with precision on the white parts of her dress.

Elizabeth waited outside the stable and, after a few minutes, Simon drove up in a small buggy looking every inch the Southern gentleman. Elizabeth shook her head in wonder. How was it he always managed to look so at home in each period they traveled to? He held the reins to the large chestnut mare with one hand and held out the other to her.

Thankfully, the buggy seat wasn't nearly as high as the buckboard had been, and she could reach the cast iron buggy step without having to lift her skirts up to her waist. But the buggy horse was a little restless and the whole shebang kept moving back and forth a few inches just as she was ready to try to get in.

"Shhh, easy," Simon said to the horse soothingly and it stilled.

Elizabeth managed to get in without much of a problem after that, and Simon helped her tuck her voluminous skirts in between them. He shifted the reins back to his left hand, picked up a long thin whip with his right and gently urged the horse to walk.

"Where on earth did you learn to do that?" Elizabeth asked.

Simon smiled and then turned his attention back to the road. "I'm English."

Elizabeth suspected being stinking rich and running with the horsiest of the horsey set probably had more to do with it, but she let it slide. She had more important things on her mind, like the mission.

They'd agreed to follow the list they'd found tucked inside Simon's grandfather's journal. Whether or not these were official Council for Temporal Studies approved missions didn't matter. The Latin inscription at the top that read, *"In the absence of light, darkness prevails"* summed it up nicely.

Simon's name had been first on the list and his grandfather Sebastian had traveled back to 1929 to save him. And now, Simon and Elizabeth had picked up where he'd left off. They'd saved Alan Grant in 1933 Hollywood and now they'd moved on to the next name on the list, Mary Stewart.

Unfortunately, the list only told them the most basic who, when and where. The what, why and how was up to them to figure out as they went along. In the end, all they really knew was that someone needed their help and whatever it took, they'd give it.

"What do you think it's about?" Elizabeth asked. She'd asked that a dozen times before they'd left and the answer was always the same.

"We'll know when we get there. And," Simon added craning his neck to see over the next rise. "Unless I'm mistaken, that won't be long now."

The road had wound its way out of town and up and over a few rolling hills. As they crested the last, Elizabeth felt a tingle of anticipation. This was where it would all begin. Of course, they might not find out anything today, she reminded herself and smoothed down her skirt to give her hands something to do. They were there a day earlier than the one given on the list, just to get the lay of the land. She had hoped they might learn more about Mary Stewart before tomorrow, too.

The research they'd done at home wasn't very helpful. The name Mary Stewart was common enough to muddy the results and the historical records of the period were pretty limited. They'd also tried to find out if the date listed—May 5, 1852, 9 p.m.—was historically significant at all. Research didn't turn up much on that front either. It was, as far as the public record was concerned, an uneventful day. That left the location, Catholic Hill. It had been easy to find on the old maps, but knowing where it was didn't tamp down her unease.

"There it is," Simon said as they came out from under a canopy of trees and out into the open.

Elizabeth pushed out a bracing breath as they drove into the city cemetery.

CHAPTER TWO

SIMON PULLED THE BUGGY off the road onto a grassy patch of shade just outside the main wall to the cemetery. He got out of the carriage and picked up the twenty-pound, iron bell-shaped hitch weight and lead rope from under the seat. Running his hand along the horse's back to calm her, he attached the lead rope to her bridle and set the weight down on the ground. With no groom or hitching post, the weight would act as an anchor and discourage her from straying. He hoped.

"Good girl," he said, giving the horse's cheek a friendly rub.

While he'd settled the horse, Elizabeth had managed to extricate herself from the buggy. She stood looking over the low, stone wall at the graveyard beyond, as unsure as he was as to just what exactly they were looking for. Doing a little early reconnoitering of the area was undoubtedly a good idea, but what they expected to find here, he wasn't sure.

He joined Elizabeth and expected her to fall into step with him as he approached the gate. When she didn't, he turned back. "Something wrong?"

She wrinkled her forehead in worry and shook her head.

He tried to suppress his smile as he walked back over to her. "Don't tell me you're afraid of graveyards."

Her frown deepened. "Not afraid. I just don't like them."

He was about to tease her when she looked up at him. The sadness in her eyes brought him up short.

She saw the concern in his face and shook her head. "It's okay. It's just … they're so full of endings, you know?"

Simon turned to look out at the grassy expanse, dotted with large oak trees and worn pathways.

"It feels like the only place on earth where hope doesn't belong," she said.

The tiny thread of pain in her voice was something Simon hadn't heard before. He started to ask her about it when she started for the gate. "We should go before we lose the light."

He watched her for a moment, concerned, and then lengthened his stride to catch up.

They walked up one of the paths toward the center of the cemetery. There, they found wooden signs marking the various portions including Jewish Hill and Catholic Hill. Catholic Hill housed a special section of the cemetery set aside for the paupers and the less fortunate and was the location on Sebastian's list. The afternoon sun bathed the grounds in a warm glow and long shadows began to stretch out from the trees and larger monuments. Small groups of people gathered at various gravesites to pay their respects. But the only sound was the wind coming off the river from across the road.

Simon looked down at Elizabeth as they walked along the well-planned paths between rows of gleaming white headstones and large mausoleums. Whatever had troubled her at the gate still lingered. No one else would have noticed the subtle change in her body language or felt the slight undercurrent of unease. To anyone else, she would have appeared as her usual self, open and curious.

Feeling him watching her, she turned and smiled up at him. It was a genuine smile and not one sent to simply assuage him. Simon put away his worry, for now.

The grand mausoleums and obelisks gave way to simpler headstones until they reached a section set off from the rest. It was covered with small wooden anonymous crosses. As they moved closer, Simon realized that the people in the distance were not visiting, but conducting a funeral.

An elderly priest and two women stood at the foot of a freshly dug grave. Simon and Elizabeth watched from afar as the priest finished and nodded solemnly to the two women before walking away. The older of the two women wore a simple black dress and dabbed at her eyes with a handkerchief. The younger, clearly wealthier woman, judging from the silk of her dress, patted the other woman's arm consolingly and then led her away from the grave.

Once the women were out of sight, Simon and Elizabeth continued on. It wasn't until they were close to the grave that they could see how small it was. A child's grave.

Simon felt Elizabeth's hand slip into his. The pall she'd carried with her since they arrived settled heavily on his shoulders.

A man appeared at the graveside and began to shovel the mound of dark fresh earth back into the grave. The clumps of heavy dirt cascaded and drummed against the wooden lid of the small pine box inside. It was a wholly unsettling sound.

Despite that, they stood transfixed. It felt wrong to watch and yet somehow disrespectful to turn away.

With such a small grave, the man's work was quickly done and he patted the earth down with the back of the shovel. He took off his hat and wiped his brow before bowing his head and saying a silent prayer. When he looked up again, he nodded to them in greeting and then looked sadly back at the grave. "Such a wee thing," he said with a gentle Irish lilt. "Did you know the gal?"

Simon shook his head and the man nodded again. The three of them stood in silence at the grave for a moment before the man tipped his hat and quietly walked down one of the paths.

"What was her name?" Elizabeth asked suddenly.

The man stopped and turned back. "Mary, ma'am. Mary Stewart."

CHAPTER THREE

Elizabeth couldn't explain what had prompted her to ask the child's name. The words had just come out. And yet, some part of her knew what the answer would be.

"Mary Stewart?" Simon repeated.

The man nodded, tipped his hat once more and resumed his way back toward the main road.

"It's a common name," Simon said. "We must have come across a dozen or more in our research."

Elizabeth looked over at the grave. "But how many of them are here on Catholic Hill?"

Simon didn't have an answer for that. "Perhaps a relative of the girl? One of those women?"

It was possible, but Elizabeth knew that wasn't going to be the case. She could hear in Simon's voice that he didn't really think so either. He was more pragmatic than she was and giving himself over to the illogical, no matter how much he knew it to be true in his heart was difficult for him. He'd come to accept it though. Elizabeth could feel the truth of it. It vibrated inside her like a living thing. "It's her," she said.

Simon looked like he was going to argue the point further, but instead he sighed and frowned down at the grave. His fingers brushed against Elizabeth's and took hold of her hand.

How on earth were they going to help someone who was already dead?

ELIZABETH TUGGED OFF HER gloves and laid them on the cloth-covered table as Simon ordered dinner and a bottle of wine. She leaned back in her chair, running her bare fingers over the dark wood and upholstered velvet armrests. The setting was rich and for the rich. The table legs, to the extent they were visible beneath the starkly white starched tablecloths, had deeply carved legs with lion's heads and huge clawed feet. The lighting was warm and a little smoky. Candles burned in their holders on the table and in the huge crystal chandeliers above and oil lamp sconces flickered against the dark wooden walls. The restaurant was lavishly furnished with early and very elaborate Victorian detail.

"I hope claret's all right," Simon said.

"Honestly, I could use a bourbon after this afternoon."

Simon hmm'd in agreement and shook out his linen napkin before slipping it onto his lap. "If you're right—"

"I am."

Simon ceded the point with a nod. "Then this mission will be challenging."

"Unlike the others," Elizabeth said with a grin. She took a sip of water and was grateful for the cooling sensation it brought. Although it hadn't been a hot day, wearing all of these clothes was beginning to take its toll.

Simon smiled back and then cocked his head to the side. "Are you all right?"

Elizabeth plucked at the lace collar of her dress. "Just a little hot."

"I'm sure, but I meant, about earlier," he said, treading carefully in a way he seldom did with others.

Elizabeth wrinkled her face into a frown. It wasn't something she liked to talk about. "It just makes me think about daddy."

She'd told Simon about her gambler father, of course, and even how he'd died when she was just seventeen. But what she hadn't spoken about was how that made her feel. How standing in the dry dusty cemetery in Texas as they lowered her father into the ground had been the loneliest moment of her life. No matter how loved she felt now, she could still feel the bite from the cold wind and taste the dust in her mouth. That singular moment when she realized she was completely alone.

Simon reached across the table and covered her hand with his. His hand was warm and strong. She could tell from the look in his eyes that he wanted to know more, that he wanted to help, to take away the pain of the memories, but he loved her and trusted her enough to wait until she was ready.

Nestled next to the comfort he offered was a mirror to her pain. Simon was no stranger to loss, she reminded herself. He'd buried both his parents and his grandparents and had spent the better part of his life alone. She was hardly a special snowflake.

Feeling suddenly embarrassed at her indulgent self-pitying, Elizabeth squeezed his hand and gave him a sniffley smile. "It's silly. It was years ago…"

"Some moments never fade," Simon said. He lifted her hand to his lips and kissed it. "Not all of them bad though."

Elizabeth nodded and let go of his hand as the waiter arrived with their wine. As Simon approved it and their glasses filled, a gentleman and two very attractive women entered the restaurant. They must have been well-known, because a few of the patrons stared and whispered appreciatively. Judging from their make-up, so much rouge and lipstick were hardly de rigueur for the typical Southern woman, they might be from the showboat that docked at the landing earlier that day. One of the women even winked at Simon as they passed by.

Simon coughed to hide his embarrassment.

"Too bad Jack isn't here," Elizabeth said not bothering to hide her amusement. "He would have enjoyed that."

Simon took a sip of wine. "No doubt, but I think he made the right choice in staying home. He needs some time to himself."

That was probably an understatement. Jack's broken heart had a long way to go before it healed. If it ever did, Elizabeth thought sadly. Since they'd returned from 1930's Hollywood, Jack hadn't been the same. Oh, he'd dated. A lot. But his heart wasn't in it. He'd sacrificed his chance at love to protect the timeline and the wounds were still raw even a month later.

"He'll be fine," Simon said as if he'd read her thoughts. "And, after all, we'll be back before he has a chance to miss us. Or miss you, at least."

"You're probably right," Elizabeth said. "But it wouldn't have been the worst thing in the world to have another set of eyes on this."

"It is a bit of a puzzle, isn't it?"

The waiter arrived with their meals—stuffed chicken and new potatoes for Elizabeth and roast mutton and asparagus for Simon. They both smelled delicious. Now that she'd had a chance to cool down and recover from the day, she realized she was actually starving.

She took a bite of chicken and then washed it down with a little wine.

"If she is our Mary, what are we supposed to see tomorrow? I mean, who goes to visit a grave in the middle of the night?"

"Someone who doesn't want to be seen."

"The two women we saw there today didn't mind being seen. We should track them down tomorrow."

"Agreed," Simon said. "They were an odd pair, weren't they?"

Their clothes were definitely from different social strata. "Neither of them looked very motherly."

Simon swallowed a piece of his mutton and wiped his mouth with his napkin. "You could tell that from twenty yards away?"

"Maybe. You have to admit, neither of them looked like you'd expect a mother to if she'd just lost her child."

Simon nodded. "True."

"Did you see all of those children's graves? Can you imagine?" The memory of it made her shudder.

"Considering the infant mortality rate is nearly one in ten and worse still until adulthood, I'm surprised there weren't more." He took a long drink from his wine glass. "But, no, I can't imagine."

The topic settled like a lead balloon on the table between them. The idea of burying her own child chased away Elizabeth's appetite. She reached for her wine.

"We should start with the priest tomorrow," Simon said, neatly closing the door to that topic. "I'm sure he can tell us where we might find those two women."

"Good idea." Elizabeth put her glass down and ran her finger along the stem. "I've been thinking. If she is our Mary, why don't we go back earlier in time," she continued, "and help her before she…"

"Dies?" Simon finished for her. He frowned. "I've thought about that as well, but however tempting, I don't think it's wise. We have no idea the repercussions a change like that might bring to the timeline."

Elizabeth sighed. "I know. I just…" She shook her head.

Simon reached across the table and gave her hand a comforting squeeze before letting go. "We have to trust that we've been given this window, here, now, for a reason. We have to trust my grandfather. We have to trust the list." He picked up his wine glass and stared into it before meeting her eyes again. "No matter how difficult that might be."

He was right, of course. She'd known that in her heart already. But knowing it didn't make it any easier.

The rest of dinner was subdued. The thought of what they might face tomorrow preoccupied them both. And things lingered unsaid.

SIMON STOOD AT THE window of their hotel room and watched the morning street traffic. Horses and riders varied as much as cars and drivers back home. Instead of a beat-up pickup truck, an old sway-back or ancient mule carried a poor tenant farmer. In place of a luxury sports car, a high-strung thoroughbred pranced among the carts and wagons with a wealthy planter astride. The more things changed… he thought.

A particularly large cart stopped just beneath the window. The driver barked orders to some unseen men who appeared and began to unload the supplies in the back. A large crate was mishandled and dropped to the sidewalk with a thunderous crash.

Simon spun around to see if the noise had awakened Elizabeth. He smiled to himself and shook his head. She continued to quietly snore away. That woman could sleep through anything. He'd always envied her that. Always a restless sleeper and early riser, he'd gotten used to being up well before she opened her eyes. Those quiet moments in the morning, before the whirlwind that was life with Elizabeth, gave him a chance to reflect and consider. It gave him time to thank the powers that be for sparing him from the life he'd felt sure he was destined for. He could still feel the shadow of that world, but the loneliness that used to pull him under was gone. Never in a thousand years had he thought he could be part of something, or more to the point, *want* to be part of something outside himself. Now, he couldn't imagine life any other way.

Elizabeth moaned softly and rolled onto her side. Her arm flopped onto the side of the bed he'd vacated. She must have been expecting to find him there and the shock of finding an empty space instead pulled her from sleep. She blinked against the morning light streaming through the tall window where Simon stood.

"Good morning," he said.

She mumbled something unintelligible and blinked rapidly several times.

"Natchez," Simon supplied, having gone through the same confusion an hour earlier when he'd awakened.

Elizabeth nodded and smiled sleepily.

Simon turned back to the window. "It's a beautiful day. Not too warm, I hope."

He heard Elizabeth slide out of bed and pad over to join him. She leaned against his back and her warm hands slipped inside his half-buttoned-shirt. He covered them with his own, and turned around in the circle of her arms and kissed the crown of her head.

She nodded sleepily against his chest. "Morning."

He chuckled, and led her over to a small table with a pitcher and washbasin. He poured some fresh water into the bowl for her and left her to splash water on her face and come fully awake.

While she did that, Simon slipped on his vest and took his pocket watch off the wooden stand on the side table. He checked it, as a force of habit, and slipped it and key fob into his vest pocket. "The desk clerk will probably be able to tell us where we can find the priest. If I remember our research correctly, there weren't many Catholic churches in Natchez, so he shouldn't be hard to find."

"Breakfast first," Elizabeth said as she pulled off her long cotton nightgown and tossed it onto the bed.

Simon watched her naked form appreciatively for a moment before turning back to the window. They had a long day ahead of them and couldn't afford a late start no matter how tempting.

He heard her rustle around in her trunk, grumbling as she did. "Crotchless drawers. I feel trapped and half naked at the same time."

He didn't envy her. All that clothing must have been incredibly cumbersome. He was grateful all he had to do was wear a three-piece woolen suit.

"I'm going to need your help with this…thing again," Elizabeth said, as she held out her corset in front of her like it was a live snake. She walked across the room and sat in front of the small vanity.

Frowning at herself in the mirror, she poked at what was left of her hairdo. "Do you know how to braid?"

"Darling," Simon said. "I will help you get dressed. I will most happily help you get undressed. But doing your hair is where I have to draw the line."

Elizabeth laughed. "Fair enough. I see why people had ladies' maids. The whole kit and kaboodle is designed to keep you reliant on others." She raised her tiny fist and shook it in mock anger. "Down with the man!"

Despite Elizabeth's protests, she managed quite well and before too long they were ready to face the day, and more importantly, that night.

After a quick breakfast, they went to the church and eventually found the priest they were looking for at the building site of the new cathedral in town. He was more than happy to help them.

Mary Stewart, as it turned out, was an orphan and the two women at her burial were associated with the orphanage. Mrs. Nolan ran the Children's Home and Miss Catherine Stanton was one of the Female Charitable Society volunteers.

The orphanage was a fairly large building on the edge of town. Its stern Federal-style architecture gave it an aura of institutionalized living that the sign out front echoed loudly and sadly. *Natchez Children's Home, Orphan Asylum for Destitute and Abandoned Children.* All of that was in bold opposition to the beautiful old maple and sycamore trees that surrounded the property and the sound of children's laughter caught on the breeze.

Elizabeth squinted up at him, shading her eyes from the bright morning sun that promised a hot day ahead and reached for his hand.

"Remember, we can't save them all," Simon warned her. With her heart, she'd want to adopt every child and take them back to the future. She nodded reluctantly, but he was worried about how the experience might affect her. And, if he were honest with himself, how it would affect him.

Ever since Father Connelly had told them about the orphanage, Simon had been tense. He was not a sympathetic man by nature. Unlike Elizabeth, who threw herself with abandon at every lost cause, he was far more cautious. For the most part, he kept his heart neatly bound. There were few things that tugged at his heartstrings. Among them, however, were children. Perhaps it was the loneliness of his own youth, the lack of nurturing parents or hard lessons taught on cold nights at boarding school. Whatever the cause, Simon felt his heart constrict at the thought of a wounded or lonely child. Here on the footsteps of a 19th century orphanage, he knew he would see nothing else.

Elizabeth squeezed his hand, and together they walked up the short set of steps to the front door. Just as Simon was about to ring the bell, the door opened and a dozen or so young boys burst out into the sunshine. Like prisoners furloughed for the first time, they whooped and hollered with joy at the sheer freedom of being outside. They shoved each other and scuffed at the dirt as they formed two rough lines at the bottom of the steps like a ragged bunch of little soldiers.

In their wake, a large plump woman with a ruddy complexion and a bellowing voice followed. "Good. Stand up straight, Clayton James," she said sternly at one boy who immediately pushed back his shoulders. "Y'all be back in your room in two hours. I've got a switch and I'm not afraid to use it. Isn't that right, *Jimmy Davis?*"

One of the boys, presumably Jimmy, looked up to face her. The angry set of his jaw faded into reluctant submission as the woman glared down at him from the top step.

He was slightly taller than the others and reed thin. Most of the children's clothes were ill-fitting hand-me-downs, but his clothes were easily two sizes too small. His jacket strained to keep just one button closed at the front and pulled tightly against his chest and shoulders. His dirty, dark brown boots, ankle high, still didn't touch the hem of his pants and pale gangly legs showed through the gap. Subconsciously, the boy reached around and rubbed his bottom and nodded.

"Good," she said with a firm nod and then crossed her arms over her ample bosom. "Now, go on and don't come back until y'all are good and tired, you hear!"

Once the boys had all run off, the woman seemed to see Simon and Elizabeth for the first time. She narrowed her eyes at them as if she didn't have time for more disobedient children. "And you would be?"

"You must be Mrs. Nolan," Simon said with his most gracious smile. "Father Connelly told us of your good work and we came to see it for ourselves. Very impressive." He gestured to where the boys had stood. "We're hoping to emulate your success. In England and perhaps elsewhere."

The compliment had the desired effect and the woman's expression softened. "England? Really?"

"I know you must be terribly busy, but if you could spare us just a few moments," Simon continued. "My wife and I would be most grateful."

The woman preened at her hair and tried to control its unruly curls. She had better luck with the children. "Of course, I can spare a few minutes."

Mrs. Nolan did more than that. She gave them a tour of the entire building, from the kitchens to the laundry. She spoke very highly of their private benefactors, but no matter how generous, they were always in need of more.

While the orphanage wasn't as Dickensian as Simon had feared it would be, it was far from the home these children deserved. Whether they'd been left parentless from cholera or yellow fever, accident or disaster, there were over fifty children here and many more in other orphanages around the county.

Simon had read about the orphan trains from large cities like New York where thousands of homeless children were shipped off like cargo to farming states in hope of being taken in. In rural places like Natchez, the healthy boys were probably "adopted" out and trained as farm hands locally. The girls faced a more difficult path. Women had few options in the 1850's and a poor woman fewer still. The future for these poor children was anything but bright.

"And this is our boy's dormitory," Mrs. Nolan explained as she led them into a room lined on each side with a dozen small beds. "We can expand and house up to seventy-five children, but that puts a strain on resources in a most dire way."

A few of the boys looked up and stared at their visitors, their eyes already hardened by a life of disappointments. One small boy just looked frightened and confused and quickly hid under his blanket and Simon felt a surge of guilt for having thought his childhood compared to this. He'd wanted for nothing but affection. These children had nothing, nothing at all.

Elizabeth slipped her arm through Simon's and gave his bicep a comforting squeeze. "Simon?"

The understanding and warmth in her eyes were almost his undoing. She tugged on his arm slightly and nodded toward the doorway. He cleared his throat and gave the boys one last look before following Mrs. Nolan on the rest of her tour.

They ended in the girls' dormitory, a mirror of the boys on the opposite end of the building. Elizabeth took the lead then, asking questions and finally circling around to their intent. "We understand that you lost a child recently. A Mary Stewart?"

Mrs. Nolan's face dropped in genuine sadness. As much of a drill sergeant she'd been with the boys outside, it was obvious she cared for the children in her charge. "Poor girl," she said as her eyes drifted to an empty bunk at the far end of the room. "She'd just come to us, too. Perhaps a month. Passed away just a week before her eighth birthday."

"What happened to her family?" Elizabeth asked.

"Mother abandoned her, near as I can tell. Doctor Walker brought her to us, but she was ill and there was nothing to be done, I'm afraid. The ague, you see."

Elizabeth cooed her understanding. "And the father?"

Mrs. Nolan shook her head. "Nowhere to be seen, I'm afraid."

Of course, her father could be dead, but there was a much more likely possibility that he'd never been present at all. The thought of it made Simon's temper flare.

A loud crash came from another room followed by a scream and then peels of laughter. Mrs. Nolan frowned. "Will you excuse me for just a moment?"

"Of course," Elizabeth said and Mrs. Nolan hurried, trying to look like she wasn't, toward the door. She closed the double doors behind her, but it did little to muffle her angry rebukes.

Elizabeth stifled a laugh and turned her attention to a nearby bed where a little girl with big round eyes sat playing nervously with her doll. "Hello, my name's Elizabeth's. What's yours?"

The girl answered softly. "Megan."

"And who's this?" Elizabeth asked pointing at the girl's broken doll and sitting down on the bed next to her. The girl was shy at first, but Elizabeth could charm the birds from trees and it wasn't long before the little girl was smiling and delightedly telling her everything about her doll, Annie. A few other girls gathered around.

Simon lingered by the door. The girls were clearly far less enamored with him than with Elizabeth. Except for one. He'd seen her when they'd first come in. She stood apart from the others, halfway in and halfway out of the door at the far end of the room. Her hair was long and straight and a lovely shade of chestnut. Her little round face was pale and sad. She stood on tiptoe, nervous and frightened, as if she wasn't supposed to be there at all. When she saw him, her expression was almost one of surprise. She'd quickly hidden herself behind the doorway, but he saw her peeking out, watching him. He could see a small blue ribbon tied to her wrist. After a few minutes, when he caught her leaning further into the room, he offered her a smile.

Slowly, almost afraid to let it come, she smiled back. Emboldened, he took a step toward her when the doors behind him opened and Mrs. Nolan came bursting back into the room. "That Wilkins boy will be the death of me yet! I'm so sorry to have kept you waiting."

"That's all right," Elizabeth said as she gently touched little Megan's cheek. "We were fine on our own, weren't we?" she said more to the girls than to Mrs. Nolan. The girls nodded vigorously and Simon wondered just what she and the little girls had been talking about.

They said their goodbyes to the girls and Simon's eyes sought out the little girl at the far end of the room, but she was gone.

Mrs. Nolan led them back into the main foyer. "As you can see, we have a long way to go before we are where we need to be, but we do our best."

"Very impressive," Simon said. "And I'm sure the Female Charitable Society is quite pleased with the work you do."

Mrs. Nolan waved away the compliment, but it was clear she was pleased. "They give more than money. Some of them. Miss Stanton in particular. Fine woman. Hard worker. Not afraid to march on the front lines."

"I'd love to talk to her. Do you think that would be all right?" Elizabeth asked.

Mrs. Nolan laughed. "Oh, she'll talk. It's getting her to stop that's the trick." She jotted down an address and handed it to Elizabeth. "She's not home today, over in Port Gibson until tomorrow. But I'm sure she'd be happy to speak to you."

"Thank you."

While they'd talked Simon had dug around inside his wallet. He'd brought more money than they would need. Despite its remarkable number, he felt almost ashamed not to offer more as he held out a five hundred dollar bill. "I'm sure you'll put this to good use."

Mrs. Nolan's eyes bulged and she barely restrained herself from snatching it from his hand. She managed to compose herself and said, "That's very generous of you, Mr. Cross," and then added to include Elizabeth, "both of you."

They gave their thanks for the tour and walked out into the now midday sun. It was hot and still.

Simon let out a cleansing breath.

"Are you all right?" Elizabeth asked.

He nodded.

"We can't help them all," she said.

He looked down at her. "But we can help the one."

Elizabeth smiled and leaned into his side. "That we can."

CHAPTER FOUR

ELIZABETH FOUND A SMALL twig that looked a little like one of Tim Burton's characters and stuck it into the soft, moist dirt just outside the bark house she'd built. The little hut was the perfect size for a fairy or a borrower or the spider crawling up her arm.

She stifled a scream and shook the spider away.

Simon shushed her and glowered from under the hood of his cloak. Elizabeth whispered her apology and, abandoning her mini-construction site, shifted her position on the large roots of the large oak tree. Score one for the petticoats. If she'd been wearing anything else, her bum would have been sore and cold by now.

They'd been at the cemetery less than an hour so far, but patience and stillness were not on Elizabeth's resume. Unsure how long the trip from town would take them at night, they'd allowed themselves a large buffer to ensure they arrived well before 9 p.m. They'd made very good time and were there with an hour to kill. They secreted their horse and buggy well away from the road in the woods behind them, and then settled behind an enormous oak tree. Its broad trunk, at least seven feet across, great gnarled roots and location, just off to the side of Catholic Hill, made it the best spot to wait for…whatever it was they were waiting for.

This particular section of the cemetery wasn't ideal for a stakeout. Not that any part of a cemetery was, but the poor section of Catholic Hill was nearly bald and they were forced to hide at least twenty yards away. Luckily, the moon was three-quarters full and the clouds hadn't settled in for the night.

The plaintive cry of a young female fox pierced the night, startling Elizabeth. Again. As if to answer, a whip-poor-will began its whistling song. Elizabeth pulled her cape more tightly about her shoulders. The hot day had given way to a cool evening, although it wasn't the cold that made her shiver.

No matter how much she'd seen in her life, sitting in a graveyard at night was just down right eerie. The moonlight touched the marble headstones in the distance and made them appear to glow like ghosts in an old black and white movie, coming and going as clouds traveled across the face of the moon. Trees seemed to shift positions, branches reaching out like arms. Odd sounds from the forest behind her all provoked her imagination to a series of unhelpful thoughts.

Through it all, Simon sat remarkably still. His large dark cloak made him look as mysterious as the world around him. Sadly, he hadn't appreciated her witty Dred Pirate Roberts reference at the store and Elizabeth made a mental note to show him *The Princess Bride* when they returned home.

Carefully, Elizabeth peeked around her side of the large tree trunk and scanned the night. It was disconcerting not knowing what they were waiting for. Considering their past adventures and some of the things they'd read in Sebastian's journal, *anything* could be out there.

Apprehensively, her eyes skimmed along the grass looking for pale zombie fingers clawing their way up through the earth. *Please don't let it be zombies, or vampires,* she added silently. Once was enough.

Despite the cold, dead feeling of the surrounding landscape, it was fertile ground for her imagination, and she could feel her pulse begin to race.

Simon glanced over at her and she could see his reassuring eyes deep in the shadows of his hood. It was enough to stop the Kentucky Derby that was threatening to start in her chest, but the anxiety of waiting was starting to prickle along her skin like an electrical current.

Elizabeth felt another wave of the fidgets coming on when Simon sat up a little straighter and reached a hand out to still her. Just over a small rise on the far side of Catholic Hill, Elizabeth could hear something approaching from the North. Even on the soft grass and dirt, there was no mistaking the sound of a horse's footfalls as it slowed from a trot to a walk. At least, she hoped it was a horse and not a minotaur or something half this and half that.

She and Simon carefully peered out from their hiding place and strained to see more clearly in the dark. A cloudbank had settled in front of the moon and what light there was became diffused and shallow. Slowly, a rider emerged from the shadows. She felt awash with relief. It was a man.

He pulled up his horse and eased out of the saddle. Looking around furtively, he hurriedly walked over to Catholic Hill. He wore a large hat and an oversized overcoat; the night's shadows obscured his face.

Simon and Elizabeth kept as still as possible. The last thing they wanted was to be seen, and judging from the man's late-night appearance and nervous body language, he felt the same way.

Even though anonymous crosses marked the graves, the freshly turned earth made it easy to discern which was Mary's. The man walked directly to her grave, clearly there to visit hers and no other.

The man was closer now, but Elizabeth couldn't make out his face. He was still too far away and it was far too dark.

The man stood solemnly over the grave for a long moment before reaching inside his coat. Elizabeth felt Simon tense next to her. She knew his hand had shifted slightly under his cloak and was now gripping the handle of the Colt-45 they'd brought with them.

The man unbuttoned his jacket and pulled out a small bouquet of flowers he'd kept safely tucked away. Slowly, almost painfully, he knelt down and laid them on the grave beneath the cross. As he stood up, something in their direction caught his eye. He looked over quickly to the woods behind where Simon and Elizabeth hid and then stood frozen in place.

Elizabeth spun around to try to see what he'd seen. Her eyes and imagination must have still been in four-wheel drive, because she could have sworn she saw a little girl in a white dress peering out from the wood.

Elizabeth looked back to the man, who was still staring past their hiding place toward the forest beyond. When Elizabeth looked again the fox she'd heard earlier poked its face out of the woods and then disappeared. Elizabeth shook her head and let out a slow breath. Darn fox.

The man shook himself out of his stupor and then, with new urgency, hurried back to his horse. He mounted in one easy step, reined his horse around and rode straight for them.

Elizabeth's heart raced. Had he seen them? Simon's arms pulled her close. He pressed them both into the base of the tree and covered her quickly with his cloak.

The hoof beats grew louder, closer, until it sounded like he was right on top of them. Suddenly, the horse whinnied and shied. He tried to urge the animal on, but it refused, and reared and pranced around nervously. From under the edge of the cloak, all Elizabeth could see were the horse's legs and the man's boots in the stirrups as he dug his heels into the horse's flank. But still, the animal refused to move. It snorted and cried.

Elizabeth wrapped her fingers around one of the oak tree's roots and tried to slow her heart. If he just looked down, he would see them. For a moment, she felt just like a little hobbit hiding from the Nazgul. Except, luckily for her, this rider appeared to be flesh and blood. She hoped.

After a long moment that hung heavy in the damp air, the man grunted in defeat and eased his horse back away. The horse and rider slipped from her narrow view under the cloak. Elizabeth could hear the horse begin to calm, and and then the man urged it on and both horse and rider disappeared into the distance and into the darkness.

A few moments passed before Simon shifted and peered out from the safety of their hiding spot. Elizabeth followed suit. The cemetery was as empty and as still as it had been before the man arrived. Slowly, Simon stood and helped Elizabeth up.

"That was close," Elizabeth whispered.

Simon flipped back the hood of his cloak. "Too close. Could you see what drew his attention?"

Elizabeth shook her head. "I think it was a fox, back there in the woods. I'm not sure. I think my imagination was getting the better of me."

"This is the place for it."

"You were as calm as a toad in the sun."

"Appearances can be deceiving. I was busy praying that it wouldn't be zombies," Simon added with a wink.

Elizabeth laughed. "Funny."

Simon worked the kinks out of his legs and rolled his shoulders to loosen them. "Let's take a look at those flowers, shall we?" he asked as he nodded toward Mary's grave. He took Elizabeth's arm and helped her walk up the soft grass to the grave. Once there, he knelt down and picked up the small bouquet of blue and purple flowers.

"Whoever he was, he cared enough to leave those," Elizabeth said.

Simon gently placed the flowers back exactly as they had been and stood. "Yes, but did he do it out of love or out of guilt."

He looked around the empty graveyard once more before nodding to the woods. "We should go."

Elizabeth was more than happy to head back to the warmth and security of town and their hotel. They walked down the hill and into the woods.

"By the way, did you notice his clothes?" Simon asked as he helped Elizabeth pick her way through the woods. "I could only make out the edges of his overcoat and trousers, but the coat was frayed and poor quality. The trousers, however, were something a wealthy man would wear."

"And his boots. They were like yours. Expensive."

Simon nodded thoughtfully. "So we know he's a man of means, and one who did not want to be seen visiting Mary's grave."

"That's not much to go on."

"It's more than we had this morning," Simon said.

They reached the small clearing where their horse and buggy waited patiently and Simon helped Elizabeth onto the seat.

"So, tomorrow?" she asked.

Simon retrieved the anchor weight and rope from the horse's harness, and slid in next to her. "Tomorrow we find Miss Stanton and see what more we can learn about Mary." He deftly eased the carriage down the dark path. "And with any luck, meet a few of the local aristocracy and worm our way in."

"Worming's good."

"It's an incestuous society. If our mystery man is among them, our paths will cross."

The lone fox screamed again and their horse unsettled before Simon calmed her. Elizabeth shivered. "I don't think I'll ever get used to that sound. It's so anguished."

Simon nodded. "Yes, it is, isn't it?" After a pause, he urged their horse on and they started down the narrow path.

Elizabeth looked into the trees as they left the woods and turned onto the road. She half-expected to see the fox looking back, or a pale faced little girl in a white dress, but there was only darkness.

Chapter Five

SIMON TIPPED HIS HAT as two of Natchez's elite walked past them on the sidewalk followed closely by a nanny who was pushing a rather gaudy velvet-covered pram. The women smiled and dipped her heads in polite greeting.

Because it was such a beautiful day and the address wasn't too far away, they decided to walk. It felt good to stretch his legs and work out the cramps from last night.

The streets of Natchez proper were laid out in a perfect grid. Clusters of enormous houses sat on the streets on and near the bluff, just above the landing where they'd arrived. Under-the-Hill and above it might be separated by hundreds of feet, but they were worlds apart. Elite planters of the early 1800's had spent fortunes on massive estates both in town and out on their plantations. Each was a testament to their power and wealth. Catherine's family was apparently one of the one percent of the one percent that made up the Natchez Nabobs.

"I think this is the house," Elizabeth said at his side as she stopped and checked the address scribbled on the note Mrs. Nolan had given them yesterday.

Catherine Stanton's house was definitely more than just a house;

it was one of the grand homes of Natchez. Simon looked up at the imposing façade of the Stantons' Cypress Hill estate. The three-story square, red brick building with its four gleaming white Doric columns and impressive, projected pediment stood set back from the street with a wrought iron gate that kept the unwanted away. Tall magnolia trees in full blossom stood on either side of the path that cut through the lush, green lawn.

"Catherine does all right," Elizabeth said.

"Someone does." Simon opened the gate for Elizabeth and followed her up the brick path.

They were just nearing the steps leading up to the front door when it opened and a man, every inch the definition of a dandy, from his black top hat and elaborately tailored tight-fitting tail coat to his silk and velvet vest, appeared with a flourish. He turned back toward the door and was joined by an older man in a conservative black suit and grey vest. His face was hewn from stone, back ramrod straight, even his beard stood at attention. Despite being several inches shorter than the younger man, the older man cut a powerful figure and one used to getting his way.

The younger man made a sour expression on his already pinched face and forced an unnatural smile. His voice had an unnaturally high pitch. "I'm sure you understand how embarrassing this is, Colonel. I simply cannot have such disrespect shown by a fiancée."

Colonel? A military man, Simon thought. That was fitting.

The Colonel forced a thin smile to his lips. His voice was deep and resonant and angry. "Of course."

The younger man clapped him on the shoulder. A gesture that was not welcome, but endured. "You can hardly be blamed for your daughter's lack of social graces," the younger man said. "But I'm sure you understand that a man such as myself cannot have a wife who runs off, unaccompanied no less, to such places as Water Street."

The Colonel's natural frown deepened. "I will speak with her about that, you can be assured, Archer."

Mr. Archer smiled broadly. "Of course." He tipped his hat. "I'll give Father your regards."

The Colonel grunted and managed another forced smile.

Mr. Archer nodded and hurried down the stairs. He bowed and tipped his hat to them as he passed and walked briskly to the street.

The Colonel stood at the top of the stairs and noticed Simon and Elizabeth for the first time. He put his fists on his hips. "And you are?"

Elizabeth started to speak, but Simon managed to beat her to it. "Good morning," Simon said removing his hat. "We were wondering if Miss Catherine Stanton is at home."

The Colonel's eyes narrowed and he took a step forward. His keen eyes darted to Elizabeth and he frowned, before addressing Simon. "You're one of them, aren't you?"

"Pardon me, I—"

"Get out!" he said turning on his heels and starting for the door.

"Sir, I think you—"

The Colonel stopped and turned back. He nearly charged down the stairs. "You and," he said, looking at Elizabeth with what could only be described as disdain, "your kind, filled her head with your suffrage nonsense. Independence! The vote!"

He said the last two words as though they were the most absurd things he'd ever heard. Simon could feel Elizabeth begin to simmer next to him and hoping to preempt an explosion, put a gentle, but restraining hand on her arm. "Sir, I'm afraid you're mistaken. We are not suffragists."

The man gave Elizabeth another appraising look. He was clearly skeptical of Simon's claims.

"We simply came here to ask Miss Stanton about her work at the orphanage. Her charitable works, but I can see we've made a mistake." Simon took Elizabeth's arm and turned away. They'd taken several steps down to the path when the Colonel spoke again.

"Wait!"

They stopped and slowly turned back. The Colonel glared at them for a moment and was about to speak again when a young, broad shouldered black man wearing a maroon and buff livery appeared in the doorway. "Colonel?" he asked anxiously.

"It's all right, Abraham." The Colonel waved him away before turning back to Simon and Elizabeth. "I must beg your pardon," he said and judging from the pained look on his face, he was not used to doing so.

"Of course," Simon said. "It was presumptive of us to call without prior notice. My card." Simon pulled out a silver cardholder and handed the Colonel his card.

The Colonel took it and offered his hand. "Colonel William Stanton."

They shook. "Simon Cross and this is my wife, Elizabeth."

Elizabeth offered him a small curtsy and her most disarming smile.

The Colonel bowed, but still wasn't warming to Elizabeth. "Mrs. Cross." He glanced at Simon's card. "Sir Simon?"

"A minor baronetcy," Simon said as though he were talking about something thoroughly insignificant.

The Colonel was impressed, no small feat it appeared, and tucked the card into his coat pocket. "My daughter is not home at the moment, but I will tell her you called." Apparently, their audience with him was at an end. He bowed and waited for them to get the message.

Simon smiled graciously and tipped his hat. "Colonel." He escorted Elizabeth down the path to the street.

When they reached the sidewalk and shut the gate behind them, Elizabeth said, "I'd like to suffrage him."

Simon chuckled. "Is it that or that we may have met the first man ever who is immune to your charms?"

Elizabeth frowned.

"You still have my heart," Simon said, stifling another laugh as her expression soured. "Come along," he slipped her arm into his. "I hear there are wanton women on Water Street."

ELIZABETH WAS STILL STEWING over the Colonel's attitude toward women as they approached the section of town where they hoped to find Catherine Stanton. With an effort she put the Colonel out of her mind as the neighborhoods rapidly changed. The divides of the class structure were easy to see.

They traveled from the beautiful, stately residential streets of the wealthy planters and powerful businessmen to those busy with commerce. Storefronts of all sorts lined the wide dirt streets offering everything from dry goods to the latest hats from Paris. Apartments of varying sizes and cost above the stores housed some of the middle class—smaller merchants, lesser public officials and professionals of moderate income. Others in that class left the city, such as it was, for the quieter spaces of small country homes on the outskirts of town or ran small farms dwarfed by their larger neighbors.

Next were the skilled laborers, mechanics, artisans and tradesmen. That left the bottom two classes of society. Tucked away on the periphery of the aptly named fringe of society were the common whites, the poor laborers, landless tenant farmers and others struggling to make ends meet, beneath them, at the very bottom of the heap, the slaves.

Simon drove the buggy around a corner and they'd arrived on Water Street. "This must be it," he said looking at the street sign.

A row of old, dilapidated homes, most of them boarding houses, lined the street. Interspersed among the boarding houses were smaller places with slanted roofs and pillars of rough-hewn wood. Porches sagged in the middle or slanted to the side as their foundations decayed. The sun-faded wooden planks on the sides of the houses showed signs of paint lost long ago, as the small patches that remained peeled and bubbled.

The street was busy with traffic. Mule carts and other large two and four horse wagons laden with heavy piles of lumber and other goods rumbled down the dirt road. The smell of manure and sewage was heavy in the air.

This was where the working class lived—the warehouse worker and bartender, the manual laborer and the prostitute. Most could not afford homes of their own, no matter how small, and so they rented rooms in one of the many boarding houses. A saloon sign hung angled from a broken hinge and an out of tune piano clinked out some song inside for the midday drinkers.

Simon and Elizabeth and their fancy hired buggy stood out, painfully. A man sitting on a split rail fence watched them with narrowed eyes from under his straw hat. He spit a short brown stream of tobacco juice through a hole where a tooth used to be and watched them warily as they drove past.

"Perhaps, I should have left you at the hotel," Simon said softly.

Elizabeth glared at him. He sighed and nodded, but she could feel his tension mount. She looked down the busy street. "How are we going to find her?"

"Get out!" a voice bellowed nearby.

Elizabeth turned and saw a large man with a jiggling belly and outrageous whiskers push open the swinging doors to a saloon. "I warned you about coming back here."

A well-dressed woman was roughly escorted from the premises by two other men and shoved out onto the planked porch in front of the heavy-set man.

"I don't think that's going to be a problem," Simon said as he pulled their buggy over.

The woman was tall and thin. The sort some people would describe as handsome, but not pretty. Her features were sharp and bold, and she stood erect with a pride that bordered on aggression.

Two dancehall-type girls in very low-cut dresses and men with drinks in their hands appeared in the doorway and watched the scene with amusement. Simon and Elizabeth climbed out of the buggy, but kept their distance. For now.

Catherine Stanton straightened her hat with incredible calm and stood regally before him. "Sir, these ladies—"

That won a raucous chorus of laughter. "Ladies?" said the fat man.

Catherine held her ground and even smiled graciously. "These women have a right to know that there is change coming and they will be able to be full citizens with all the commensurate rights, if they will just read this material." She tried to hand the girls a few single-page flyers.

The fat man shook his head and moved toward the girls. He slung his meaty arms over their shoulders and pulled them close. "Now why would they want that? When they got me to take care of 'em? Ain't that right, girls? 'Sides, women ain't got the brains a man does. I'm doin' 'em a favor," he added with a quick swat to their behinds.

Catherine's eyes narrowed. "The current state of inequality is neither just for women nor advantageous for men," Catherine said. "Surely, a man of your towering intellect can see the wisdom in that."

The jolly fat man's face fell and the undercurrent of laughter from the people around him stopped instantly. "You're trying to insult me."

"I'm not trying; I'm succeeding. Although, there's not much to it," she added with a shrug.

Elizabeth loved her gumption, but the fat man was less than amused. He took a menacing step forward. Simon mirrored his movement.

"I warned you once," the fat man said, "and you come back. I won't warn you again. You stay away from my girls and away from my place. You understand?"

Catherine didn't flinch. She kept her chin up and eyes fixed on his. "This is the future, sir. You cannot stop progress." She held up the hand holding the raft of flyers.

The man swung his arm and knocked the papers out of her hand. They were instantly caught on the breeze and fluttered into the street.

"That's what I think of your progress."

Catherine turned and started to gather her papers. She scurried after them as they danced over the dirt street.

The next few seconds happened in a blur. Before Elizabeth understood why, Simon ran from her side. "Look out!" he cried.

Elizabeth turned in time to see the fast approaching wagon, but too late to do anything about it. Catherine had bent down to pick up some of her papers and the heel of her shoe became tangled in her petticoats. As she struggled to stand, the wagon, whose driver saw her too late and couldn't stop the heavy load in time, bore down on her with frightening speed.

Suddenly, Simon was at Catherine's side. The wagon was nearly there. Three thousand pounds of horse thundered toward them.

Simon grabbed her under the arms. Onlooking women gasped and men called out. Simon, holding tightly to Catherine, dove to the ground and disappeared from sight behind the horses and wagon. For a sickening moment, Elizabeth couldn't tell if they were safe or not. It wasn't until the heavy wagon fully passed that she saw them again. They were lying in a heap on the dirt road. Elizabeth felt the unstoppable rise of panic. Heart in her mouth, she ran to them.

Simon was already starting to extricate himself from the tangle of limbs when she arrived.

"Are you hurt?"

Simon looked up at her, and she could see the fear in his eyes. It had been too close, but he wasn't hurt. "I'm fine."

He knelt and reached out to Catherine who rolled over, her eyes just as wild. "Good heavens," she said.

"Are you all right?"

She nodded and looked down the street to where the wagon finally managed to stop at least another thirty feet down the road. The driver jumped off and ran back toward them, joining the growing crowd.

Catherine held out her hand and took Simon's offer of help. "I told my father these clothes might be the death of me, I just didn't realize I actually meant it."

Elizabeth laughed nervously and Catherine joined in. "Thank you, sir," she said, still short of breath. "That was very stupid of me and very brave of you."

Brave, yes, Elizabeth thought, and crazy. Was that how Simon felt each time she leapt before she looked? She'd have to apologize for that later.

Simon smiled graciously and dusted off his pants leg and then bent down to pick up his hat. "You're sure you're not hurt?"

Catherine blew out a long breath. "Just my pride." Her eyes darted over Simon's shoulder and then looked to the sky for strength. "Of course."

Elizabeth followed her gaze and saw a black man, Abraham, the house slave from Cypress Hill, pull his horse to a stop from a full gallop and dismounted. "Are you all right Miss Catherine?"

"I'm fine," Catherine said. "I suppose father sent you to spy on me."

Abraham's worry, which seemed to be truly genuine, subsided and was replaced with mild amusement. "Now, Miss Catherine you know he only ask me to come because he worry about you."

Catherine pursed her lips. "You worry about me more than he does."

Abraham smiled, almost shyly. "We both do and you find new ways to give us cause every single day."

Maybe it was because Elizabeth's senses were heightened with still pulsing adrenaline, but she saw that there was something more than mistress and slave between the two. There was an ease she didn't expect and what appeared to be genuine friendship.

Catherine held out her arms. "As you can see, I'm perfectly fine." Abraham glanced down at the wagon and arched an eyebrow. "Well, I am thanks to… I'm sorry, I don't even know your name."

Simon smiled again and bowed slightly at the waist. "Simon Cross and my wife, Elizabeth. We met your father earlier today."

"And you came away unscathed!"

"We called this morning hoping to speak with you about your work at the orphanage," Elizabeth said. "And heard you might be here and hoped to catch you."

Catherine grinned. "And that you did. I am most grateful to you."

"Perhaps you can spare us some time to discuss your work, when you're feeling up to it," Elizabeth said.

"I can do better than that. Unless you have another engagement, you must come to Cypress Hill for dinner this evening. We're having a small party and I'm sure father would be even more displeased with me than usual if I didn't ask you as a small measure of gratitude."

A party with the Colonel and his wealthy friends would be the perfect place to start their investigation into the man at the cemetery. Things were looking up. "We'd be delighted."

CHAPTER SIX

IKE AN OLD-FASHIONED VALET service, two grooms stood at the curb in front of Cypress Hill waiting for carriages and buggies to arrive. One of them held the horse as the other offered a white-gloved hand to Elizabeth and helped her out of the buggy.

"Don't let Catherine bait you into conversations about women's rights," Simon said. "We need to make friends, not enemies tonight."

Elizabeth didn't like it, but knew he was right and took his offered arm and let him escort her up the path. The front door opened at their arrival and they stepped into the enormous, arched entry hall. The maple wood floors were covered with long runners and Doric columns that mimicked those out front stood on either side of large arches. Dozens of candles and wall sconces made it feel more warm and welcoming than Elizabeth feared it would be.

She liked Catherine. What was not to like? She was a rebel suffragette in the Deep South. She risked life and limb to help spread the word and had a tongue as sharp as her wit.

Catherine's father was a different matter. He was old school, like one-room-schoolhouse old school. Elizabeth tried not to judge, no matter how easy it might be. She'd spent enough time in other periods to know that the world of 1850 was born of what had come before. Many modern sensibilities weren't even a glimmer in anyone's eye.

The same house slave they'd seen earlier in the day took their hats and gloves and disappeared again.

"Hello," Catherine said holding out her hand to Elizabeth and coming to greet them at the door. She squeezed Elizabeth's hand. "I'm so glad you could come."

She seemed inordinately pleased. Not that Elizabeth and Simon weren't scintillating guests, but Elizabeth had a feeling there was something more at work here.

"Thank you for inviting us. I'm afraid we don't know many people in town," Simon said oozing charm from every English pore.

Catherine waved to her father who excused himself from other guests down the hall and joined them by the entry. He shook Simon's hand and gave Elizabeth a modest nod of the head. "My daughter tells me I owe you a debt."

Simon smiled, but didn't deny it. Smart cookie, Elizabeth thought. Put that one in your pocket for later.

"We're honored to be here and have a chance to enjoy your beautiful home. The hotel is adequate, but we are a bit weary of traveling."

The Colonel nodded and grunted in agreement. "Long campaign."

"Yes."

The silence lingered until the Colonel grunted again and said, "Bourbon?"

"Thank you," Simon said and the Colonel led him away.

Elizabeth's instinct to follow was cut off at the pass by Catherine's arm slipping through hers. "He'll be all right. I think your husband can handle dear old papa. Let me introduce you around and then we can eavesdrop for what scandalous things they're saying about me."

Catherine led Elizabeth into a large, ornate parlor where a half-dozen guests mingled. Opulent didn't begin to describe the room. A six-foot-tall intricate gold-framed mirror hung over a large marble fireplace. Deep maroon damask curtains draped gracefully over ten-foot high windows with gold-colored, detailed cornices.

Through the open pocket doors Elizabeth saw Simon and the Colonel in the adjoining parlor. They were busy drinking their bourbon and deep in discussion with another man.

"There you are, Eli," Catherine said, pulling Elizabeth's attention back. They approached a tall good-looking man in his late-twenties. He had warm brown eyes and an easy smile. And, unlike the others in the room, who all smiled as Catherine entered, Eli's smile appeared genuine.

"Cat," he said in greeting as he excused himself from another couple. "I'm so glad to see you in one piece. I heard that you were nearly killed today."

"Nearly. I was thrown out of a brothel on Water Street," she said in challenge and then added, "Run by a large fat man. I think you know the one."

Eli coughed, and although he was trying to hide a smile, his eyes darted nervously to Elizabeth. "Cat."

"Oh, it's all right," Catherine said. "She was there." And then added in response to his raised eyebrows, "Outside and on unrelated business."

Eli bowed his head. "Mister Elijah Harper, at your service."

"Don't get too excited," Catherine warned in a friendly way. "Elizabeth, this incorrigible flirt is a dear friend and fellow trouble-maker. Elijah, this is Mrs. Cross."

Eli's face fell into a boyish pout. "Oh," and then it brightened. "Widow?"

Catherine slapped his arm and Elizabeth couldn't help but laugh. "No, but please call me Elizabeth."

Eli took her hand and kissed it with a flourish. "Our dear Cat here has a penchant for trouble, Elizabeth. I'd be careful, if I were you."

"Some have said the same about me," Elizabeth said.

Eli arched an eyebrow in appreciation.

"Oh, my dear," a woman said from behind. "We just heard about Mr. Archer. Mr. Goode and I are just shocked. That's all, just shocked to our core. We heard his mother isn't sick at all and they *chose* not to come after your father was so kind to them. It's akin to standing you up at the altar. You must be shattered."

Catherine took Mrs. Goode's hand and patted it sympathetically. "Oh, my dear Mrs. Goode. I would rather be dragged through a briar patch in nothing but my bloomers than be married to a man like Stanley Archer."

Mrs. Goode spluttered in shock and fluttered about helplessly. "You shouldn't say such things."

"And yet I do," Catherine said with a sweet smile. It was all Elizabeth could do to not laugh out loud.

Mrs. Goode forced a confused smile and wandered off. So, Mr. Archer, nee of this morning, was more upset than Elizabeth had thought, and had been there for something more than just a casual visit.

"Come meet my brother and his wife," Eli said. "If your reputation is going to survive, you'll need something to counteract this one," he said with a nod toward Catherine.

The three of them joined Eli's brother and sister-in-law. James was a slightly shorter, much more tightly wound version of Eli. His clothes were impeccable. From his neatly trimmed mustache to the shine on his boots, everything spoke of a man in control of his environment. If Central Casting needed a Southern Belle, they couldn't do better than his wife, Rose Harper. She was so composed and gracious Elizabeth felt like an elephant seal by comparison.

Despite Rose's conservative clothes and hairstyle and its strict middle part and severe control, she had a natural, easy grace about her. It helped that she was downright stunning as well, with strawberry blonde hair, pale porcelain skin, and hazel eyes the color of amber.

Rose smiled kindly at them as they joined their group. "We heard about your accident, Catherine."

Catherine arched her eyebrows, an amused smile lifting the corners of her mouth. "My exploits do travel, don't they?"

James frowned and tugged at his ear. It was clear he didn't approve of Catherine's exploits any more than her father did, but Catherine didn't seem the least bit bothered by his grumbly show of disapproval.

Rose glanced up at her husband, then turned to Catherine and said with genuine affection, "We're just pleased you weren't injured. You shouldn't go to those sorts of places alone."

"She shouldn't go at all," James said unable or unwilling to curb his tongue.

Catherine's eyes narrowed. "Traveling alone can be perilous. Perhaps next time, I should ask to be escorted by one of the many men I know who frequent those sorts of places. I'm sure I'd be much safer in the company of someone like Judge Crane."

James's scowl deepened and Rose blushed. Eli didn't bother to hold back his laugh, but that merely won him a set of daggers from James.

In the brief silence that followed, the temperature in the room plummeted. Elizabeth tried a quick change of subject. "My husband and I were hoping to speak to Miss Stanton about her work at the orphanage. I understand from Mrs. Nolan that you and Mrs. Harper have been quite generous in your support."

"Yes," James said, thawing slightly as he warmed to the subject. "We're quite happy to help such a worthy cause. Mrs. Nolan does a fine job."

"The children are well cared for," Catherine said. "But nothing takes the place of family, no matter how fractured it might be at times."

"We heard about the girl who passed away recently," Elizabeth said. "Mary Stewart, I think. Her mother abandoned her?"

Rose brought her hand to her throat, and shook her head. "Can you imagine?" she said. "To leave a child…"

"There was no other family?" Elizabeth asked. "Aunts or uncles…"

Catherine shook her head. "Hard to say. The mother was gone and the girl was ill when she came to us." She reached over to a shelf and picked up a daguerreotype photograph that had several colorful ribbons hanging over the frame. She lifted the ribbons and then pointed at a girl in the photo. "Here, that's Mary."

Mrs. Nolan and about a dozen children were in the photo, some blurry, as they couldn't stand still for the long exposure. Mary sat in a chair, her legs primly together, her hands clasped on her lap. Elizabeth noticed a ribbon tied to her wrist. "What are the ribbons for?"

Catherine ran the loose ribbons through her fingers that hung from the frame. "It's just a little thing I give the girls to make them feel special. I remember Mary chose blue to match her eyes. That one foot of silk ribbon and her doll were all that child had in the world."

"That poor girl," Rose said, distressed. "Do you have any children, Mrs. Cross?"

"No," Elizabeth said. She looked over to where Simon stood with the other men in the far parlor before turning back. "We…not yet."

"If I could, I would have the house filled to the rafters with children," Rose said her lovely face slightly drawn. "To think of our Louisa in such a place…"

James cleared his throat. "I'm afraid this subject is distressing my wife."

"I'm all right," Rose protested, but James took hold of her arm.

"You mustn't upset yourself, my dear," he said in a tone that made Elizabeth cringe. Rose looked as though she might protest, but glanced quickly at Elizabeth, then smiled at her husband, and subserviently lowered her eyes.

The little exchange was not lost on Catherine who arched an eyebrow. James looked at her challengingly until Eli stepped in. "Who needs a drink? I think now's a good time for one. Or two. Cat?" Eli added as he lifted a nearby decanter.

Catherine looked ready to loose a salvo over James' bow when her father called for her from across the room.

"Catherine?" the Colonel called out. "Would you?" he said as he waved her over.

After a beseeching look from Eli, Catherine didn't argue and put the photo back. "We can talk more after dinner," she said to Elizabeth and then excused herself and joined her father.

James and Rose declined Eli's offer for a drink, and as much as she could use one, Elizabeth demurred. Eli shrugged and poured one for himself.

"Tell me, Mrs. Cross, are you and your husband planning to stay in Natchez?" James said, forcibly changing the topic of conversation.

Elizabeth was ready for this. She and Simon had practiced their backstory. She shook her head sadly. "No, not for too long, although it is nice to rest. Simon and I have been traveling for months. England to New York to Ohio and then down the river to Natchez. We were going to stop at New Orleans, but I just had to spend some time on dry land."

"To our great pleasure," Eli said as he raised his glass in her honor. "I do hope you'll come visit us at River Run while you're here."

"River Run?"

"Our plantation," James said. "We're just on the bluff above the river about six miles upstream."

Elizabeth didn't want to seem too eager, but this was exactly what they'd been hoping for—a chance to mingle with the mighty. "I've never actually seen a plantation."

"Then you must come visit us at River Run," Rose said as she put her hand on Elizabeth's forearm. "There is no more beautiful place on God's earth."

When the servant announced that dinner was ready, the dozen guests gathered in the hall. Catherine took Elizabeth's hand and led her over to Colonel Stanton's side, whose eyes shined brightly with bourbon.

He frowned at them both.

"Papa, since Mrs. Archer and her son," she added with a hint of contempt in her voice, "couldn't make it this evening, why not have the Crosses take their places as guests of honor?"

Elizabeth felt for Catherine. Pulling out of an invitation, especially one where you were the guest of honor, was a big old kick in the social pants. On the other hand, Catherine didn't seem the least bit bothered, and having a chance to be the guests of honor at a hoity-toity dinner would all but ensure their spot at future swanky dinners. She smiled up at the Colonel hoping to find the perfect mixture of humility and flattery.

The Colonel frowned more deeply than ever, but recognized that he'd been cleverly maneuvered and had no option but to gracefully accede. He held out his arm stiffly and led Elizabeth to the head of the table and to the seat to his right. She barely managed to remember not to pull out her own chair. She did, however, manage to step in front of the Colonel forcing an awkward do-se-do that only ended when he stepped back and glowered at her. Couple after couple joined them in the elegant dining room.

"Hello again," Eli said as he took his place behind the chair on Elizabeth's right.

The ladies took their seats and the men remained standing, until Catherine and Simon came in. He held out her chair and then sat to her right, catty-corner across the long table from Elizabeth.

Like the other rooms, this one had a warm fire-lit glow to it.

A large chandelier hung above the table, the light from the candles catching the crystals that hung beneath them. Dozens of candles and a few oil lamps lined the side tables and a low fire burned in the fireplace behind her. Elizabeth thought it was lovely, but couldn't help wondering if they had fire insurance back then.

Eli noticed her looking at the fireplace. "If it gets too warm for you, I'll have them move the screen over." He indicated a needlepoint tapestry held in a wooden frame, almost like a mid-sized freestanding mirror. Elizabeth had read about them. Some women wore beeswax-based make-up and the heat from the fireplace would melt it away. These tapestry screens helped keep their faces in the right place.

"Thank you," Elizabeth said glad she'd worn only a little lip rouge.

Eli smiled and then turned his attention to the man on his right. Elizabeth smiled at the Colonel. He smiled back, but looked more like a man with a gallstone than a guest.

"Beautiful table," Elizabeth said, hoping to start a pleasant, innocuous conversation mending whatever fence she'd apparently busted. "Are these plates French?"

The Colonel grunted, mumbled a yes and then turned and joined a conversation with Mrs. Goode to his left. Elizabeth floundered for a moment. Each guest at the table was involved in a conversation with a partner or two except for her. She fiddled with her water glass

"And that is why I can no longer have Claret," Mrs. Goode intoned. "And I do so love it. My one vice, you understand."

Eli offered his condolences to Mrs. Goode for her brave fight against gout and gave Elizabeth a wink.

As was Victorian custom it seemed, dinner was an endless affair of soup, salad, fish, mutton, and roast chicken. House slaves in spotless liveries brought the food out on silver chargers in wave after wave. It took Elizabeth a few times of twisting awkwardly the wrong way, but she finally got the hang of serve-from-the-left and remove-from-the-right.

Elizabeth made a few more attempts to engage Colonel Stanton and each one floated like a pricked balloon to the floor. That was until she remembered some of the stories Gerald had told her when she and Simon had stayed with the Eldridges in 1906 San Francisco. Before Gerald had been rescued by Evan Eldridge, he'd served with the 21st Infantry Regiment in the Battle of Stoney Creek during the War of 1812. Elizabeth dropped a few details and must have asked the right questions, because the Colonel actually responded with more than a grunt.

By the time their last course had been taken away, Elizabeth's corset was feeling decidedly smaller than it had at the start. What she wouldn't give for some comfort clothes right now. Sadly, her lucky sweatpants were a thousand miles and one hundred and fifty years away.

The men and women split into groups each retiring to their own adjoining parlor. The ladies were offered cordials and brandy. Mrs. Goode declined sadly, but took out a small snuffbox and inhaled half of it.

Two of the women Elizabeth hadn't had a chance to talk to much during dinner were happily gossiping about the next entertainment that was going to arrive in town and how it had to be an improvement over Tom Thumb, who *was* shockingly small, but bereft of much other talent.

Rose told Elizabeth about River Run and Catherine offered stories about young Eli that made Rose blush. Whatever Catherine's proclivity to get a rise out of everyone whose path she crossed, she had a genuine affection for Rose. Although she hadn't known Rose for long, Elizabeth couldn't help but feel the same way, as if she were a small china doll that needed protecting.

After an hour the gentlemen joined them in their parlor. Eli slipped next to her on the small sofa forcing Simon to sit opposite. Simon arched an eyebrow, but didn't force the issue.

When a discussion on politics broke out, everyone including Mrs. Goode had an opinion to offer, everyone except Simon and Elizabeth, who remained as silent as possible on all topics. When a serious argument between Dr. Parish and Mr. Cobb erupted over whether Stephen Douglas or James Buchanan should receive the Democratic nomination for the presidency, Elizabeth knew they'd been wise to stay on the sidelines. The names might have changed, but little else about politics had.

Elizabeth caught Simon's eye. He smiled and subtly raised his glass to her. She did the same and took a sip of her port. Her eyes dipped down to her glass briefly before flicking back to Simon.

But it wasn't Simon that grabbed her attention. Standing just beside his chair was a pale little girl, the little girl from the woods. The little girl in the white dress with the ribbon tied around her wrist. Mary.

ELIZABETH GASPED, BUT SO softly only Eli, who was sitting right next to her, heard. He turned and asked her if she was all right. Elizabeth blinked and caught her breath, turning to him. "I'm fine."

When Elizabeth turned back to look at Simon, the little girl was gone. It was clear no one else had seen her. She was pretty sure if anyone else had they'd be using smelling salts right about now. Heck, she could use a whiff herself.

"There aren't any children here tonight, are there?" she asked Eli.

"No," he said drawing out the word in that way people did when they thought the questioner was half-nutty.

Elizabeth smiled and rubbed her temple. She glanced around the room. She'd only glanced away for a moment; there was no way a child could have gotten out of the room so quickly. It was Mary. She was sure of it. It was definitely the girl from the photograph Catherine had shown her. Why was she here? And why was she staring at Simon?

"Are you sure you're all right," Eli asked.

Honestly, she wasn't sure, but announcing that she'd just seen a freakin' ghost probably wasn't the best idea. "Just tired, I think. All the travel."

Eli nodded, concerned.

"Perhaps I should call it an evening?" Elizabeth stood and Eli reflexively followed suit.

Simon caught her eye as she approached and rose from his seat, his face full of worry. She smiled, but there was no way she could hide the fact that she'd been shaken, not from him.

"What's wrong? Are you unwell?"

"I think perhaps we should go."

"Elizabeth—"

"Now," she said quietly and very insistently. "I'm afraid the day is catching up with me," she said for the benefit of the rest of the room.

They begged off citing the fatigue of travel and so much good wine and food and politely, but quickly, made their goodnights. Rose Harper reminded them of their promise to visit River Run tomorrow and a groom was dispatched to bring their buggy around.

"What is going on," Simon said, tense and worried.

Elizabeth glanced over her shoulder. "Not until we're away from here."

She could hear Simon grinding his teeth, but he kept his questions to himself.

Once they were a few blocks away from Cypress Hill Elizabeth let out a shudder and a deep breath. "Oh, boy."

"Are you going to tell me what happened or should I just let my imagination continue to run wild?"

Elizabeth took a bracing breath and shifted in her seat to face Simon, fighting the urge to look for the ghost at every turn. "I saw Mary tonight."

His eyes shot to hers. "In a photograph or—"

"Well, yeah, but that's not the only place I saw her."

"Elizabeth—"

"She was *there* in the parlor," Elizabeth said almost afraid to let the words out.

Simon's hands tightened on the reins. "What?"

She couldn't help but feel a chill creep up her spine and nervously looked around expecting to see the child floating along beside them. "Mary Stewart was standing in the parlor right next to you."

Elizabeth expected some remark about her corset perhaps being too tight, but instead Simon asked, "What did she look like?"

"She was pale, ghostly pale. About this tall," she said holding her hand about three and a half feet high. "With big blue eyes and a round little face. She had on a white dress and a little ribbon—"

"Blue ribbon tied to her wrist," Simon finished.

Elizabeth's goosebumps got goosebumps. "How did you know that?"

Simon shook his head. "I didn't think anything of it at the time. I thought she was just another one of the girls at the orphanage."

Elizabeth felt a chill grip her stomach. "You mean you saw Mary there?"

"Apparently."

Elizabeth pulled on her gloved fingers nervously. "I guess I should mention that I probably saw her in the woods at the cemetery too," Elizabeth added and cut off Simon before he could chide her, "I wasn't sure; it was dark and I thought my eyes were playing tricks on me. I promise though, if I see anything else, you'll be the first to know."

"How can you be sure the child we've seen is Mary?" Simon asked. She told him about the photograph Catherine showed her.

"And no one else saw her?"

Elizabeth shook her head. "No, I don't think so. It all happened so fast though. She was there one minute and poof the next."

Simon eased the buggy off the main road toward the livery stable. "Was she doing anything? Gesturing?"

"Like charades?"

Simon rolled his eyes and pulled to a stop.

Elizabeth conjured the image in her head again. "No, she was just standing there. Staring."

"At what?"

Elizabeth felt a fresh chill. "You."

Chapter Seven

SIMON PUT THE GLOBE back on the freshly lit oil lamp and closed the door to their hotel room behind him. Elizabeth fought the urge to check under the bed for ghosts.

Simon placed the lamp on the bedside table and slipped off his jacket. "It's remarkable really."

"It's creepy is what it is."

"Elizabeth," Simon said not unkindly.

She turned her back to him and he began to work on the long row of hooks at the back of her dress. "It is, after all, why we're here."

"I know."

Simon helped her lift the dress over her head and hung it in the armoire.

"Maybe I've just seen too many Spanish horror movies," Elizabeth said as she stepped out of petticoat after petticoat.

Simon unbuttoned his vest. "No doubt."

"It's just the way she was looking at you," Elizabeth said with an involuntary shiver.

"How do you mean?"

"All," Elizabeth said, wiggling her fingers in the air. "Ghosty."

Elizabeth unhooked the front of her corset and sighed happily as it fell away.

"As opposed to?" Simon asked.

"I don't know." She scratched her ribs to ease the sudden itch of finally being unconfined. "That...now, I'm here, now I'm not. Corporeal, non-corporeal. It's disconcerting."

Simon pulled down his bracers and sat down on the edge of the bed. "I imagine it's far more so for her."

Elizabeth stopped fussing with her clothes and plopped down next to him. "You're right. I'm sorry."

Simon squeezed her hand. "Don't be. We're dealing with something new. It's difficult to accept."

"You do, don't you? Accept it, I mean. That what I saw was a ghost."

"Yes," he said simply.

"That's not like you." Simon was usually the Scully and she was the Mulder.

"No, it's not," he said with a frown. "And I can't explain why exactly. I just...know it."

Poor Simon appeared utterly flummoxed at the idea of having taken something on blind faith instead of relying on his usual rigorous examination of the facts. Elizabeth kissed his cheek. "I'll be the cynic this time."

Simon laughed outright at that and then tried to pull off his boot, but it wouldn't budge. "Would you?"

Elizabeth gripped the heel of his boot and, with some effort, pulled it off, before moving to the left. "What do we do now? Wait for her to contact us again? How will we know what she needs from us?" She placed the boots by the armoire and then crawled into bed.

"We'll keep doing exactly what we have been doing." Simon finished undressing. "Learn as much as we can about her life and death and identify that man from the cemetery. Find the connection between the two."

He pulled back the covers and slipped into bed next to her. "Right."

"But now, we'd better get some rest. We have a long day ahead of us tomorrow."

Elizabeth nodded and Simon blew out the last candle. He leaned over and kissed her. "Good night, darling."

"Good night, Simon." Elizabeth rolled onto her back and sighed. "Good night, Mary."

It was a little before one in the afternoon when Simon and Elizabeth's buggy neared River Run, or at least, Simon hoped they were near. The sun blazed down onto the black roof of their little carriage and only the breeze of the journey brought relief. They'd been on the road for nearly two hours and he cursed himself for not having thought to bring along something to drink.

The road wound along the bluffs above the Mississippi, but seldom gave them a view. Tall oaks and maple trees or the grounds of a large estate obscured most of it. The inland side of the road was mostly pasture land and freshly plowed soil for the farms and plantations beyond.

Elizabeth watched another empty field go by. "I remember some of the cotton farms when I was little back in Texas. Just fields of white as far as the eye could see. Most of it's oil or gas land now."

"Everything changes," Simon said and then spotted the sign he'd been looking for. An engraved wooden sign on the edge of the road pointed down a side road. Simon eased the buggy down it.

"Well chit my chitlins and corn my pone," Elizabeth said in wonder.

The entrance to River Run was magnificent. They drove under an enormous wrought-iron arch with "RR" at the top in a fanciful script and onto the main drive to the house. Each side of the road was flanked by a row of one-hundred-year-old oak trees, their branches reaching out to each other and forming a canopy over the road. Streams of sunlight broke through gaps and gave the whole thing a golden, slightly ethereal feel.

"When they said it was beautiful, they're weren't whistling Dixie."

Simon had actually been looking forward to Elizabeth's bad Southern jokes and painful puns. Her silliness and his feigned admonishment had become part of their routine and, honestly, they both loved it. He knew she'd be disappointed if he didn't play his part and offered his best admonishing, but amused, "Elizabeth."

She simply shrugged and smiled.

It took them another minute or so before they could fully see the house beyond. Bright white and three stories tall, it was a classic ante-bellum home in the traditional Greek Revival-style. Eight massive Doric columns lined the front of the house; behind them a double-sized gallery with black trimmed railings ran the length of the house and appeared to wrap around each side. Tall black shutters stood on either side of French doors, four up and four down.

King Cotton had certainly been good to the Harpers.

Simon helped Elizabeth from the buggy and then up the steps to the oversized front door. He turned the lever for the doorbell. A few moments later the door opened.

"Mr. and Mrs. Cross calling to see the Harpers," Simon said.

The slave, an older black man with grey hair and simple black livery, bowed and invited them inside. Just as they entered the towering main foyer, Rose Harper appeared at the top of the grand staircase. "Hello, so wonderful to see you both," she called out and then quickly made her way down the stairs.

Simon hadn't had much of a chance to speak to Rose at the party last night, but she was every bit as attractive and warm as Elizabeth had said. Men had called her the most beautiful woman in Natchez. As she glided down the long staircase, tall and slender, her full skirts swaying musically, he had to concede she was quite comely. Her distinctly Southern grace and the elegance of River Run would be missed when the Old South ceased to be.

Rose reached the end of the stairs. "I was just putting Louisa down for her nap. I'm so pleased you could come."

She took Elizabeth's hands. "Are you feeling more yourself today?"

"Much better, thank you."

Seeing them together struck Simon. Despite Elizabeth's claim to the contrary, she was as lovely and as lissome as Rose. Although, perhaps, he was slightly prejudiced in his wife's favor.

"You both must be parched after that long ride. How about a nice glass of sweet tea?"

"That sounds perfect," Simon said.

Rose led them through the long main hall. "James and Elijah are on the porch out back."

As they got closer to the rear of the house Simon heard their voices, raised in argument.

"You're a fool, James. That Southern Pacific stock will triple in five years. More than that!"

"It is not your decision to make, little brother."

"The future is in the West. The first men to get there will profit, but the men who help the rest get there will be kings."

It was fascinating to hear a conversation straight from the history books. Men like Cornelius Vanderbilt and the Big Four including Huntington and Stanford were just some of the railroad barons who made a virtual mint out of the nation's westward expansion. Older brother might do well to listen to his little brother, Simon thought as he emerged onto the back veranda where the men were arguing.

"I won't give you the—" James stopped mid-sentence and cleared his throat, embarrassed. "My pardon, I didn't realize..." He glared at Elijah who didn't appear ready to let the argument drop, but a pleading look from Rose bent him to her will.

Rose called to a servant, who lingered obediently close by, and asked for fresh tea. She smiled graciously at Elizabeth and Simon and looked out at the land behind the house with unabashed affection. "Welcome to River Run."

The rear porch was really just a continuation of the massive double-deep gallery that ran all the way around the house on both upper and lower levels. The back gallery overlooked a well-manicured lawn with lush, ornamental gardens on either side. Tall trees lined the edges closest to the house and a few outbuildings were barely visible. It was an impressive estate. Every aspect was a show of power and wealth, but unlike Simon's home in England, Grey Hall, it managed to feel like an actual home as well.

Elizabeth walked to the railing and breathed in deeply. "It's beautiful."

Rose joined her. "I think so."

Shortly, the servant brought out a tray with glasses of sweet tea. It was far too sweet for Simon's taste, but it was cool and wet so he drank it gratefully. Elizabeth hummed happily and held the cold class against her cheek. "Heaven."

Eli leaned casually against the railing. "I was going to ask if you were feeling better, but I can see that you are," he added with a broad smile.

Simon swallowed his displeasure with another sip of tea. The sweetness did little to change his disposition toward Elijah Harper. It was too soon to tell if he was simply too charming for his own good or potential trouble. He had never liked men who played games with other people's affections, whether it was for business or pleasure. Whatever Elijah's end game, his attention to Elizabeth set Simon's teeth on edge.

"I can't decide which of you is prettier," Elijah said to the two women. He scratched his chin as though pondering one of the great mysteries of the universe.

Both Rose and Elizabeth blushed at the compliment. Simon felt a reflexive flash of jealousy, but ignored it. He knew he had no rival for Elizabeth's affections, but Elijah would bear watching.

James cleared his throat and forced a smile. He gestured to a set of wicker chairs and a settee. "Why don't you two rest for a few minutes? Elijah and I have some business to attend to," he added with a pointed look at his brother. "But, it shouldn't take long and, if you'd like, I'm happy to give you a tour of the plantation. If that would be of interest."

"Very much," Simon said. "Thank you."

James and Eli excused themselves, and Simon waited for Rose and Elizabeth to take seats before sitting down next to his wife.

"You have to forgive, Eli," Rose said. "He's harmless. I think he does it just to provoke my husband. Brothers, you understand. When the rest of them are here, it's a miracle the house doesn't fall down around us."

"How many Harper brothers are there?" Elizabeth asked.

"Two others surviving, although they live so far away now we don't see them very often. There were six boys when I was a girl. Of course, the Lord has seen fit to take a few to Him since then. All three Harper sisters have been lost to us."

"Nine children?" Elizabeth said. And five of them dead now, Simon thought.

"Yes," Rose said. "I also come from a large family. Seven brothers and three sisters. They're all in Charleston and Richmond and spread all over. I do miss them, dearly." She looked down at her hands folded neatly in her lap. "I always wanted a large family myself, but some things are just not meant to be."

The melancholy in her voice was palpable.

Both Simon and Elizabeth were only children. It was difficult to imagine growing up in a household with so many siblings, although, large families were much more commonplace in this time period. A woman could easily give birth every year or year and a half for ten or twenty years.

"I hope we'll get a chance to meet Louisa later," Elizabeth said.

Just the mention of the girl's name and Rose shed her grief. "Yes, of course."

As promised, James and Elijah returned to join them about twenty minutes later. Simon could still feel the tension between the two men; perhaps it never abated. Rose had a minor crisis with the house staff that had to be taken care of and begged off and the rest made their way around the back of the house and through one of the gardens.

"River Run is just under 2000 acres right now. We have one hundred field hands and can produce nearly 1000 bales of cotton per season. Although, I hope to do better," James said as he gave them the overview of the plantation. He was particularly proud of his slave-to-bale ratio and overall crop value when it came time to market.

Simon was about to ask a question, when he felt Elizabeth squeeze his arm. He looked down and she nodded toward a patch in the garden with the same blue flowers they'd seen at Mary's grave. Without knowing more about the scarcity of the flower, it was hardly conclusive evidence. For all he knew, those flowers could be in every garden in Natchez.

"Of course," James continued. "We have other holdings. My brothers grow rice in Yemassee, South Carolina and sugar over in the Ascension Parish. But my heart is here in River Run."

They had emerged from the garden and into a clearing with multiple outbuildings, including, Simon realized, a massive stable.

James spoke to one of the grooms, who hurried inside. He turned to Simon and Elizabeth. "I assume you both ride."

"Have you met a Texan who can't?" Elizabeth said with a smile.

What on earth was she thinking? There was reckless and then there was Elizabeth. Why did she always seem to go out of her way to find dangerous situations to explore? Simon shot her a sharp look that she studiously ignored.

"Very good." James said.

He glanced at Simon who nodded, reluctantly. "Something gentle for my wife, please. Her skills are not as sharp as her wit." He ignored the face she gave him.

Elijah and James walked into the stables leaving Simon and Elizabeth alone.

Simon leaned down and said in a tense whisper. "Exactly when did you learn how to ride?"

Elizabeth shrugged diffidently, but Simon knew she was putting on an act. "I've ridden," she said. "Some."

Maybe the heat had finally gotten to her?

"My father and I used to practically live at the race track," Elizabeth said too casually. "The trainers used to let me ride the horses all the time."

Simon narrowed his eyes. "A small girl on a racehorse?"

"Okay, so they led the horse around the paddock, but technically I was riding." She patted his arm in an attempt to soothe him.

Simon snorted.

James and Eli came out of the stables discussing the health of one of the horses. It seemed James' horse was nursing a sore leg and wasn't ready to be ridden yet. Two grooms led several horses out behind them.

"If you think I'm going to be left behind, you can forget it," Elizabeth whispered. "And I rode a pony at the fair once, too," Elizabeth added with arched brow as she started toward them.

"In a dress?"

She stumbled a bit and glared over her shoulder before continuing on. Simon would have laughed if it weren't her neck on the line.

James had chosen a handsome chestnut for Simon and a large broad-backed strawberry roan for Elizabeth. The groom led Elizabeth's horse to a mounting block. Simon saw her swallow hard as she looked at the two horned, off-center sidesaddle.

Simon came up behind and whispered in her ear. "Put your right leg over the top pommel and the ball of your left foot in the stirrup. Keep your hips square to the horse; don't lean to the left."

"Right. The chalice from the palace has the brew that is true."

"Elizabeth."

She lifted her skirts and climbed up the stairs. Thankfully, the old roan was as still and as calm as could be. Elizabeth mounted and managed, barely, not to slide off the other side.

"Easy peasy," she said with a shuddering wiggle in her seat.

Simon patted the horse's neck. "Let him do the work. At least he knows what he's doing. And for God's sake, be careful."

Finally, she seemed to hear the genuine distress in his voice and nodded reassuringly.

Not reassured, but with little choice, Simon mounted his horse as James and Elijah did. It wasn't until then that Simon noticed Elijah's black mare. It had a broad white blaze down the center of its face. Remarkably like the one on the horse they'd seen the man riding that night in the cemetery. Of course, like the flowers, a white blaze was hardly unique. Simon hadn't been able to get a close enough look to be sure it was the same one. Separately, each clue was hardly incriminating, but together…

Simon looked to Elizabeth to see if she'd noticed, but she was distracted by Elijah turning circles around her.

"This way," James said and led their little procession from the stable and paddock area. Behind the long buildings was an expansive vegetable garden.

They passed through a courtyard complex where separate buildings housed the kitchen, which was separated from the main house for fear of fire, the smokehouse, chicken house, store house, dairy, laundry and a large cistern with water reserves. Beyond them were several barns and holding pens.

"This is our ice house," James said proudly, nodding toward a single-story brick building with a pitched roof. "All brick, even the pit. Took months to finish, but it provides far better insulation against our Southern summers. Ours is one of the largest in Mississippi, I understand."

It was constantly surprising how primitive some things were in this time. It was such a little thing in modern life, but with no refrigeration, Southerners had to import blocks of ice from the North and store them in large underground ice houses. Only the wealthy could afford such a luxury as ice in the summer.

"Have you ever had a real mint julep?" Eli asked Elizabeth as he rode beside her. "Don't answer that, because you haven't until you've had one of mine. I'll make you one later that'll put tears in your eyes."

Elizabeth laughed, delighted. Simon gripped his reins more tightly and reminded himself that they were there to help someone, not to murder someone.

They left the house yards and passed the cotton gin house where the seeds were pulled out of the cotton lint. It was a corkscrew-like contraption with a shingled roof and a box at the bottom. Two long, wooden beams angled down from the top toward the ground.

"What's that?" Elizabeth asked.

"Our cotton press," James said. "We hitch mules to the buzzard wings and it turns the screw, pressing the cotton down into bales. We hope to have another by next fall."

They turned onto a long dirt road. One side was pastureland and the other held a row of small, identical buildings.

"Our slave quarters," James said. "We take pride in taking care of our people."

Simon hardly considered the hovels he saw before him as anything he would consider taking care of someone. He supposed there were far worse slave quarters to be seen elsewhere though. At least these appeared to be well-maintained, for what they were.

Each house was roughly fifteen-feet square with thatched roofs and a single chimney. Fences separated small pigpens and gardens between them. A group of thirty or more slaves stood in a line in front of an open tent just ahead. Each slave took off his hat and bowed his head respectfully as their party passed.

"We provide clothing twice a year and our doctor," James said nodding toward the end of the tent, "Dr. Walker, comes once a month to make sure they're all fit and healthy. A sick slave can lead to twenty before you know it and half your crop rots in the field."

Simon grunted in agreement and swallowed the bile in his throat. It was hard to accept. To look at these men and women, and, God help them, children, and know their fate and be helpless to do anything was more difficult than he ever could have imagined. If he hadn't known better, it would be easy to look at them as poor workers, hardly different in any age, except for one glaring detail. They lacked one essential right—freedom.

"Excuse me for a moment," James said. "Dr. Walker!" He steered his horse over to the front of the tent.

A large man came out of the tent wiping his hands on a dirty towel that he casually tossed, without even looking, toward one of the slaves that stood nearby. His hair and beard were streaked with grey and Simon guessed his age at late-forties, perhaps fifty. His crisp white shirtsleeves were rolled up to the elbow. He carried himself with an assurance that crossed well over the border into cocksure. A single glance over his shoulder at the slaves waiting their turn had them nervously and quickly averting their eyes. It was abundantly clear that they feared him. If it was possible to dislike a man before meeting him, this was the one.

"James," he said, in a deep melodious voice, as he reached up to shake Harper's hand.

"I hope you'll be staying for dinner," James said.

"You know I can't turn down Missy's crackling bread. Or your good bourbon." He patted a hand over his stomach.

"Good. We'll see you back at the house then," James said and with a tip of his hat rejoined them on the dirt road.

The doctor called out sharply for the next slave who shuffled reluctantly into the tent.

They left the road and cut across the property. Although cotton was River Run's cash crop, there were hundreds of acres set aside for fodder crops for the livestock—hay, barley, corn and wheat. Other fields were earmarked for cultivating vegetables such as sweet potatoes, pumpkins, peas and collard greens. Other than the farm equipment, items for the big house and the slaves' clothing, about which James made a point of detailing the great effort and cost he took to import from Boston, the entire plantation was self-sufficient.

"All of this and the fields back behind that copse of trees," James said as they stopped alongside an enormous field with row after row of upturned soil, "will be cotton in the fall. All except that swamp over there. Nothing grows in the swamp."

Simon could see it in his mind's eye. The tall brown stalks with tufts of white as far as the eye could see. Dozens of field hands doing the backbreaking work of hand-picking each boll.

"Our land is perfectly suited to its aim," James said, shifting in his saddle. "We are out-producing most of our neighbors by ten percent. There's a tract of land just up river that would allow us to expand our operation and increase that divide. With more slaves and some hard work, we could be a 2000 bale plantation by next year. Of course, ready capital is always in short supply."

So that was it, Simon thought. At first, he'd simply thought James was proud to show him around their plantation, but Simon knew a pitch when he heard one. He glanced over to Elizabeth who was being distracted and entertained by Elijah. Perhaps that had been part of the plan all along. Eli would occupy Elizabeth leaving James free to woo Simon and his money.

"Two thousand," Simon mused aloud, baiting his own hook, "and the price per pound?"

"Fourteen cents. That'll rise this year, I'm sure. And with an average of 500 pounds per bale…"

Simon did some quick math. "At fifteen cents for 2000 bales, that's…$150,000."

James looked off at the distance. "Mm-hmm. All there for the taking." He turned his horse around. "Should we start back?"

This was a fortuitous change of events, Simon thought. In an instant, he'd gone from burdensome guest to potential investor. Now, James' rush of hospitality made more sense and it gave Simon leverage in the relationship he'd sorely needed. One could only push their host so far, but a wealthy, would-be partner could demand much more. Invitations, access, and information suddenly became much easier to acquire. Simon allowed himself a small smile.

They stopped to water their horses at a small, clear stream that fed a shady pond hidden back in the woods off the main road. It was late afternoon by the time they returned to the house. Simon dismounted and walked over to Elizabeth who was busy trying to figure out how to get down.

Simon held up his arms. "Just make sure your dress doesn't snag." He caught her as she slid down the saddle with an audible "oof".

She'd done well, but he could see from the pained look on her face that it had come at a cost. "They don't call it a charley horse for nothing," Simon said.

"Very funny. I'm going to need a long bath and an even longer massage if I'm ever going to be human again."

Simon leaned down and whispered, "I can't promise you the bath, but the massage…"

Elizabeth smiled and made a thrumming sound that made Simon's pulse race. Maybe he could find that bathtub after all? Did they make tubs for two in 1850?

"Did you find out anything interesting from James? All Eli wanted to talk about were his racehorses and how beautiful I am."

"Poor butterfly."

Elizabeth shrugged and tried to look pious. "I struggled through."

Simon chuckled. "I didn't find out anything interesting about Mary, but I think we've found our 'in' to local society."

Elizabeth arched an eyebrow, but didn't ask any questions as James came over to them. "Shall we go back to the house?"

When they walked up the back steps to the house Rose met them. "I was wondering when you all would come back. Did James take you all the way to kingdom come? You must be exhausted," she said to Elizabeth. "Come upstairs for a rest. I'll have some lemonade sent up." She turned to Simon, offering him a knowing smile. "I'm sure you men have plenty to talk about."

Chapter Eight

Elizabeth felt silly having a stranger help her take her dress off, but considering how hot and tired she was, she probably would have let Jack the Ripper do it if it meant a little freedom from her clothes. The housemaid helped her out of her dress and then, mercifully, loosened her corset just enough. She closed the heavy drapes and left a tray with cool lemonade on it, finally shutting the door to the upstairs bedroom behind her and leaving Elizabeth alone in the quiet.

She drank down a glass and looked around the room. Like everything else at River Run, it was beautiful with pale blue walls and a large four-poster bed. There was also a long chaise, called a fainting couch, and now she knew why. Between the heat, her layers of clothes and the corset, she was ready to plotz.

She sat down on the couch and lay back. The room was still and quiet and the heat still pressed down on her. It was only moments before she drifted off to sleep.

The doctor had finished his work and joined the men on the back porch for a drink and a smoke while the ladies rested. Eli and James continued to prod each other. There was genuine brotherly affection there, but also a genuine animosity. The doctor, knowing which side buttered his bread, sided with James on almost every point, although his interest in the subjects was minimal at best. His focus stayed on the drink in one hand and the cigar in the other.

"I understand," James said to Simon, "that you are a baron of some sort."

"A baronet."

"Should we call you Sir?" the doctor asked with more than a twinge of sarcasm.

"No," Simon said. "When I took an American wife, I took the country as well. I don't see the need for an artifice such as a title." He glanced over at the doctor. "A man commands respect by who he is and not what someone calls him, Doctor." Simon saw the flint in the doctor's eyes and turned his attention back to the brothers. "I appreciate that in America a man is who he makes himself to be for good or for bad."

Eli raised his glass in salute.

"Within reason, I suppose," James said. "There is a downside to so much freedom. Too much in some cases. Your people, the English, know their places. The lower classes don't expect to live like kings, the workers know their work and they take pride in it. Here, everyone's got their heads in the clouds. Better yourself, of course, but within reason. Your class system keeps things in line. Keeps expectations where they should be. Keeps people from reaching for things they will never have."

Simon was quite familiar with this line of thinking. Nobles and Lords had used it for years to justify the antiquated system that kept them in power. "No one loves the status quo quite so much as the people at the top of the pyramid."

"Why shouldn't they reach?" Elijah asked.

James shook his head. "Imagine the chaos if dockworkers suddenly decided to be councilmen or the farmers turned lawyers? People are made to be what they are."

"I'm not sure I agree with that," Simon said.

Elijah sat up a little straighter and couldn't keep the smile from his face.

"We've all known wealthy, well-positioned men who are, to put it kindly, imbeciles, have we not?"

They all smiled and nodded.

"How do you think my father made all of his money?"

They all laughed and Simon continued, "Conversely, there are men who were born to a lower station, but are capable, with hard work, of achieving more. I think a man should always seek to improve himself and his fortune."

Elijah raised his glass in salute. "Here, here." He drank it down and slumped back into his chair.

Simon glanced at him and then back to James. "I also have no patience for the idle rich. Hard work is not just a poor man's burden."

James glared at his brother and then smiled at Simon. "You're quite right. Of course, all of this is entirely different for Negroes."

The doctor rolled his cigar thoughtfully between his meaty thumb and forefinger. "Slaves lack the natural ability to understand their situation in all its complexity. Give them difficult choices and a slave trembles in fear and self-doubt. I have seen it. They have neither the mental acuity nor the moral cohesiveness required for such things."

Simon had to bite his tongue to keep himself from skewering the doctor for spouting such appalling idiocy.

James nodded in agreement with the doctor. "Exactly. Those factories in the North take advantage of those simple, poor souls. I've heard stories that would make your skin crawl. Worse than pigs to slaughter. Giving *them* false hope of things beyond them is cruel to my way of thinking. We have an obligation to care for our lessers, to provide for them."

Simon knew it would be impossible to change the man's mind, and he could ill-afford to make him an enemy. "A happy and healthy workforce is a productive one?"

"Precisely," James said. "Productive. And everyone wins."

Everyone sitting here certainly does, Simon thought. One saving grace of this patriarchal attitude of James', Simon realized, was that it also led to charity. "I was glad to hear that your generous nature extends beyond your people to the rest of Natchez. Your generosity to the Children's Home, for instance."

"A worthy cause," James said modestly. "Dr. Walker volunteers there as well."

Dr. Walker took a puff from his cigar and narrowed his eyes slightly. "I do, on occasion."

"Mrs. Nolan spoke about the good doctor on our tour," Simon said. "My wife and I heard about the home and wanted to see it for ourselves. We have more money than we need and are considering establishing one like it in Texas or perhaps England."

The doctor nodded, disinterested.

"Mrs. Nolan praised your hard work, Doctor. Even mentioned that you brought in one of the children yourself, a young girl, not long ago," Simon said and pretended to search his memory. "Mary Stewart, I think it was."

The doctor found the bottom of his glass far more interesting and didn't bother to look up from it. "I do what I can. I am a skilled physician," the doctor said with no trace of humility false or otherwise, "but even some things are beyond my abilities."

"She'd been abandoned?" Simon said.

"It's possible, but I really don't remember."

"She *died* three days ago," Simon said, feeling his anger rise. "Does that jog your memory?"

"As a doctor, I deal with death on a regular basis. I am hard-pressed to remember them all. Cherub-faced or not." The doctor bowed his head toward James. "Your lovely daughter excluded, of course."

Simon couldn't think of anything to say that wasn't punctuated with a fist in the good doctor's face. "Of course," he said and let the topic shift again. Between Elijah's indolence and improper attention to Elizabeth, James' bigotry and weakness, and the doctor's possible sociopathic tendencies, Simon felt the distinct beginnings of a headache coming on.

ELIZABETH WOKE FROM HER nap and rang for the housemaid. Once she was strapped back into her corset and fluffed and primped enough for polite society, she left her room to rejoin Simon and the others. She had just closed her door when she saw a little girl poke her head out of a room at the far end of the landing.

"Hello?"

The little girl smiled and moved out into the doorway. She stood there biting her lip and twisting at the waist as little girls sometimes do when they're curious and unsure. "Hello."

The girl was pretty and a little pudgy. She had a little girl potbelly and a heart-shaped face. "You must be Louisa," Elizabeth said as she walked over to her.

The girl gnawed at the inside of her lip and nodded.

"My name's Elizabeth. My, that is a pretty dress. Did your mother pick it out for you?"

Louisa nodded again and plucked at the small tulle flowers that decorated the front of her dress. "Mama ordered it all the way from Paris, France. That's in Europe."

"That's really far."

Louisa took Elizabeth's hand and led her into her bedroom. "I went there once when I was a baby, but I don't remember it."

The bedroom was white and bright, and filled with toys and dolls and everything a little girl's room should be filled with. A dark mahogany children's bed with a tall backboard and white gauzy mosquito netting sat in the far corner of the room. A pint-sized table and chairs were frozen in mid-tea party.

She dropped Elizabeth's hand. "Do you like dolls?"

"Very much. Some of my best friends are dolls."

Louisa ran over to the tea party and introduced Elizabeth to each doll. Each doll had a finely hand-painted porcelain face and a dress as fancy as any Elizabeth had. Finally, Louisa lifted the covering over a miniature pram and pulled out an odd cloth doll. It had a rough hand-sewn quality to it and the clothing was coarse material in bright colors. It looked almost Mexican or even Caribbean.

"Who's this?" Elizabeth asked.

"Jammy," Louisa said. "She came all the way from J-Jam…"

"Jamaica," a voice said from the door. Rose smiled and said it again. "Jamaica. Your father brought that back for you, do you remember?"

Louisa smiled and nodded.

"Did you rest well?" Rose asked Elizabeth.

"I did, thank you. Louisa was just kind enough to give me a tour of her beautiful bedroom."

Rose walked over to her daughter and touched her hair. She smiled down at the child with such love and tenderness it made Elizabeth feel awkward and perhaps a little envious. "It's time for supper, darling. I'm afraid I have to take Miss Elizabeth away."

"Can she come back? I didn't even get to introduce her to the rest."

Rose smiled patiently and then looked to Elizabeth. "I hope so."

Rose not only sounded sincere, but there seemed to be a bit of longing in her voice as well. Elizabeth could only imagine how lonely it must be as the only woman at River Run. "I'd like to very much."

"I was going to ask you later, but we are having a few festivities this weekend to celebrate the end of the planting season. We'd love to have you come. Stay for the long weekend? Saves you that horrible drive back into Natchez."

"Thank you," Elizabeth said. "I'll have to check with Simon, of course."

"Of course," Rose said with a hopeful smile.

Elizabeth winked. "But I think I can handle him."

Rose laughed, but when she spoke there was a twinge of envy. "I have no doubt."

THE SUN BEGAN TO set on the far side of the river and James and the doctor excused themselves to go over the doctor's reports of his examinations before dinner. Elijah asked to join them, but James insisted he not leave their guest alone. Simon assured them he'd be fine and wished to stretch his legs with a walk before dinner. Thankfully, they agreed and left him to his own devices.

Simon was not used to being so social and he'd had just about his fill of the Harpers and Dr. Walker. God help him, he didn't know how he was going to tolerate dinner. Elizabeth would have to carry them both tonight. He was completely out of small talk.

The grounds of River Run were just the tonic he needed. They were quiet and peaceful and not one of the trees had an opinion or wanted his. He stopped and leaned against a magnolia and breathed in deeply. The magnolia tree's sweet, lemony scent filled the air. The heat from the day was dissipating and a cool breeze began to blow. The yellow light of the setting sun made the Spanish moss hanging from the trees look like spun gold. It was beautiful and he wished Elizabeth were with him. She'd be sorry she missed it.

He pushed himself away from the tree and started to turn toward the garden when he saw her. A small round face poked out from behind a tree and then hid again as though she were playing hide and seek and afraid of being caught. Mary.

Slowly, he walked toward the tree. She peeked around the edge again, blue eyes wide and frightened. His heart beat so fast in his chest he was sure she could hear it. He swallowed and took a deep breath to calm himself before saying, "Hello."

Her eyes grew even wider, but she didn't hide again.

He stopped walking. "My name is Simon. You're Mary, aren't you?"

She just continued to stare at him as if he was the ghost and she was the living being.

"Mary?" he said again.

Slowly, she stepped out from behind the tree. She was so small and frightened and pale. He hadn't gotten a good look at her at the orphanage. What he'd thought was a white dress was a nightgown and her body wasn't just small, but frail and trembling.

"I'm here to help you."

Her eyes danced all over his body, trying to take all of him in, torn between wonder and disbelief.

"Can you speak?"

She didn't answer. It wasn't even clear that she knew what he was saying.

"If I'm going to help you, you're going to have to do more than stare at me."

Mary looked around the woods, her eyes searching for something, until, suddenly she ran off toward the garden. Simon stood and followed after her. She weaved in and out amongst the flowers until she reached a small pergola with vibrant blue flowers. The same flowers the man left at the cemetery. He even noticed a freshly cut stem. The flowers had come from River Run. But why? Who was the man and what did Mary mean to him?

Simon knelt down. "I don't know how to help you. Help me understand."

Mary took an uncertain step forward. Slowly, she lifted her hand and reached out to him. Simon held out his hand to mirror hers. Tentatively, she took a small step forward and their hands moved closer to each other.

"I won't hurt you."

Her tiny fingers brushed against his and Simon felt an overwhelming rush of emotion. He closed his eyes to try to keep it away. He'd never felt so much sadness and confusion. It was like a wave crashing over him. A dark wave of despair so heavy it took his breath away. His heart beat faster, louder, the sound echoing in his ears, until the rush of blood and her pain were almost all he could hear and feel.

"Mr. Cross!"

In an instant, the connection was gone. Mary was gone. The oppressive emotions that had choked him moments ago faded quickly. Simon turned around to see a slave standing over him, shaking him by the shoulder.

"What are you doing?" Simon bit out, knocking his hand away.

The slave took a step back. "I thought maybe you was ill, suh. I'm sorry, I…"

The sense of anguish felt like no more than a dream now, but Simon still had to struggle to control his emotions. "I'm fine."

"I been standin' right here while you was talkin' to the flowers—"

"I'm fine," Simon said more sharply than he meant to. The poor man was obviously frightened he'd done something wrong and would be punished for it. Simon lowered his voice. "Thank you, I'm sorry. I'm fine."

It took Simon a moment to realize, too, that if the man had been standing there, right behind him, he should have been able to see Mary, but he hadn't.

"They ask me to come find you," the man said. "Dinner be ready shortly."

Simon clasped the man on the shoulder in an effort to reassure him. He could feel the man wince in anticipation of a far less friendly gesture.

"Thank you," Simon said. "I'll be right there."

The slave nodded confused and still uneasy, and hurried back to the big house.

Simon lingered for a moment, but he knew Mary wouldn't be back. Not tonight. But he spoke to the empty air regardless. "I will help you, Mary. I swear it."

CHAPTER NINE

"ARE YOU SURE I can't get you more?" Catherine asked.

Elizabeth shook her head. Catherine had kindly invited them over to Cypress Hill for lunch and Elizabeth had eaten more than her share. She sipped the cool sweet tea and enjoyed a breeze as they sat in the garden.

"Thank you though," Simon said. "It was very kind of you to have us."

Catherine laughed. "I'm not sure if you've noticed but I'm not the most popular girl in Natchez. More people are going than coming. I'm pleased to have the company. And I do hope you'll come to the ball next week. My father takes the Veterans' Spring Gala quite seriously."

Elizabeth smiled. "We'd be very pleased to. Everyone's been so kind and it's so beautiful. All of Natchez is," she said and then, feeling an opening, added. "There's an odd feeling to it though. Maybe it's the river or I've read too many stories."

Catherine frowned, confused.

"My wife believes in ghosts," Simon said with a tolerant sigh that set their plan into motion.

After his encounter with Mary, he and Elizabeth had discussed the best way to ferret out more information about any other local supernatural occurrences or paranormal specialists. If they'd been in New Orleans, they could have simply visited Marie Laveau or any of a dozen other voodoo priestesses or mystics. But Natchez was not New Orleans and a more circumspect approach was needed.

"I assured her there are no such things," Simon said convincingly. "The noises we heard along the road…"

Catherine leaned back in her chair and tilted her head. "Don't be sure. Now, I've never seen one myself, but I have heard stories that make you wonder."

Elizabeth leaned forward eagerly. "Stories?"

"Her other weakness," Simon said with a smile.

Catherine's eyes lit up and she rang the bell on the table summoning a servant. She asked that Abraham come out to speak with them. "There's a story he told me when we were little together. I haven't forgotten it, but he tells it better."

A moment later, Abraham came out and stood by the table.

"Abraham, you remember the Crosses," Catherine said.

The way she said it was so familiar, so casual, as if all four of them were old friends.

Abraham nodded and waited, obviously wondering why he'd been summoned.

"Tell them the story of Osay," Catherine said.

Abraham shook his head and glanced back to the house. "Now, Miss Catherine, your father warned us about that. He doesn't take to those sorts of stories."

"It's a good thing he isn't here then, isn't it?" She waved him on and it was clear he had no choice.

Abraham cleared his throat and began. "Osay was a great African warrior and leader to his people. They loved him and he loved them. But he loved no one as much as his wife and unborn child. He loved the child so much he would speak to it every night and one night, the unborn child spoke back to him. It said, 'The water will take you home.'"

Abraham frowned and shook his head. "Now, Osay didn't know what that meant, but the words, they stayed with him all that night and all the day. He kissed his wife goodbye and he and a few other men went out on a hunt to feed their families, but they never come back. Men captured them and drug them to the river. They put Osay in shackles that cut into his wrists and his throat. The river gave way to the great ocean and a great ship. Osay and his men, and women and children he had never seen before, sailed across the world in the darkness of the ship's belly. Many people died, but Osay lived and he heard his unborn child's voice every night, 'The water will take you home.'"

Elizabeth was starting to feel the chills as Abraham continued the story, more Osay than Abraham now. "Months passed without the sun, until finally Osay was pulled from the dark below into the dark above and the frightened men and women children cried as they were pulled apart. Osay was sold to a man up river from here. A cruel man who kept them chained. Osay labored for his master during the day and dreamt of his home during the night, until one day he could stand no more."

Abraham stood up a little taller, his eyes bright with anger and passion. "Late one day, while the white bosses argued with each other, Osay turned and whispered to the man chained next to him and on down the line it went. Tears filled some of their eyes, but they nodded. Slowly, Osay led them into the swamp whispering 'The water will take us home.'"

Abraham stopped for a moment, as if the images were too vivid and too painful. He swallowed hard and kept on. "The masters didn't realize until it was too late. Osay led them into the shallow waters. The white men yelled at them, but they gave no heed. They all were saying it now, together, as they walked deeper into the water. 'The water will take us home.' Then, the chains and the voices stopped and the white men watched as Osay and his people sank into the dark water, never to return."

Elizabeth's heart was pounding and Abraham broke from the spell he'd wove. "To this day, they say you can hear the chains at night in that swamp. That you can hear their voices whispering, 'The water will take you home.'"

Catherine shivered. "I know people who have heard those voices. Up by River Run."

Simon and Elizabeth exchanged quick, uneasy glances. Had other people seen Mary or were there more ghosts to contend with?

"Thank you, Abraham," Elizabeth said. "I knew there was something up there. Do you know any other stories?"

Abraham shifted uncomfortably. "I know a few, but if you want to learn more about haints and such, Old Nan is the one who should do the tellin'."

"Old Nan?" Simon asked.

"She's an old slave over on the Parson's plantation. Bit of a local legend," Catherine said. "Do you think we could see her?"

Abraham gave Simon and Elizabeth a shrewd and appraising look. "I suppose, but you have to promise you won't tell the Colonel, Miss Catherine. He wouldn't like it. Not like it at all."

The Stantons' fancy barouche carriage, with a driver at the front and Abraham standing on the back, took them to the Parson's plantation. When they arrived Catherine got permission for the four of them to go visit Old Nan in her cottage. She'd been the nanny to the current owner when he was just a boy. One summer he nearly died from Scarlet Fever and might have, if Old Nan hadn't taken care of him. She caught the disease and then some sort of brain fever had caused her to go blind. Elizabeth knew that like Mary Ingalls, Nan had suffered from viral meningoencephalitis. Either way, the result was the sadly the same. The family had taken care of her, setting her up in a small house near the other slave quarters and ensuring the others cared for her.

They approached the small, wood cabin and Abraham asked them to wait there. He disappeared inside and then returned and invited them in. They climbed up the wobbly, planked steps and into the dark room. A frail old woman, who looked like she was in her seventies, waved a thin hand at Abraham and he lit two candles that sat on the rough-hewn mantle above the small fireplace.

It wasn't cold inside, but Elizabeth shivered anyway. She felt like she'd walked onto the set of Beloved. Hopefully, their story had a happier ending.

Old Nan's eyes were milky white, but she sought out Simon and Elizabeth and looked them up and down before speaking. "You are strange to me. In and out at de same time, here and not here."

As if she could see their confusion, she nodded and smiled patiently as she leaned back in her chair. "Abraham say you come to hear about de ghosts. You one of dem writer people from de newsypaper?"

"No," Elizabeth said. "I just, we—"

She wasn't sure how to ask what was needed.

Nan nodded. "You take Miss Catherine and you wait outside, Abraham."

He looked nervously to Catherine and Simon who assured him that they'd be fine.

"Yessuh," he said and started for the door, shuffling a reluctant Catherine back out the door.

Once the door had closed, Old Nan smoothed out the blanket that covered her legs and rocked back in her rocking chair. "Now, your heart can speak."

Elizabeth cast an unsure glance at Simon who nodded encouragingly.

"You come 'bout a child," Nan said.

Elizabeth swallowed hard and nodded, then realized the woman couldn't see her. "Yes, how did you know?"

"You carry it with you."

Elizabeth looked around the room quickly. "The ghost?"

Old Nan laughed. "No, child. Your burden."

"I don't understand," Simon said.

"I sure you don't," Old Nan said. "But you will. In time."

Simon frowned. "We were told that you were knowledgeable about such matters and could help us with our quandary."

Nan frowned and tilted her head to the side.

"We were told you could help us," Elizabeth clarified.

Nan nodded slowly and stopped rocking. Her pale eyes drifted between Simon and Elizabeth. "I see what others cain't. Dey's dis world and d'other. I don't see so good in dis one, but I can still see. And de spirits, dey know and come to me sometime when dey sad or feelin' lonesome."

Elizabeth remembered Simon's description of his encounter and her heart ached for the child. "Has Mary come to you?"

"Mary?"

"Mary Stewart. She died a few days ago and yet," Simon said. "I've seen her. We've both seen her."

Nan nodded again. Elizabeth could tell Simon was growing anxious. He was impatient under the best of circumstances and cryptic mystics definitely pushed his buttons.

"We think she needs our help," Elizabeth said. "We'd like to help her, but we don't know what to do."

Nan brought her fingers to her lips in thought and then slowly started to rock again. "Sometimes de children don't know what be wrong. Dey's scared and alone. I show dem de way when I can. But some is needin' somethin' I cain't give. Mary, she be in de wrong place. She need you to help her be somewhere else."

"How? Where?" Simon asked.

Nan looked at Simon and then at Elizabeth. If she didn't know better, she would swear the woman could see. Nan shook her head. "Don't rightly know yet. And time ain't on our side."

Elizabeth didn't like the sound of that. "What do you mean?"

"It take a whole passel a strength to be here, where dey shouldn't be. Dey sorta fade away and once dey's gone, we cain't do nothin' for 'em."

"What happens to them?"

Nan stopped rocking again. Her pale eyes seeking out something invisible in the distance. "You ever feel a cold chill on a warm day? Or hear a cry caught in de wind?" She looked back at them. "Dat's all dat's left. Po things. Dey's betwixt and between forever."

Chapter Ten

Both Simon and Elizabeth were content to let Catherine do most of the talking as they rode back into town. It was nearly dark by the time they arrived. Simon and Elizabeth thanked Catherine and Abraham again, retrieved their buggy and drove back to their hotel. Neither spoke much. The visit with Old Nan had left them both feeling a little introspective.

Simon stopped at the restaurant and ordered food to be sent up to their room. Thankfully, he'd had the foresight to take a bottle of wine and two glasses with him to tide them over until the food arrived.

As he opened the bottle, Elizabeth shed her layers of clothing, put on a robe and splashed her face with water to cleanse it from the day's dust.

Simon handed her a glass of wine. "Better?"

Elizabeth nodded and sat on the sofa in their sitting room. She tucked her legs up under and sipped her wine. Elizabeth tried to ignore the feeling of melancholia that had settled over her, and judging from Simon's thoughtful expression, it had taken him, too. It wasn't bad enough that poor Mary had died so young, but now, if they couldn't find a way to help her, she might be lost forever.

Simon sat down on the sofa and sighed.

"I've been thinking about Old Nan," Elizabeth said. Simon hmm'd in agreement. "Do you think she's some sort of psychopomp?"

Simon nodded thoughtfully. "Like Anubis or Charon? A guide for souls to the afterlife." He paused for a moment. "It is possible. There are stories of guides or doulas in virtually every culture. I had always considered them…wishful thinking, a chimera to ease the fear of the unknown."

"And now?"

Simon smiled and shook his head. "After what I've seen, what I've felt, the last few days, I think I was, as you might say, full of it."

Elizabeth laughed. "I wouldn't say that." Simon glared playfully at her and she laughed again. "It's normal, and rational, by the way, to disbelieve until shown otherwise. I've always thought I was the nutty one for believing things without any proof at all."

Simon didn't argue with that. He just smiled and took a sip of his wine before setting it on the side table.

"You're supposed to say, no, darling, you're not nutty at all."

Simon chuckled. "Am I?"

Elizabeth narrowed her eyes.

"No, darling, you're not…nutty at all."

"It's too late now."

Simon faked a wounded expression. "How can I make it up to you?"

Elizabeth pulled her legs from underneath her. She shifted on the sofa and stuck her legs out toward him and wiggled her toes. Simon chuckled and pulled her feet into his lap. His strong warm hands started to massage the aching arch of her left foot and Elizabeth practically purred. Dr. Scholl could not be born soon enough.

She relished the feeling for a moment before coming back to the matter at hand. "If Old Nan is a doula for the afterlife, I hope she can help us understand what Mary wants."

"To be somewhere else," Simon recited.

"Yeah, but does that mean somewhere else in the afterlife, like crossing over or somewhere else here?"

Simon's forehead creased in thought. "Another grave?"

"You mean like grave robbing?"

Simon stopped massaging her foot and looked at her like she was a backward child. "Of course not. Just relocating."

"Maybe we're being too literal. What if she needs to be elsewhere emotionally, spiritually?"

Simon's hands stopped moving as he thought. "She is frightened and confused."

A dark cloud covered his face and Elizabeth could see him struggle with his emotions at the memory of his encounter with the girl.

He stared off, unfocused. "She's so terribly sad and so very small."

Elizabeth shifted and scooted down the sofa. Simon lifted his arm and she snuggled into his side and rested her hand on his chest.

Simon let out a deep breath and pulled her closer. "Why did it have to be a child?"

SIMON STEPPED ASIDE AS the man stumbled through the front doors of Smiley's Saloon. The man reeked of cheap whisky and even cheaper cigars. His cheeks were flushed as he struggled to stand and stuff in the tail of his shirt. He grinned sloppily at Simon and tripped his way down the steps to the street below. It was eleven o'clock in the morning.

More than ever, Simon was glad Elizabeth wasn't here. It was definitely for the best. Not that she shared the opinion. She'd made that loud and clear this morning.

Last night they'd agreed that they couldn't afford to wait for Mary to make another appearance. Even if she did, there was no guarantee they'd learn anything more than they had before. If she couldn't communicate with them, all they'd gain was another touch of her pain. Simon needed no reminder of her misery. With little hope learning from her in death, that meant, investigating her life. Starting with her parents.

Simon and Elizabeth visited the catholic priest they'd first seen at the cemetery. He knew little of Alice Stewart. She had no friends he knew of, certainly if she had, they would have been at her child's funeral. All he knew was that she had apparently worked in a local saloon as a hostess. It was his understanding that she hadn't worked there in some time though, but a cold trail was better than none.

It had taken some persuading to convince Elizabeth that she shouldn't come along. A woman like her in a place like that would draw far too much attention. Finally, she'd seen the wisdom in it, although knowing it was the right approach did little to calm her frustration. After listening to a diatribe on the general failings of men as a gender, Simon had promised he'd be careful, and set off to the seedier side of town.

Watching the drunk weave his way down the street, he knew he had certainly found it.

Simon pushed open the swinging door and walked into the smoky main room. It was as he'd expected, as he'd feared it would be. Despite it being a large room, the stench of stale beer and spilled whisky assaulted him. Smoke curled up toward the rafters and the second floor landing. Two men slept with their heads resting on the tables between cards scattered from last night's game, while a few others sat on stools along the long wooden bar, drinking and commiserating.

Two women wearing tired expressions and tired dresses leaned against the far end of the bar waiting for fresh meat. They both perked up at the sight of him.

Simon steeled himself as they sharpened their claws in anticipation of a rich meal. He smiled and approached them. "Ladies."

They both giggled. "You're an English man, ain't ya?" the bleached blonde said with wide eyes that were so painfully delighted and ravenous at his presence it was a wonder they didn't roll out of her head.

"Yes," he said. "Guilty."

They giggled again and Simon smiled.

"You must be lonely so far from home 'n all?" the other said as her fingers walked up his chest.

"I am hoping for company," he admitted and then, as her eyes lit up hastily added, "to talk."

"Oh sure," the blonde said with a knowing grin at her friend. "We can talk and things."

Both girls were barely out of their teens and unlikely to know Alice's history. "You're not quite my type," Simon said.

The brunette laughed while the blonde huffed and then smiled again, saccharine sweet. "I can be anything you want, honey."

"He said you ain't his type," the brunette said, practically shoving the other girl out of the way and stepping close to Simon, resting her hand on his chest.

"Neither of you," Simon said, "are quite what I'm looking for. Is there someone older?"

"If it's experience you're lookin' for," the brunette said as her hand wandered down his chest and toward his pants, "I can do things you ain't never dreamed of."

Simon stilled her hand and pulled it away. "I'm looking for someone more mature?"

"Don't be in such a hurry, honey," the brunette said again. "I'm older than I look."

"Please—"

"Can I help you?" Simon turned as a woman in her early thirties was coming down the stairs. She caught the eyes of the two girls and jerked her head to the side. "Beat it."

Judging from how hastily the two girls left and hurried over to the other men in the bar, this woman was in charge. The older woman slowly walked down the last set of stairs, sizing up Simon with each step. The slow predatory smile that spread across her face told him she liked what she saw.

"My name's Genevieve," she said, holding her hand out. "Maybe I can help you."

Simon took her hand and bowed slightly.

She smiled seductively and cocked her head to the side in anticipation.

"Have you worked here long?" Simon asked.

Her smile tightened and the veil of her pretense fell. "If it's a virgin you're lookin' for mister, you come to the wrong place."

"No," Simon said, feeling his neck color in embarrassment and anger at the awkwardness of his situation. "Is there somewhere we can continue this? Somewhere with a bit more privacy?"

Genevieve's eyes flashed at the prospect of a well-heeled client. "I have a room upstairs."

Simon inclined his head and Genevieve showed him the way. He could feel the eyes of the other girls watching as they ascended the stairs, but did his best to ignore them. Genevieve led him along the second story landing and down a hall. She opened the door to a room and stepped inside. Simon followed her in and closed the door behind them.

"You want a drink first?" she asked holding up a half-empty bottle.

"No, thank you."

Simon glanced around the sparse room. The wallpaper had long faded and begun to peel along the seams. Curtains that might have been bright red velvet were no more than a dull pink now. A small dresser with a tarnished mirror, a single wooden chair and an unmade bed were the only furniture.

"What do you like?" she asked, turning to face him and unlacing the front of her bodice. "It might be extra—"

It took Simon a moment to realize she was beginning to undress. "Please, don't."

She arched an eyebrow and shrugged, then hefted up her heavy skirts and put one foot on the chair. "I can keep 'em on, but it's more fun—"

"I'm here to talk, not…"

She let her leg fall to the floor and frowned. "Look, mister—"

Simon hurriedly took out his wallet and pulled out a twenty-dollar bill. He held it out to her. "Just talk."

She looked hungrily at the money and then again at him, sure there was some catch, some trick. Apparently, it didn't matter in the end. She snatched the money and stuffed it down the front of her dress.

"I'm looking for information about another girl who used to work here. Alice Stewart."

Genevieve poured herself a few fingers of whisky. "Yeah?"

"I'm hoping you might be able to tell me something about her."

She drank down half the glass. "What's to tell? She worked here and now she don't."

"Did you know her?"

She shrugged. "She worked here when I was just comin' on. She was all right. Better than that lot down there," she said with a nod toward the door.

"Do you know anything about her child, Mary?"

"She's dead."

Simon sat down on the edge of the bed. "Yes, I heard."

Genevieve finished her glass and poured another. "You sure you—"

Simon thought it might make her feel comfortable and accepted a small glass. He took a sip. It was noxious and burned all the way down.

"Why are you so interested in Alice?"

Simon pulled out his wallet again and put a ten-dollar bill on the bed next to him. "Does it matter?"

She shrugged and took the money. "She worked here, like I said. She got pregnant with the kid and left."

"Any idea who the father was?"

Genevieve arched both drawn on eyebrows and laughed. "This ain't a hotel. We don't exactly keep a registry."

"Where did she go?"

Genevieve shrugged. "She lived over on Canal in a boarding house. A few of us did. She was just about to have the kid and she disappeared. Ended up in a house up river."

Simon looked into his drink. "Disappeared?"

"Few days before she's ready to have the kid, she just left."

"Did she go to hospital?"

"No," she said, shaking her head, "although she did see a doctor. I don't know why. She was as healthy as a horse and twice as crazy."

"Crazy?" Simon prompted.

"High strung, like one of them racing horses. She was never fit for harness." The bitterness in her voice was clear, but she tried to shrug it off. "Next I hear, a few weeks later, she's had the kid and they're living in a little house up river. She was beautiful in her day. Maybe one of her regulars wanted to keep her to himself."

"Any idea who that regular might have been? Did anyone stand out?"

She laughed. "Honey, you all stand out."

Simon almost smiled. "I mean, there wasn't one man in particular who fancied her?"

She took another long swig of whisky and frowned in discomfort as it went down. "I don't think so," she said. "You all love us just the same."

ELIZABETH HAD READ THE sampler on the wall five times. *Home is where the heart is.* What she wouldn't give for a crinkly old issue of People Magazine or better yet, GQ. Was there an 1852 equivalent? Southern Gentlemen's Quarterly? If there were it should be required for any doctor's office waiting room.

She'd sat at the hotel while Simon went off to the brothel. He'd been right, darn him, that it was better that she didn't go, but that didn't mean she had to sit on her duff either.

Simon's version of the doctor and the one she'd seen at dinner didn't quite jibe. While he hadn't exactly been Mister Charm, he wasn't as recalcitrant and flinty-eyed as Simon had painted him. Maybe he just didn't take to Simon, or perhaps he needed a woman's touch to relax him into spilling a little more information. Either way, in the ten minutes she'd sat in their hotel room after Simon had left, she'd hatched her own plan. Visit the doctor and see what she could pry out of him.

So, here she sat, in Dr. Walker's waiting room in his home office. The house was attractive and well-kept, but a far cry from the fancy, schmancy mansion Catherine and the Colonel lived in. As she looked around the room more carefully, she could see that it could use a little sprucing up. All of the furnishings were expensive, but a little beyond their prime. Even the nurse who sat behind a large desk busily going over paperwork had seen better days. Maybe the doctor's practice was on the wane?

"Thank you," a slightly overweight middle-aged woman said as the door to the office opened. She fluttered about in the doorway for a moment, waving her handkerchief anxiously and dabbing at her throat. "Are you sure this will help?"

Dr. Walker appeared and gestured toward the waiting room. "I'm sure." He turned to the nurse. "Would you make sure Mrs. Turnbull has a follow-up appointment for two weeks from today?"

Mrs. Turnbull fluttered again. "You'll be quite well by then, I assure you." He pointed to a small bottle she clutched in her hand. "Two drops before every meal."

"Will that be enough?" Mrs. Turnbull asked with a sigh that threatened to blossom into a swoon.

"Yes," the doctor said, irritation tinting his voice. "Quite."

With that he shuffled Mrs. Turnbull off to the nurse. Elizabeth could see him reign in his frustration as he turned back toward his office and heard Mrs. Turnbull argue with the nurse about her "continuing and unrelenting suffering."

Elizabeth rose from her chair. "Doctor Walker?"

"Mrs. Cross?" he asked as he checked his pocket watch. "Did we have an appointment?"

"No, I'm sorry. I was hoping you could spare a few minutes?"

Dr. Walker glanced at the nurse who nodded and returned to soothing Mrs. Turnbull.

The doctor held out his hand to usher Elizabeth into his office, leaving the trilling complaints of Mrs. Turnbull behind. Once inside, he gestured toward a chair by the desk.

Elizabeth took her seat. "Is she all right?"

"Mrs. Turnbull?" The doctor arched an eyebrow and took his

chair behind the desk. "Like so many of my female patients, the only diseased part of her body is her mind." She could see him consider the wisdom of saying more. "Hysteria. A plague upon the rich and indolent."

His gaze fell on Elizabeth's expensive dress and from his expression he felt she fit the bill on both counts.

"Common sense and hard work can bring one money," she said, "but it is seldom the other way around."

The doctor smiled appreciatively. "Indeed."

"I may be guilty on one count, my husband is wealthy, although I hope you'll forgive me the transgression of marrying well," Elizabeth said as she pulled off her gloves. "I am however, like you, I think, in the other respect."

"Are you?"

"We share a common interest. You give of your time to the Institute, the orphanage and others. I'm assuming that's how you came upon that girl Mary Stewart. Her mother was somewhat of an unfortunate. One of your charitable pursuits?"

The doctor leaned back in his chair and a smile creased his eyes enjoying the challenge. "Yes. She actually came to me when she was first with child. Asking for…help," he said delicately. "I assured her that I could do no such thing. Sadly, just as wealth does not a clever man make, having a child does not always create a mother."

He leaned forward and pushed some papers into a tidy stack on his desk. "I did what I could for the child, but she was always sickly and uncared for. Perhaps it's a blessing that she has to suffer no more."

"Yes," Elizabeth said, wishing that were the case.

"But," the doctor said, reaching for a notebook. "You surely didn't come here to talk about my other patients, hmm? Are you feeling unwell?"

"I'm not sure."

"What are you symptoms?"

"Just a little tired really. A few headaches. I'm sure it's nothing."

The doctor hummed and made a few notes. "Is your husband here with you?"

"No," Elizabeth said. "I didn't want to worry him over nothing."

The doctor nodded. "He's quite emotional for an Englishman. No offense intended."

"He is passionate."

The doctor jotted another note down. "Cambridge man, isn't it?"

"Oxford," Elizabeth said, getting the distinct feeling this was some sort of test.

"Yes, that's right." The doctor came around his desk. "Stand up, please?"

Elizabeth did and he gently probed her neck and examined her head for bumps as he spoke. "I knew a man who went to Oxford, about your husband's age. Always complaining about a Professor there. Haverford, I think."

Elizabeth smiled innocently. "I'm afraid you'll have to ask Simon about that."

"Of course," the doctor said. "Turn your head. Any feelings of nausea or other discomfort?"

Elizabeth shook her head. "No, not really."

The doctor turned her head to look her in the eye. "Now, Mrs. Cross you must be honest with me if I'm to help you."

"A little cramping," she said feigning embarrassment and touching her stomach. She'd planned her symptoms well.

"Sit," he said as he took her wrist and took out his watch. He took her pulse. "A bit fast."

She wasn't surprised, what with all the dissembling and deceiving she was doing. Not to mention that he seemed to be examining not just her, but her story as well.

He circled back around his desk and sat down again. "You needn't be embarrassed, Mrs. Cross. I am well acquainted with issues common to the female. Including pregnancy."

Elizabeth's eyes went wide with shock. "Pregnant?" She'd been hoping to give the impression of general malaise, take two aspirin and call me in the morning vagueness, not pregnancy.

"Possibly."

"No," Elizabeth said with a small forced laugh. She was definitely not pregnant. "I'm not."

"It could be something else, a tumor perhaps. A full examination should tell us more."

Elizabeth shifted in her seat. "It's nothing. I'm sure. I'm sorry I wasted your time." She started to stand, but the doctor held up a hand and waved her back into her chair.

"Hardly time wasted, my dear." He walked over to the door, pulled it open and called to his nurse. "Would you help Mrs. Cross undress?"

"Cross!"

Just as he was about to climb into his buggy, Simon turned to find James and Elijah Harper pulling up in their barouche.

"What are you doing here?" James said amiably.

"Business, I was just returning."

Eli arched an eyebrow, but kept silent.

"Fortune is on my side today. I was just thinking of you," James said. "We're going down to the landing to supervise the arrival of some new equipment. I was hoping to show you our warehouse facilities. Since you expressed an interest the other day," he added hastily.

Simon could see the hopeful gleam in his eye and was happy to oblige. He joined them in their carriage, ignored Eli's smirks and made small talk as they neared the end of Water Street and the road down to the landing.

"Elizabeth has found her current trousseau inadequate," Simon said. "Is there someone in town who can help rectify the situation or do we need to wait until New Orleans?"

"I'm afraid, I stay out of such matters," James said. "But I'm sure Rose can help your wife."

"Thank—"

A loud boom interrupted and Simon barely suppressed a flinch. He and Elizabeth had heard that sound a few times since they'd arrived, but it had never been quite so loud. "What the bloody…"

"Our cannon," James said, gesturing up river. "It announces every steamboat's arrival. For some, it's still something of a novelty."

Right on cue, a dozen or so boys ran toward the bluff, dashing across busy streets and hopping fences. They clustered at the top of the hill to get a good view of the ship as it came up river to the landing. It was a majestic sight.

Two tall twin stacks with crowns on their tops belching out black smoke while two smaller stacks billowed steam from the engines. The great paddlewheel at the back churned the water and people gathered on the decks to watch the landing.

"For me," James said looking out at the river. "It's prosperity coming up river. Money flows faster than water on the Mississippi."

Simon had to agree. The volume of commerce in the harbor was astonishing, goods and people in constant motion. "Impressive."

James puffed up a bit and took them down the landing to one of the large warehouses. He gave Simon a tour of their contents and his plans for expansion. James did everything he could to prime the pump and present Simon with a sizable investment opportunity.

James excused himself and went over a shipment manifest with the warehouse manager, leaving Eli and Simon alone together. During the tour Eli had seemed impatient and sullen. Perhaps this was yet another area the brothers didn't agree upon.

"So, Mr. Cross," Eli said. "How are you enjoying Natchez?"

"Very much."

Eli pushed back the brim of his hat and eyed Simon. "Your *business* this morning was satisfactory?"

There was definitely more than a hint of accusation in his tone. Did Eli know where he'd actually been?

"Quite," Simon said curtly, hoping to stop the conversation there.

"I'm sure it was."

Simon clenched his jaw and turned his attention back to James. A large, heavy-set man with a large flowing mustache had interrupted his conversation with the warehouse manager. It was clear from James' body language that he was not happy to see this man. After a tense moment, James pulled the larger man aside and cast a nervous glance around. He saw Simon and Eli watching him and offered them a rictus smile.

James and the heavy-set man's conversation was brief, but tense. James pulled out an envelope from his inner jacket sleeve and gave it to the other man. The big man tipped his hat and left. James tugged on his waistcoat in annoyance and tamped down his anger as he rejoined Simon and Eli.

"Trouble, brother?" Eli asked, almost hopeful.

James answered with a glare and turned his charm back on for Simon. He smiled broadly and gestured for them to leave the warehouse. "We have a manufacturing facility just outside of town. Twenty spindles working now, but we have room to expand."

Simon managed to escape the textile tour and assured them he would see them at the races tomorrow near River Run for the start of their weekend celebration.

He didn't like leaving Elizabeth alone for too long. When he returned to an empty hotel room, he realized he'd been right to worry. Not finding her there meant an immediate surge of adrenaline. He felt the sharp prickle of it as it shot out through his veins. It was reflexive. It always would be where Elizabeth was concerned. She was a veritable magnet for trouble, but he reminded himself, there was no reason to assume anything untoward had happened. Perhaps she just went for a walk. He pushed out a cleansing breath, and looked for a note.

He found it resting on one of the end tables and sighed in relief. It was short-lived, however. The note read simply: *Gone to see the doctor. Love, E*

Simon read the note again. Had she taken ill while he was gone? It wasn't as if she could call him and let him know. If she had, why didn't she say more in the note?

He stuffed the paper into his jacket pocket and strode for the door. Perhaps the desk clerk knew where she'd gone.

Simon gripped the door handle and yanked open the door only to find Elizabeth attached to the other side. She stumbled into the room and he caught her as she fell against his chest.

"Criminy, where's the fire?" Elizabeth said as she disentangled from him.

Simon clutched her arms and held her away from him, searching for signs of injury. "Are you all right?"

She took off her now-lopsided hat and her eyes flashed with exasperation. "I'm fine, but you look a little crazy around the edges."

"Elizabeth," Simon said, trying to shift from worry to wonder. "Why did you go to the doctor? Are you ill?"

She tossed her hat onto a table and waved him off. "Don't be silly."

"Of course not." Simon closed the door to their room.

"You'll be happy to know I am quite salubrious."

He shook his head. This woman was maddening. He dug into his pocket and produced the note. "*Why* did you go to the doctor?"

"To do some investigating," she said as though it should have been obvious.

A retort stood at attention on his tongue, but he swallowed it. "It would have been helpful if you'd mentioned that."

"Oh!" The light finally blinked on for her. "You thought…" She came to him and patted his chest. "I'm sorry."

Simon crammed the note back into his pocket and nodded.

She pushed up on her tiptoes and kissed his cheek.

"I'm glad to hear at least," he said, "you're in good health."

"And, I have superlative birthing hips."

Simon frowned and shook his head. "Perhaps you should start from the beginning?"

Chapter Eleven

Elizabeth looked around the fairgrounds and decided she definitely needed more clothes. She was already repeating and, judging from the sea of frills and lace surrounding her, that simply wouldn't do.

She and Simon nodded and smiled as they passed through the crowd looking for the Harpers. They'd been invited to be guests at the Jockey Club's private pavilion at the racetrack. The track was a far cry from the shabby ones she used to tag along to with her father in Texas. The atmosphere was more, definitely more, Ascot than Amarillo. A cluster of food stalls at the entrance gave way to the enormous field that held both the tented pavilions and the half-mile track.

The stables and paddock area were a hub of activity as horses were warmed up and prepared for races. Adjacent to that were corrals for horse trading. From plow horses to young thoroughbred colts, there was something to entice every level of society.

The whole thing felt more like a county fair celebrating Spring and the end of planting season than a regular old horse track. There were food stalls and jugglers and musicians, and even a few buckboards with people drinking and eating in the back. A sort of 19th century tailgate.

She and Simon were nearing the large white tents of the Jockey Club when Elizabeth saw Catherine and the Colonel. Catherine waved happily toward them and the Colonel remained as stone-faced as ever.

Just as they were crossing a path to join them, two tenant farmers and their mules came between them. The men bellowed at the two teams of mules as they tried to convince the animals to head to the paddock area. They yelled and begged, whipped the reins down on their backs and slapped their flanks with their straw hats, and argued with each other until the mules heehawed and went on their way.

The Colonel might have actually harrumphed as he glowered after them. "Commoners and Negroes racing," he said. "Mules for God's sake. It's desecrated the club." Almost as an afterthought, he bowed his head and greeted them. "Cross."

"Colonel. Miss Catherine," Simon said.

Catherine rolled her eyes at her father and then smiled at Elizabeth. "So good to see you. Are you feeling…well?" she asked with a slight wiggle of her eyebrows.

How could she possibly know that she'd seen the doctor yesterday?

As if reading her mind Catherine added, "Since her husband's death Mrs. Turnbull has little more to do with herself these days than gossip."

The Colonel grunted in displeasure. "And what's your excuse, Cat?"

"Touché, father." Catherine looked as though she were going to follow up with a volley of her own, but resisted the temptation. Barely.

"I'm fine, thank you. No news to report," Elizabeth said, hoping to stop any Stanton family war before it started.

That won another grunt from the Colonel. Maybe there were nuances to his grunts like lowland gorillas.

"Do you have a horse here today, Colonel?" Simon asked, clearly hoping to put the conversation back on safer ground.

The Colonel's chest puffed a bit and he fought down a proud smile. "Yes." He gestured to the stables, urging Simon to walk with him. "Are you a good judge of horseflesh, Cross?"

Simon bowed to the ladies and let himself be led off by the Colonel.

"I'm sorry about before," Catherine said. "It's none of my business."

"It's all right."

"It isn't," Catherine said. "I hate it when father's right."

Elizabeth laughed and Catherine joined her. She wound her arm through Elizabeth's and they started toward the main tent. "Be sure to try the applesauce cookies."

They found the Harpers under their own white canopy shading them from the warm Spring sun. Tables and chairs had been set up in a comfortable living arrangement, complete with a rug underfoot. Rose oversaw several slaves as they rummaged in large wicker baskets and set the long table for luncheon.

"Hello," Rose said, giving one final instruction to the slave. "I'm so glad you could come. Would you like something to drink?"

"Thank you, no. I have wagers to make!" Catherine said and then whispered to Elizabeth. "Despite what my father might say, the smart money is on Lionel Duncan's filly." She winked and promised to find them later.

"Would you like something?" Rose watched Catherine go with an amused smile, before turning her attention fully to Elizabeth. "Sweet tea?"

Elizabeth gladly accepted. Between the ride over and the walk through the dusty concourse she was sure she had half of Natchez in her throat.

"Sit, please," Rose said, offering Elizabeth a chair.

They both sat down and Louisa hurried over to her mother's

side. "Look," she said, showing her mother a beautifully carved and painted horse, "Uncle Eli got him for me. Isn't he beautiful?"

"Manners, darling," Rose said with a firm, but encouraging smile.

One of the slaves handed Elizabeth a cool glass of sweet tea.

Louisa gave Elizabeth a quick, shy smile and bobbed a curtsy. "Hello."

Elizabeth grinned and leaned forward. "Hello. Your horse is very handsome."

Louisa beamed and her mother pulled her daughter against her side. She examined the wooden animal carefully. "Oh, he is fine looking, isn't he?"

The girl nodded and rested her head on her mother's shoulder as she stared adoringly at the little wooden horse and ran her fingers over its mane.

"Do you like horses very much, Louisa?" Elizabeth asked.

She chewed her lip and nodded. "Daddy says when I'm old enough I can get a pony."

Rose frowned, but only for a second. "We're still discussing that, darling."

"I'm going to be eight next week and that's plenty old. Daddy said I can ride as well as any boy twice my age and that I'm twice as pretty too."

Her mother stifled a laugh and hugged her. "Your father has a way with words."

"Are my ears burning?" James said as he appeared at the edge of the tent.

"Mrs. Cross," he said as he took off his hat.

"Elizabeth, please."

He smiled and leaned down to kiss his wife's cheek. Rose tilted her head to present it, but there was something in her body language, the tilt of her head, the way she looked away that struck Elizabeth. She'd sensed some underlying tension between them at dinner at the Stantons', but had thought perhaps it had been her unfamiliarity with the etiquette of the time. Now, however, she felt sure there was more to it than primness.

"Look, daddy!" Louisa said proudly holding out her horse.

"What have we here?" James said as he scooped his daughter up into his arms.

"From Uncle Eli!"

James admired the horse. "An impressive specimen. But he's a little small to ride, don't you think?"

Louisa giggled.

"I did see a pony…" James said.

Louisa squealed in delight and Rose stood, clearly not happy with this development. "James."

"I haven't bought him."

"Yet," Rose said.

James readjusted Louisa on his hip and turned to Elizabeth. "What is a man to do when he's torn between the two women in his life? Someone's going to have quite the birthday." He kissed Rose on the cheek and then nibbled at Louisa's neck until she broke out into a fit of giggles. Rose smiled adoringly at her daughter, but Elizabeth hadn't noticed her look at James the same way. They seemed happy enough. While James was certainly madly in love with both of them, there was something reserved about Rose when she was with James. Something changed when he came around. She pulled back just the tiniest bit. Elizabeth could see it now in her eyes, something not quite wary, but ill at ease.

"Are you coming to my party?" Louisa asked Elizabeth.

Rose smiled almost apologetically at Elizabeth. "I do hope you will."

"I'd love to," Elizabeth said. "And you're going to be eight?"

Louisa nodded vigorously.

Rose reached over and tried to tidy Louisa's slightly unruly curls. "Louisa, I swear, your hair has a mind of its own."

"Leave the girl be," James said, twisting so Louisa was out of her reach. "We like it just the way it is, don't we darling?"

Louisa nuzzled into her father's neck and Rose cast a quick uneasy smile at Elizabeth and sat back down.

Simon had listened to the Colonel expound upon the virtues of good breeding for what felt like hour upon hour. His horse, Bucephalus, had come from the line of Little Venus who had run at Columbia in under eight minutes. Simon alternated between polite attention and aggressively obvious indifference. Neither seemed to matter to the Colonel who only needed himself as an audience.

Finally, the Colonel was called away to tend to Bucephalus and offer advice to the jockey before the afternoon match races began. Simon graciously let the Colonel attend to business and turned to search for the main Jockey Club pavilion.

Simon took the moment of peace to observe the crowd and enjoy the ambiance. He hadn't quite realized he'd missed the country until now. Life in Santa Barbara wasn't exactly the cement jungle of Manhattan, but it was still a city. Between the grounds of Grey Hall and his grandfather's estate in Sussex, Simon had spent a fair amount of his youth in the country. Standing here with the familiar and pungent aroma of a stable and trees merely giving way to more trees, he found he missed it.

Just as he began to wonder if perhaps he and Elizabeth should buy a country house somewhere to escape to on occasion, he noticed Doctor Walker in the crowd. The doctor craned his neck, clearly looking for someone. Abruptly, he stopped walking. A short, thick-chested man with shabby clothes, perhaps a day laborer or stevedore, approached him. The doctor did all of the talking. The other man merely nodded.

A voice beside Simon broke him from his silent observation.

"Lost her already?"

Simon turned and saw Eli suddenly at his side, casually leaning against the corral fence. Simon bit back a terse reply. He turned back to look for the doctor, but both he and the other man were gone.

"She's probably in our private tent," Eli said. "Just before the last turn."

Simon nodded curtly and started off in the direction indicated, but Eli grabbed his arm as he passed.

"You should be more careful. Someone just might find her."

Simon glared at Eli's hand and tensed his arm. "I beg your pardon."

Eli let go and leaned back against the fence, his elbows resting casually on the top rail. "I don't like to tell another man his business—"

"Then don't."

"But when a fine woman's reputation is at stake, I feel inclined to intervene."

Simon's jaw set. What in bloody hell was he going on about?

Eli dipped his head forward to speak more softly. "Natchez is a small town. What a man does here is seldom secret and never for long. I would hate to see your beautiful wife become the subject of gossip and ridicule because of *your* indiscretion."

So Eli had known about his visit to the brothel. Simon had suspected as much when he'd run into them the other day, but had hoped it was just general dislike. That, at least, was mutual. He couldn't possibly explain why he'd been there. His silence though, he knew, was damning.

Simon's jaw clenched tighter. "And I suppose for a price you'll stay silent on the matter?"

Eli shook his head. "You can keep your money. My brother's the one who wants it. I'm merely thinking of your wife."

Simon clenched his hand into a fist. "Are you?"

Eli started to say something and then smiled and pushed off from the fence. "If she were my wife, I would think of little else." With that he tipped his hat and disappeared into the crowd.

ELIZABETH WAS BURSTING WITH questions and, well, other things. She knew she shouldn't have had that second glass of sweet tea, but she'd been thirsty and it had been so cool going down. Now, however, she was faced with the modern woman's 19th century nightmare—the outdoor privy.

She shuddered at the thought, but she had little choice. Between the tea and the corset squeezing her bladder to the size of pea, she couldn't wait any longer. She excused herself and got directions from one of the slaves. It seemed the ladies' john was back near the woods. Setting it apart from the rest of the grounds was undoubtedly wise, but it didn't help her situation any. She smiled and casually walked as quickly as she could to a small wooden building discretely hidden behind a small copse of trees at the edge of the woods.

Feeling much better, she started back for the Harpers' tent when a hand clamped down over her mouth and another grabbed her upper arm in a tight grip. The man pulled her back against his chest and dragged her behind the trees. She could smell the alcohol and tobacco on his breath. She struggled against him, but his hands were like iron bands digging into her flesh.

He shook her to stop her fighting and tightened his grip even further. His breath was hot against her neck. Elizabeth felt a fist of panic rise in her belly.

"This is a warning," he said in a soft, rasping voice.

Elizabeth tried to catch her breath. At least he wasn't going to kill her. You don't warn someone and then kill them, right? She tried to think of a way to break free, to call for help, but he was too strong and her damn clothes weren't made for kicking a man where it counts. She took deep breaths through her nose, but the stench of rotten fish on his hands nearly made her gag.

"You and your husband been asking questions that ain't none of your business," he said. "Best keep your pretty nose to yourself, if you want to keep it. You understand?"

Elizabeth held still.

Not liking that, he shook her again. "I said, you understand?"

She nodded.

"Good."

She thought he might let her go then, but he moved his hand up and covered her nose. She couldn't breathe. Instantly, she started to struggle. She twisted in his arms, but he was too strong and the more she struggled the less breath she had. It all happened so quickly.

She felt the darkness start to come. Like a camera shutter closing, the world dimmed to a small circle of light. Sounds of her own struggle were muffled like they were underwater. Her body felt oddly weightless, like she was draining away from herself.

Just as the final curtain of darkness was coming down, she hit the ground. The shock of it brought her around and she gasped for air. Blessedly, it came. She pulled in deep lungfuls of air and the world around her slowly came back into focus. As she regained full consciousness the shock of what had happened hit her. She felt the prickling rise of panic and pushed out a few quick breaths to keep herself under control.

As quickly as she could, she stood. She looked around for the man, but there was no sign of him. Her arm ached and she rubbed it to get the circulation moving. He hadn't meant to kill her, she realized. If he had, she would be really, most sincerely, dead.

She hurried away from the trees and out into the open. No one was around. No one had seen. She started back toward the pavilion.

Her hands trembled and she clasped them again and again to try to stop their shaking. She wiped her mouth trying to rid it of the taste, of the stench of him, and shuddered at the memory. Pulling her handkerchief out, she did her best to rid herself of any evidence of the attack. The last thing she needed was to try to explain what happened to Rose or James. She cleaned her face as best she could and discarded the smelly handkerchief.

Dusting off her dress, she took a few calming breaths before she neared the Harpers' tent and prayed Simon would be there.

He was, thank God. Simon stood at the far side of the tent and listened to James expound on the need for warehouses in Liverpool. He saw Elizabeth enter and smiled. But his smile faded instantly as he sensed something was wrong. Immediately excusing himself from James, he started toward her.

Elizabeth forced a smile. "Do you mind if I steal my husband for a few minutes?"

"Of course," James said.

Elizabeth wound her arm through Simon's and led him away from the tent.

"What's wrong?" Simon asked.

Once they were well out of earshot Elizabeth stopped and took a deep breath. "First, I could really use a hug."

Simon frowned, but didn't hesitate to take her into his arms. "What's happened?"

Elizabeth enjoyed the comfort and safety of his arms for a long moment before pulling away. "I was coming back from the bathroom just now and someone grabbed me."

"What do you mean someone grabbed you?"

"A man, he must have been hiding in that small group of trees waiting for me," she said looking back toward the copse of trees.

The vein in Simon's neck began to throb and she could see him trying to rein in his anger. He looked toward the trees she'd indicated. "What man? Did he hurt you?"

"No," she said.

Simon reached out and grabbed ahold of her arms. She flinched as he inadvertently squeezed her bruise.

Simon immediately released her. "Elizabeth." His hands hovered over her arms, as if he wanted to hold her, but was afraid to hurt her again. Finally, they fell to his sides and clenched into fists. His voice was low and hard when he spoke again. "What did he do?"

"It's just a bruise," she said and, seeing he was working himself up with thoughts far worse than what had happened, hastily added, "Really. He just held my arm too tightly. I'm fine."

His eyes desperately searched hers for the truth and calmed a little when he finally believed she wasn't withholding anything. "Just now, you said?" he asked taking a stride toward the trees.

"Yes, but he's gone. It wasn't a random grab-a-woman sort of thing. It was a warning," Elizabeth said.

Simon pulled his attention away from the woods. "A warning?"

"He grabbed me and told me to keep my nose to myself. That we were asking questions someone doesn't want asked."

Simon grunted. "Damn it. Did you see his face? Would you recognize him?"

"No, he was behind me the whole time. He just grabbed me and said to keep out of it and then he was gone."

"He just walked away?"

Elizabeth hesitated to tell him the last bit of it, but keeping things from him would only be worse in the end. "I sort of passed out a little."

"You what?" Instinctively, he reached out to her again, but held her elbows gently.

"It was just part of his escape plan, I think. Better than a crack on the head."

She could see him work through it in his mind, not liking what he saw, but knowing it could have been far worse. He reluctantly nodded. "Yes."

"So," Elizabeth said, "that's my news. What have you got?"

Simon shook his head. "Elizabeth—"

"Comes with the territory," she said, wishing she could actually feel as brave as she sounded. "I'm all right and it means we're asking the right questions."

Simon started to argue with her, but stopped himself. She knew how hard this sort of thing was for him. It wasn't exactly easy for her either. Being manhandled, threatened and nearly suffocated was not her idea of an ideal picnic. But it meant they were heading in the right direction. They couldn't afford to stop now. She knew Simon's concern for her would trump everything else though, and she stepped forward and put her hands on his chest. She could feel his heart beating quickly and his chest rising and falling as he struggled with his emotions.

"We're doing the right thing," she said.

He nodded slowly and then covered her hand with his and brought it to his lips. "You are not leaving my side today. Agreed?"

Elizabeth was more than happy to oblige. She didn't want a repeat performance any more than he did. They started back to the Harpers' tent and Elizabeth noticed Eli had been watching them. He made no attempt to hide the fact and didn't move from his spot leaning against one of the tent poles as they re-entered.

"Elizabeth," he said with a broad smile that faded quickly as he gave Simon a curt nod. She made a mental note to ask Simon what that was all about later. For now, the first match race was about to get under way. The entire entourage headed out to claim spots in the grandstands for the first series, but Elizabeth hardly cared about the races now.

Chapter Twelve

THE COLONEL'S HORSE MADE it through the first two rounds, only to lose in the third. Money was won; money was lost and a pleasant afternoon passed without any more revelations or incidents. The entire party retreated to River Run, just barely beating a powerful spring storm as it rolled in.

Simon slid into bed next to Elizabeth and sighed. It had been a long day, and he felt the tension from his worry over the incident with Elizabeth finally start to fade as he lay down next to her. They went over everything they'd seen and heard that day.

"The women didn't gossip about anyone?" Simon asked. "Something you might have overlooked initially?"

Elizabeth rolled onto her side and shook her head. "Not really. It was all politics and children and then more children. I swear it's like everyone here is a Duggar."

Simon had no idea what that meant.

"Everyone here has lots of children," she explained with a sigh. "Flocks of children."

She shifted onto her back and Simon could sense there was something wrong. He waited for her to elaborate and when she didn't he pushed himself onto an elbow and regarded her in the faint light. "What's wrong?"

She looked at him, almost shyly and then back at the ceiling. Her words came out in a torrent. "I know we never discussed it and I was so busy being in love with you there wasn't room for much else and then we were traveling and I wasn't thinking about it, but now that we're here and I can't stop thinking about it." She rolled her head to the side and looked at him pleadingly. "You know what I mean?"

Simon blinked. "Not entirely."

She bit her lip and then continued. "How do you feel about children? Having them, I mean. Us having them? Together."

Simon was stunned. Of all the things he'd expected her to say that was not one of them. He stared at her numbly for a moment.

"It's okay if you don't. I just—"

"Do you want children?" he asked. He could tell by her expression that the answer was yes, but also that she was almost afraid to admit it.

"Not right away, but I think someday, I would. But—"

He reached to brush a lock of her hair away from her cheek. "You're afraid I don't, is that it?"

She nodded slowly. He could hardly blame her for thinking that. His childhood had not exactly been an advert for the joys of family. Not to mention that he'd spent the larger part of his adult life avoiding any sort of messy emotional entanglements.

His fingers brushed against her neck and then he traced the edge of her jaw as he spoke. "The only thing in this world I can imagine loving as much as I love you would be our child."

Emotions welled in her eyes. "Really?"

He chuckled softly, leaned down and gave her a gentle kiss. "Really."

She gazed back up at him with such love and tenderness his heart lurched in his chest. The thought of her with his child threatened to overwhelm him. As if she sensed it, she pulled him back for a deeper kiss, and he poured his soul into it. Someday, he thought. Someday.

As TENSE AND FRENETIC as the previous day had been, the following morning was its perfect counterpart. Hot and muggy and slow. After breakfast the entire house lay about in a dreamy haze of Southern luxury. Well before noon, Mint Juleps with plenty of alcohol were served on the veranda as slaves catered to their whims and worked as human fans to blow away the hot, sticky morning. Elizabeth felt indulgent and drowsy, and more than a little guilty. As long as her comfort came at a slave's expense, she couldn't truly relax.

They rest of them happily waited for the day to come to them. All of them, except James, who never seemed idle or without work, relaxed. This morning he pored over some papers as he had tea instead of a Julep. Eli tipped back his chair and balanced on the back legs as he told Rose and Elizabeth a story about his adventures in Jamaica. Meanwhile, Simon was the very picture of a man of leisure, power and confidence. His cream-colored suit made him look every inch the Southern gentleman. He leaned back into his deep, white wicker chair with the grace of privilege. His long legs stretched out in front of him, casually crossed at the ankles, his chin nearly resting on his chest. To the rest of the world, he looked bored, even on the verge of falling asleep. But Elizabeth knew he was keenly observing everyone and everything around him. His eyes subtly shifted to hers and glimmered with a hidden smile before resuming his quiet observation.

Elizabeth had always been too restless and engaged with the world to separate herself the way Simon could. As Eli finished his story, she shifted in her chair and took another small sip of her Julep and sighed with contentment. It was heavenly.

"I told you my Juleps were the best in Mississippi," Eli said.

"I have very few points of comparison," Elizabeth said, "but I can't imagine one better."

Eli grinned and Elizabeth saw Simon's jaw twitch. He'd told her about his conversation with Eli. What she would have given to have been a fly on the wall for that!

"Will you be joining us for the hunt this afternoon?" James asked.

Elizabeth could hardly fathom the idea of riding a hunt in her corset, sidesaddle in this heat. Not to mention the idea of chasing a poor little fox around the forest was not her idea of fun.

"I think I'll stay here, if that's all right?"

"Good," James said. "Rose could use the company."

Rose looked as if she were about to say something, but thought better of it. She smiled instead and said, "I do welcome it."

She sounded sincere, but there was definitely an undercurrent of something. Elizabeth just couldn't quite pinpoint it. Rose looked unusually pale and drawn, and her usual natural grace to all and to all things seemed a little pinched today.

Missy, the cook, appeared at the bottom of the stairs to the yard. "Your pies are ready, Miss Rose."

"Thank you, Missy. Would you bring them into the house?"

Missy bobbed her head and hurried back to the kitchen.

"Pies?" James asked.

"For Mrs. Clay."

James frowned. "Too far. Have one of the servants bring them over. You should rest."

"I want to give her my condolences in person." James shook his head, but Rose continued. "You worry far too much about me, James. I'm fine."

James ignored her and called out to one of the servants. "Sally, you tell Missy to have Jacob bring those pies over to Mrs. Clay. Miss Rose will give you a note to take along." Sally yassir'd and scurried off. "Now, I won't hear more of it," James said to Rose with a look that said he fully expected his word to the final one.

Elizabeth felt sorry for Rose. She was a prisoner of her sex, her era and her husband. James was indeed master of the big house and all in it.

Rose apparently had little choice but to let him have his way and nodded. James rose from his chair and then leaned down to kiss her cheek. "You can pay a call next week. Now, there's real work to be done before the hunt, gentlemen."

"Maybe I'll stay here with the ladies?" Eli said with a wink to them, clearly knowing the rise it would get out of his brother and Simon as well.

James glowered at his brother who sighed and reluctantly stood.

"Cross, I thought you might like to choose your own horse this time," James said. "I'm sure you'll find one to your liking."

"I'm sure."

James waited expectantly. "I'd also like to discuss a small business matter."

Simon arched an eyebrow and then nodded. Slowly, he stretched, letting James stand there waiting for him. "You'll be all right?" he asked Elizabeth as he stood.

"I doubt I can get into much trouble here," she said.

Simon snorted and brushed a kiss against her cheek. "Please be careful," he whispered before joining the men.

Rose turned to her after they'd left. "He loves you very much."

"The feeling is very mutual," Elizabeth said, pulling her gaze away from Simon.

Rose's smile faltered just a bit before she forced it back into place. "How did you meet?"

"He was giving a lecture," Elizabeth said, remembering that the truth was far easier to remember than lies. "And I raised my hand to ask a question. It annoyed him," she said with a laugh.

"He didn't stay annoyed for long, did he?"

Elizabeth smiled at the memory. "No, not for too long. And you and James?"

Rose leaned back in her chair and smiled at the memory. "I was young, barely thirteen when we moved to Natchez. I thought all of the Harper boys were terribly handsome."

"But, one more than the others?" Elizabeth asked.

Rose nodded and Elizabeth saw a slight blush steal into her cheeks. "Yes." She remained silent, lost in the memory for a moment before continuing. "James was already a man when we met. So sure of himself. He's a fine husband and a loving father."

The choice of modifiers wasn't lost on Elizabeth. "I can see how besotted he is with your daughter."

"She is very precious to us," Rose said and then looked at Elizabeth as if she were weighing whether to speak more on the subject or not. Elizabeth waited patiently for her to continue, afraid that if she said anything, Rose might reconsider sharing whatever it was she seemed about to reveal.

After a long pause, Rose spoke again. "It was a near thing, bringing her into this world. I'd lost several children before and Doctor Walker warned me that it was a great risk to try again, that the likelihood of our child surviving was…He said sometimes a child isn't meant for this world."

Her head dipped down and she toyed with a bit of lace from her dress. "But we both wanted a child so badly. We come from large families and the idea of an empty home…"

Rose shook her head and let out a shuddering breath and lifted her head. "But then Louisa came. And she was perfect. A beautiful, healthy child. That is the greatest gift a woman can ever receive," Rose said. "Perhaps some day, you'll know how it feels?"

Elizabeth knew a leading question when she heard one, but Rose's honesty and openness drew the same from her. "I hope so."

A contemplative silence followed and then was broken by a bird's song in a tree in the garden.

"A mockingbird. Teaching her chicks to sing," Rose said. "Out there in the—"

The words died in her throat. They'd both turned to look out into the garden to find the source of the birdsong, but saw something else instead. Half-hidden amongst the bushes and flowers stood Mary. She peered up at them with such sadness that it seemed nearly a living thing.

Rose gasped and looked away.

"Are you all right?" Elizabeth asked.

Rose looked back into the garden, but Mary was gone. "I'm fine. Just—" She put a quivering hand to her head. "Perhaps my husband was right," she said as she stood on shaking legs. "I am feeling a bit tired."

Elizabeth stood and helped steady her. "You seem upset."

"No," Rose said quickly. "I didn't sleep well last night, that's all. Forgive me, I'm such a poor hostess, but I seem to have come upon a headache rather suddenly."

Elizabeth debated being frank with her and asking about what she saw, but decided against it for now. "I'll be fine. You get some rest and I'll see you later."

Rose nodded and gave one last look to the garden before going inside.

Elizabeth waited until she was gone before walking down the stairs and toward the bushes where they'd seen Mary. "Mary?" she whispered. "Are you there?"

No one answered.

Chapter Thirteen

By midday, River Run was overrun with men and horses and hounds. After a frenzied gathering near the front of the big house, dozens of men and just as many dogs trotted away to a field to the North where they'd start the hunt. Elizabeth knew Simon would have much rather stayed with her, but he had his part to play and that meant riding with the Harpers. He'd chosen a handsome, high-strung roan as his mount and fell in next to James and Elijah as the group disappeared down the shadowed corridor of oak trees and out of sight.

Elizabeth watched him and the others ride away. That left her with the other womenfolk who were left behind to talk with and, thankfully, drink with. The drinks that were served on the veranda did little to quell her restlessness. Even if she hadn't seen Mary that morning, the idea of sitting and waiting for the men to return was irksome. She did her best to smile and cull what information she could out of the other guests, but there wasn't much to be gained. She found herself distracted and watching the garden, hoping for another glimpse of Mary.

The brief rest Rose had taken hadn't helped her much. She still looked drawn and tired. She smiled as she excused herself from the group, but Elizabeth could see how drained she really was.

Mrs. Turnbull watched her go and then spread out her fan with a flick of her pudgy wrist. "It is lovely here, isn't it?"

It took Elizabeth a moment to realize that she was talking to her and sat forward at attention. "Yes."

"Rose married wisely. That Elijah is handsome, I suppose, but like a lost pup when it comes to business."

"Oh, so true," chimed in Mrs. Goode. "James has a fine head on his shoulders. Her father made the right choice by her, I think."

Elizabeth sipped her drink. "Her father?" she asked casually.

"Oh, yes," Mrs. Turnbull said. "He arranged their marriage. A fine match, I think."

Mrs. Goode nodded in vigorous agreement. "It takes a strong hand to run such a grand plantation. Rose is a lucky woman her father had such foresight."

Mrs. Turnbull looked at Elizabeth. "I'm sure your father ensured that your husband was the right sort of man for you."

"Well, he is a baron, isn't it?" Mrs. Goode said enthusiastically.

Elizabeth was about to correct her when Mrs. Turnbull chimed in, "Royalty. Hard to go wrong there, I'd say. You're quite the lucky girl."

Elizabeth smiled. "Yes, I—"

"Speaking of royalty," Mrs. Goode said, as if Elizabeth hadn't spoke. "Did you hear about Virginia's last trip to Saratoga? Scandalous!"

Elizabeth waited a moment and then quietly excused herself. Having lost her appetite for their company, she went in search of Rose.

She caught her in a private moment on the side porch between tending to her guests and ensuring the elaborate dinner planned later was coming along as scheduled. "Is there anything I can do to help?" Elizabeth asked.

Rose smiled and shook her head. "You're a dear for asking, but I'm fine."

"You're sure?" Elizabeth asked hopefully, casting a glance back at Mrs. Turnbull who was busy spreading the latest gossip and prying new bits out of anyone she could corner.

Rose followed her gaze and smiled in understanding. "Why don't you go for a walk? She leaned in closely. "I would if I were you."

The thought of escaping the ladies for an hour was tempting and the idea that she might be able to see Mary again irresistible. "You're sure that would that be all right?"

"Between Mrs. Turnbull and Mrs. Goode, there won't be a moment of peace to be found here. There's a shady path near the river I like to walk when I can."

"My dear!" Mrs. Goode called. "We're out of canapés!"

Elizabeth laid a grateful hand on Rose's arms and got quick directions to the path. She made her escape and wound her way through the garden, hoping Mary might show herself. But it wasn't to be. Eventually, Elizabeth found the footpath Rose had mentioned. It ran along the bank of the river and Elizabeth headed south away from the hunt and away from the house and the swamplands farther north.

Elizabeth walked down river and watched as the current rushed past. The Mississippi was mighty indeed. It had to be over a mile across here, looking more like a lake than a river. Flatboats, keelboats, steamboats and rafts traveled up and down winding their ways around the snags and shoals that made piloting the river the stuff of legends. She could just imagine Tom and Jim or Huck riding on one of the rough-hewn rafts that hugged the shores.

The River was hypnotic. She walked on and on, pulled down river with the current that seemed to reach even on to the shore. She stopped once at a small footbridge that reached over a stream and played a game of Pooh Sticks. It wasn't quite the Hundred Acre Wood, but it was an enchanted sort of place. Calm and peaceful. It felt timeless. Maybe that was part of why the Old South thought their way of life would never change. Standing here now, she felt it too. Maybe it was the river or the heat of the day, but each moment seemed to last just a bit longer here, as if time itself was lingering, unwilling to move forward.

After another twenty minutes walking, the midday sun bore down on her with increased intensity. She'd left the cool canopy of trees as the path wound its way inland. In more sunlight than shade now, and having lost the cool breeze from the water's edge, the heat was becoming oppressive. The layers of her clothing felt suddenly heavier and constricting.

Elizabeth was about to turn back when she came across a small, quiet pond protected by a grove of shade trees. It was barely thirty feet across and clear. She could just hear the babble of a nearby stream. The pond must have been spring fed.

She knelt in the grass at its edge and scooped up handfuls of water to cool her face. Droplets ran down her neck and she wiped them across her overheated skin. A large rock sat nearby sloping down into the water. Perfect for dangling her feet. The idea of the cold water on her hot and cramped feet was too much of a temptation to pass by. She unlaced her boots and pulled off her stockings.

A contented sigh escaped her lips as her toes dipped into the water. She splashed more water onto her neck and face, succeeding in wetting the front of her dress in the process. Elizabeth unbuttoned the front of her blouse and pulled the damp edges of the cloth away from her skin and fanned herself.

It felt good, but she knew what would feel better. No one was around. No one would ever know. She'd have one heck of a time getting back into her corset though. But she hadn't had a real bath in four days and the clear cold water sang its sirens song so sweetly. Before she knew it, she'd shucked off every last layer.

Wearing only a smile, Elizabeth waded into the water, giggling at the strange sensation as her toes squished in the muddy bottom. Careful to keep her hair dry, she walked in deeper until the water came to her shoulders. She closed her eyes and listened to the quiet.

It was idyllic and just what she needed. If there were a pond like this near the house, she'd use it every day. She swam out to the middle of the pond letting the cool water renew her.

On the far side of the pond, a frog leapt onto a log and croaked at her.

"Well, hello," she said.

"Hello, yourself."

Elizabeth spun around in the water. The sun blinded her and she shaded her eyes to see who it was. A man stepped forward.

"Elijah! You scared me half to death. What are you doing here?" she demanded.

He lifted the hem of one of her petticoats that she'd flung onto a nearby bush in her haste. "I could ask you the same question."

She frowned and he chuckled.

"Aren't you supposed to be hunting?" Elizabeth said as she treaded water and tried to cover herself at the same time.

"I am," he said.

Elizabeth had a sinking feeling. Was the entire hunt going to show up next?

"I was bored and rode off," he said, walking along the edge of the pond. "Then I saw what looked like a pair of ladies' undergarments hanging from a tree. What sort of man would I be if I didn't investigate?"

He was enjoying this far too much. Not that she could really blame him. She was the one who'd gone skinny dipping in the middle of a fox hunt.

He saw her nervous look and smiled. "Your secret will be safe with me, but…" He cocked his head to the side and listened. The unmistakable sound of hounds on the chase could be heard in the distance. "The others are not far and getting closer, I think. If you stay where you are…"

She knew the end of the sentence and she couldn't let that happen. Elizabeth started to swim toward the shore, but stopped. "You need to…" She waved her hand to shoo him away.

He smiled and nodded, but then a dark frown covered his face. "Come faster," he said urgently as he strode to the edge of the pond.

Elizabeth stopped swimming. "Not with you standing there."

He stepped into the water and reached out to her. "Swim!"

He was staring at something behind her and Elizabeth swiveled to see what it was. About ten feet away, the smooth surface of the water rippled just slightly. She stared at it dumbly for a moment before it lifted its head out of the water.

Elizabeth wasn't a screamer, but she let out a shriek to wake the dead. Snakes. Why did it have to be a snake?

"Swim!" The panicked edge to his voice was all the prompting Elizabeth needed. She turned back and swam toward the shore as quickly as she could. She splashed and kicked and then dug her hands into the muddy bottom to try to stand.

Eli had grabbed a long stick and held it in one hand, and extended the other out to her. He was knee-deep in the water, boots and all. "Hurry!"

He took another step deeper into the water and grabbed onto her outstretched hand and yanked. Her feet were sunk down into the muddy bottom and didn't want to let go, but Eli pulled until they both tumbled back onto the shore. She fell on top of him and he rolled her over away from the water's edge. He scrambled to his feet and jabbed the surface of the water with the stick.

Elizabeth climbed to her feet and could just see the brown and tan striped snake as it swam away to the far side of the pond where it had come from.

"Cottonmouth," Eli said, watching to make sure it kept going.

"Is it gone?" Elizabeth said not able to suppress a shudder.

"I think so." Eli turned back and then immediately turned his head, averting his eyes.

In the excitement, she'd completely forgotten she was naked. She eeped and reflexively tried to cover herself.

"And now we have another secret," Eli said.

SIMON HAD HAD QUITE enough of the hunt and was happy to linger at the rear of the procession as it started off in yet another direction. He'd noticed Elijah veer off from the group a few minutes ago. Simon reined in his horse and broke off. He would learn nothing more following the pack and he'd put in more than enough time with James to ensure his interest in him as an investor. Not to mention that James Harper was a thudding bore. Not that he blamed the man for being obsessed about his business. It took that sort of drive to run a plantation the size of River Run, but none of that was getting Simon closer to understanding how Mary fit into all this. He'd paid his dues with James, now it was time to find out just what Eli was up to.

Putting aside Eli's embarrassing misconception about his visit to the brothel and his annoyingly persistent flirtation with Elizabeth, Elijah Harper was a man with a secret. Simon had studied him all morning and of that he was sure.

Simon urged his horse on and they broke into a canter to catch up to Eli. Although, he couldn't see him, he was sure he'd gone off in this direction.

Simon emerged from a thicket of woods when he heard the scream. It went straight to his heart.

"Elizabeth."

He dug his heels into the horse's flanks and raced toward the sound. What the hell was she doing out here? His heart beat faster than his horse's hooves and he tried to control the fear that gripped his heart. He saw Eli's horse grazing on a small patch of grass and guided his horse toward it.

Simon dismounted his horse before it had even stopped. He heard a man's voice, Eli. "And now we have another secret."

Simon crashed through the thicket to see Eli turn in surprise. And Elizabeth. Naked and frightened.

Instinct and anger propelled him forward. He closed the distance between himself and Eli in two quick strides. What the hell had he done to her? Simon grabbed Eli by the front of his shirt. His other hand coiled into a fist ready to strike when Elizabeth called for him to stop.

Simon's fist hung in the air, arm cocked like a crossbow ready to fire. Blood rushed through his head, fury coloring everything red.

Elizabeth grabbed one of her petticoats from a bush and wrapped it around her body as best she could. "He was helping me."

Simon had an idea just what he was helping himself to.

Eli grasped Simon's wrist. "There was a snake."

Simon turned to Elizabeth for an explanation. She nodded and Simon eased his grip. Eli pulled Simon's hand away and looked at him with unbridled disgust.

"I was swimming," Elizabeth said, "and there was a cottonmouth."

Simon rushed to Elizabeth's side and shrugged out of his jacket and wrapped it around Elizabeth's shoulders. "Were you bitten?"

She shook her head. "No, thanks to Eli."

Simon hated being beholden to anyone, much less a man like Eli Harper, but he truly was now. Elizabeth could have been killed. He turned to Elijah. "I am grateful for that. But I have to wonder why you were here at all."

Eli glared at him and then spoke to Elizabeth. "You don't have to stay with him, you know."

Simon stepped forward angrily. "And just what do you mean by that?"

Eli stood his ground. "A man who raises his hand against a woman doesn't deserve her."

What the hell was he going on about?

"I saw you arguing at the race," Eli said. "I saw you grab her." He nodded toward Elizabeth.

"It isn't what you think," Elizabeth said, but before she could protest further the sound of approaching riders came. She grabbed her clothing and scurried behind a large bush.

Men's voices rose in the distance and the hounds bayed in a frenzy.

"Elijah!" a man's voice said from behind the thicket.

Eli glared at Simon and made sure Elizabeth was hidden, and then answered. "Here."

The man pressed his way through the undergrowth. He was in a state of near panic. "The hounds have found something. You have to come."

"You don't need me to bring him to ground."

"It's not the fox," the man said, the color gone from his face. "It's a body."

CHAPTER FOURTEEN

Simon watched Eli and the other man ride off, torn by the desire to follow them, and needing to stay and apologize to Elizabeth and reassure himself that she was indeed all right.

"Did he say a body?" Elizabeth said as she poked her head through the bushes.

"Yes."

"You should go."

"I will, I just—"

Elizabeth's head disappeared and suddenly his jacket flew over the bush. He barely caught it before it landed on his head.

Elizabeth parted a few branches of the bush and her face appeared again. "Body. Evidence. You've got to go."

She was, of course, correct. Finding a body now, here, could hardly be a coincidence.

"All right," he said. "But for God's sake, be careful on your way home."

Once her promise was secured, Simon rode off after Eli. He found him and the other riders not far from where he'd left Elizabeth. The huntsmen struggled to control the dogs and pull them away, while most of the riders had dismounted and gathered near a young oak. Some covered their faces with handkerchiefs and as Simon neared them, he understood why. The acrid odor of decaying flesh couldn't be missed.

Simon pushed through the crowd until he saw it. Instantly, he felt the urge to wretch. Only the head and a small part of the upper torso of the body were visible in the shallow grave. Last night's storm must have unearthed it and animals had done the rest. It was already in an advanced state of decomposition. The flesh slagged off the bones and the skull had only a bare resemblance to the human it had once been. Judging from the hair and clothing, what he could see of it, it was a woman. The sickening feeling in his gut grew stronger.

James, his own face a ghostly pale, stared down at the body in shock and horror. Eli seemed one of the few to have his senses about him and had ordered a man to ride to town to get the constable.

"Who is she?" one of the men asked.

If anyone knew they weren't willing to answer.

"All right," Eli said. "I think everyone should go back to the house."

That seemed to rouse James from his stupor. "Yes, yes. I'll stay here with…" He glanced at the body again and then turned away. "With Wallace and Gaughran."

Wallace nodded, but turned and vomited.

"I'll stay," Simon offered.

James seemed to be having trouble processing and stared blankly at him for a moment before nodding. "Gaughran and Cross. The rest go with Eli."

As the others rode off, James stared down at the body, transfixed in horror. It was, of course, a natural reaction to such a thing, but Simon couldn't help but wonder if there were more to it.

"Do you have any idea who she is?" Simon asked.

"No," James said quickly and pulled himself away and then added almost angrily, "Of course not."

Gaughran wiped his mustache with his handkerchief and said, "Perhaps, we should wait upwind?"

Simon fought down his revulsion and observed what he could about the body. Forensic science was still in its infancy and any sort of identification would be difficult. From what little he knew of such things, she'd been dead several weeks, although, with the heat, it could have been more recent than that. The grave was shallow, dug in haste. He leaned in a little closer.

Her dress had been torn at the neckline, probably from scavenging animals. A thin chain from a necklace of some sort glimmered in between the gaps of torn fabric. He continued to study the body as best he could and that's when he noticed a small hole in her skull just above the temple. The hair obscured some of it, but it was clear that the bone had been cracked, and a small piece dislodged. It was possible it had happened post-mortem, but somehow Simon knew that wasn't the case. This woman had been murdered.

"She's not going anywhere," Gaughran said, waving him over to where he and Harper stood waiting.

Simon glared at him and nearly lectured him on having a little respect. Instead, he looked down at the poor woman again and made his second promise to the dead. He would find out who did this and justice would be served.

The three waited in relative silence until Eli returned with several slaves and a wagon, should the police need it to transport the body. As it would be several hours before the police could arrive, a few slaves lit torches around the perimeter of the area and were left to the grim task of waiting for help to arrive.

When Simon returned to the house, he found Elizabeth in their room preparing for the party, which, shamefully, had not been cancelled. As they changed into fresh clothes, Simon told what little he'd seen.

"She'd been there a few weeks?" she mused aloud as she laid out her dress.

"Possibly."

Elizabeth stopped fussing her clothes. "How long ago did Mary's mother leave?"

Simon paused. "Mrs. Nolan said it had been about a month since Mary had been brought to the orphanage. So just before that I would assume."

"The timing fits." Elizabeth raised her eyebrows. "And why would she suddenly leave Mary after almost eight years?"

Simon considered that. "I don't know. We know so little about their life together. It's possible something changed."

"Or she was…" Elizabeth said, not wanting to say the word.

"Murdered."

Elizabeth sighed and nodded. "That would certainly explain why Mary's so upset. Maybe she wants us to solve her mother's murder?"

Simon nodded, although he sensed there was more to it than that.

Elizabeth returned to smoothing out her dress. "Whatever's going on, a body was found at River Run. Not a coincidence."

"No," Simon agreed.

He turned to look into the mirror to adjust his tie and watched Elizabeth in the reflection. "About earlier…"

Elizabeth stopped working on her dress and turned to him. Her expression was compassionate, but also a little exasperated. She joined him by the mirror and turned him so she could work on his tie for him. "Did you really think he was attacking me?"

"I heard you scream. It…I can't say I was thinking very clearly after that."

She sighed and nodded. "I guess it did look bad. But, he's not a bad guy, Simon. He's actually—"

"Accusing me of beating you?" The memory of it sparked a fresh wave of anger.

Elizabeth's face fell and she patted his now finished tie. "From his perspective," she said as she shrugged off her robe. "It kind of makes sense."

A deep blue and purple bruise had blossomed on her upper arm where the man had held her at the race. It made his stomach roil. It also, however, was the penny drop that made him realize what Eli must have been thinking.

"He saw us arguing at the race," she said as she slipped on her corset and turned for Simon to pull the laces. "Or at least what looked like arguing. You grabbed me. I winced."

Simon tied the laces and then ran a hand gently over her shoulder. The idea that anyone could see him as the sort of man who could hurt a woman, much less hurt Elizabeth made him angry and sick to his stomach.

Elizabeth turned around to face him. "He's trying to protect me."

"From me," Simon said, the whole of it clear to him. He sighed and tried to ignore his growing sense of shame. He picked up one of her petticoats. "What were you doing there in the first place?"

"I went for a walk."

"Naked?"

"No," Elizabeth said as she motioned for him to hold out the petticoat so she could step into it. "That came later."

Simon narrowed his eyes at her.

"What? It was hot. You try wearing all this for a day," she said as she picked up another petticoat.

Simon helped her into it and then stood and faced her. While he was sorry it had happened at all, and he had reacted badly, he didn't really regret it. Considering the circumstances and Elizabeth's penchant for finding herself in dangerous situations, he'd do the same thing again. Trouble wasn't just attracted to his wife; it absolutely stalked her.

"I'm sorry," he said, hoping she wouldn't ask just what for.

Elizabeth smiled and tiptoed up to kiss his cheek. "Apology accepted."

He looped his arms around her waist and pulled her body against him. "I'm really *very* sorry."

She narrowed her eyes, but played along and arched an eyebrow. "Very?"

He nodded solemnly and she leaned up to kiss him again. He held her close and deepened the kiss. "I'm repentant," he whispered and kissed along her neck. "Remorseful." He added another kiss. "Contrite." And another.

Elizabeth purred under his kisses. "You should apologize more often."

"Yes." He scooped her up into his arms. "I'm sorry we're going to be late to the party."

Elizabeth's laughter filled the room and they were indeed late.

THE PARTY WAS, UNSURPRISINGLY, subdued, and talk of the discovery dominated conversation. Theories ranged from the romantic, a tragic end to a love triangle, to the dubious, the secret start of a slave revolt. Simon found a quiet spot away from the nattering and kept his own theory to himself. If the woman was Alice Stewart, why was she here at River Run? To which of the Harpers was she connected? And how?

At first blush, Alice Stewart's previous life as a prostitute implicated Elijah. He was clearly familiar enough with them to know that Simon had visited one. It was hardly a stretch to think he himself had been a customer on occasion. James appeared fully dedicated to his wife and child, but there was a strain in his relationship with Rose that was becoming more evident. Had he sought comfort in the arms of another woman? From Alice Stewart? If so, had Rose found out?

Simon shook his head. It was all idle speculation and no more helpful than any other supposition. They'd have to wait until the woman was identified. If she could be.

He felt his mood darken at that thought until he sensed Elizabeth arrive at his side.

"Some party, huh?" she said before she took a sip of punch.

Simon grunted, but turned to look at her. Right now, he needed the affirmation of life she provided. She smiled up at him and he felt his heart lighten.

The housemaid Rose had sent up had worked her hair into some semblance of order, but like Elizabeth herself, it refused to fully cooperate and loose curls escaped to touch her cheek. It was a departure from the severe styles of the day, Elizabeth had explained away as "the latest in Paris fashion." Her dress showed her slender shoulders and just enough décolletage to make him wish the night was over and they could be alone again. "I realize this is undoubtedly a wildly inappropriate thing to say considering the circumstances," Simon said, "but dear God you are beautiful."

Her cheeks flushed, but not from embarrassment. She'd long gotten over her surprise at being found attractive. Simon had made sure of that. The blush that stole down her neck was a reflection of his desire returned to him. He was just about to lean down and suggest they find an excuse to leave when Rose approached them.

"Hello," she said with a sad, discomfited smile. "I'm sorry the party is, well…"

She shook her head and looked back at her sullen, silent guests. The dark mood inside mirrored the weather outside where a storm had broken. Rain pelted against the window glass and the occasional thunder and lightning pulsed.

Simon felt for her. She seemed a kind and gentle woman. "Perhaps some entertainment?" he suggested.

Rose brightened at the idea and turned to Elizabeth. "Do you play?" she asked indicating the piano. "I'm afraid I'm no good at all."

Women of the upper classes of the time were expected to be proficient in everything from literature to music, all the better hostesses to make. Elizabeth looked up at him in a panic. Other than singing, loudly and rather badly, in the shower, Elizabeth did not have a musical bone in her body.

"May I?" Simon asked.

Rose's face lit with pleasure. "Of course!"

She shared a quick, impressed smile with Elizabeth before ushering him over to the grand piano in the corner of the large salon. He leafed through the sheet music, finding several pieces of Chopin and Beethoven with which he was well-acquainted. He did not consider himself skilled enough to play them as they deserved, but he doubted the guests would notice. It wasn't as if they listened to them every night. Perhaps at concerts in town on rare occasion, but in a still somewhat rural setting such as Natchez, music was more of a rarity than a regularity. Even the first phonograph was still twenty-five years away.

Simon stretched his fingers; thankful he'd taken up the piano again after he and Elizabeth had returned from 1929 New York. He hadn't enjoyed playing as a child, but as a man, he found it quite relaxing. Of course, he realized as a small crowd gathered, that had been in the privacy of his home with only Elizabeth as his audience. Not that he had stage fright, he simply preferred the intimacy of playing only for her. However, duty called.

Rose looked on hopefully and he let out a calming breath and began. The crowd listened attentively as he played "Für Elise", offering a more than polite round of applause when he finished. He followed with one of Chopin's preludes before begging off and encouraging someone else to take a turn. It had had the desired effect, and while the party was not, nor should it have been, a light affair, the oppressive pall that had settled over the guests lifted somewhat.

Simon searched for Elizabeth as he relinquished his role as the night's entertainment, but was caught by Rose, Eli at her side.

"Thank you," she said with sincere gratitude. "I would have rather canceled the party, but James was insistent. And now, I'm glad he was. Otherwise, I would never have had a chance to hear you play so beautifully."

"It was my pleasure," Simon said with a slight bow. "Have you seen my wife? I seem to have misplaced her."

Rose smiled, but Eli did not. In fact, he did not try in the least to conceal his disgust.

"I think I saw her—" Rose said, and then someone caught her attention. "I'm sorry, will you excuse me for a moment?"

"Of course," both men said in unison.

Rose disappeared into the crowd leaving Simon and Eli alone together.

Simon loathed being indebted to any man, but Elizabeth had told him the whole story of her ill-fated swim and regardless of his personal feelings toward Eli, the man had saved her life.

Simon's honor provoked an acknowledgement of the debt and he turned to face Eli. "I want to apologize for earlier today," Simon said, the words grinding out of him like grain between millstones. "I leapt to a hasty and erroneous assumption."

Eli's expression did not change.

"It also seems," Simon continued. "That I owe you a debt for saving Elizabeth's life. It is one I don't take lightly."

"Pretty words," Eli said. "But your actions toward your wife speak far louder."

Simon gritted his teeth. That again. "Now, it is you who have made an assumption."

Eli's lip curled in disgust. His gaze traveled across the room and Simon turned to see him looking at Elizabeth who was talking to Rose and James.

"She deserves better," Eli said almost to himself.

"No doubt," Simon said. "Regardless of what you may think of me," Simon continued, knowing that he could not explain away his visit to the brothel, "I love my wife and would never hurt her or any woman."

Eli arched an eyebrow. "And the bruises?"

"I can only say that I was not the cause."

Eli folded his arms across his chest. "And why are you telling me this now? I hardly think a man like you cares what I think of him."

Simon glanced at Eli before finding Elizabeth in the crowd. "I don't. But I do care what you think of Elizabeth. She is no one's pawn, least of all mine. She deserves far greater respect than that."

Across the room, Elizabeth must have felt their eyes upon her. She smiled at them, and excused herself from her conversation to join them.

She grinned charmingly as she approached. "And what are you two up to?" she asked as she slipped her arm around Simon's, leaning slightly into his side.

"Your husband was just singing your praises. And," Eli said with a quick glance at Simon, "they are well-deserved. Cross." He bowed and slipped off into the crowd.

"What was that all about?" Elizabeth asked.

"The beginnings of détente, I hope."

"How to Make Friends and Influence People by Simon Cross? Who'd a thunk it?"

Simon chuckled. "Who indeed."

MOST OF THE GUESTS had left by the time the constable arrived. He was a tall, gangly man in a dark blue wool uniform. He shook freshly fallen rain from his cap and followed James into his study. A few minutes later, both men emerged, but there was little news to be had or at least, Simon thought, little news James was willing to share.

The last guests left and eventually Simon and Elizabeth made their way up to their room. As they undressed and prepared for bed, they shared their observations of the evening.

"So Eli no longer thinks I'm under your thrall?" Elizabeth asked as she slipped under the covers.

A fresh storm had come and rain pelted the glass of the window. "I don't think so. If you had been, you would not have wandered off alone nor stripped naked during a fox hunt." Simon closed the window sash and unhooked the drapes to let them fall in front of it.

"I thought you rode in the other direction."

Simon eyed her through the dim lamplight. "Fox hunts don't work like that."

"Well, I know that *now*," she said with a lovely pout.

Simon sighed and shucked off the rest of his clothes. He pulled on his nightshirt and found Elizabeth fighting a giggle. "What?"

"Your knees are so…adorable."

Simon scowled and plucked at his long nightshirt. "I hate this thing."

Elizabeth tried again not to laugh.

"It bunches up when I sleep," Simon protested as he slid into bed next to her.

Elizabeth lost her battle and a fit of giggles ensued. "I think it's cute."

"Do you?" he asked as he caressed her neck and jawline.

The giggles disappeared under his touch and he leaned down to kiss her. He deepened the kiss and when he finally pulled away, he was gratified to see her eyes slightly glazed. She smiled up at him dreamily, all thoughts of his knobby knees gone.

Chapter Fifteen

Elizabeth rolled onto her side. She could only make out vague shapes in the darkness of their room and her head was too heavy with sleep to make sense of any of them. A flash of lightning sliced into the room through the small opening at the edge of the thick drapes that hung over the window. She waited for the following clap of thunder, listening to the stillness of the night, but none came. Only the sound of the rain as it pelted against the glass of the window and…something else. She closed her eyes and listened. It was faint, somewhere outside of their room.

Simon's arm had fallen across her waist in his sleep and she lifted it carefully and placed it on top of the covers as she slipped out from beneath it. Simon shifted slightly and she thought she might have awakened him. But his face was still slack with sleep and his breathing slow and deep.

Softly, Elizabeth tiptoed across the creaky wooden floor to the door of their room. She eased it open and stepped out into the hall, closing the door behind her. The house was sleeping. The drapes were open at the large window at her end of the landing and the light from the storm flashed down the hall. The paned glass appeared as a stretched checkerboard on the floor with each burst of lightning. Elizabeth stood on the carpet and wrapped her arms around her middle to ward off the night's chill and listened.

She heard the noise again, more clearly now than she had before. It sounded almost like a rocking chair rolling back and forth on a wooden floor. It seemed to be coming from Louisa's room at the far end of the hall.

Elizabeth walked slowly down the hall, her own shadow stretching out in front of her, long and jagged. She tread softly as she passed the Harpers' rooms and neared Louisa's. The door to her room stood ajar and Elizabeth could hear the sound more clearly now.

Elizabeth's heart began to race as she reached out and grasped the door handle. She eased the door open just a touch more and peered inside. The room was dark, but there was enough light for Elizabeth to see a small wooden cradle rocking back and forth of its own accord.

A chill swept over Elizabeth, but she stepped inside. The room was empty, save for Louisa who slept soundly in her bed. Elizabeth checked behind the door, but there was no one there. No man or ghost.

The rocking began to slow, carried only by its own momentum. Elizabeth padded over to check on Louisa. The child slept peacefully, one of her dolls cradled in her arms.

Elizabeth walked over to the cradle. The doll Louisa had called Jammy was inside, tucked in like a baby. Elizabeth reached down and stopped the cradle from rocking. The still silence of night came again. With another glance at Louisa, Elizabeth made her way out of the room. She took care to put the door back exactly as it had been. Satisfied, she turned to head back to her own room.

But at the end of the hall, stood a small silhouette against the large window. Elizabeth barely stifled a gasp. Mary. A flash of lightning came and Elizabeth could see now that the girl was facing away from her, looking out of the window. Something was different though. Mary turned and looked at Elizabeth over her shoulder. That's when

Elizabeth realized what it was. Mary was there and yet, a little not there. Her body was almost translucent.

Elizabeth glanced anxiously back at Louisa's room. "Mary," she whispered as she turned back.

But the girl was gone. Elizabeth hurried to where she'd been standing just seconds before. The stairway was empty, the hall still. Where had she gone?

Elizabeth looked out of the window and saw Mary's small figure run across the lawn. Without thinking, Elizabeth hurried down the stairs after her. Why, she didn't know, but she ran down the hall toward the back of the house. She threw open the back door and walked out onto the veranda and looked into the garden where she and Rose had seen Mary earlier that day.

There was no sign of her now, but Elizabeth could feel her close by and ran out into the rain. She could just make out the white of the girl's gown against the darkness. The little girl stopped her flight and turned back to Elizabeth. They stared at each other, the rain a blurry curtain between them. In that moment, Elizabeth felt her reaching out to her. It was a silent plea, and one Elizabeth could not refuse.

Mary turned then and started to run again. Heedless of the rain or the cold, Elizabeth ran after her. The girl had disappeared into the garden and Elizabeth picked her way through the cold grass and muddy paths.

"Mary?" she called out.

Another burst of lightning illuminated the night. Elizabeth saw a flash of Mary's white gown through the trees and raced after her. Thunder rolled overhead, growing louder and getting closer like an oncoming train.

Elizabeth searched the night for another glimpse of the child. The rain was heavy now and she had to wipe it from her eyes to see. Finally, she saw her again. Mary had stopped running and stood still, waiting for her, standing among the shadows.

Elizabeth hurried toward her. It was only as she neared that she realized that the shadows were not shadows at all, but gravestones. Mary stood among them, silently urging Elizabeth to come to her.

Elizabeth slowed as she neared the girl. "Mary?"

The little girl looked at her and then down at the ground. Elizabeth inched closer. She could feel the child's pain radiating from her in waves. Loneliness, confusion and sadness surrounded her, emanated from her and grew more and more intense the closer Elizabeth got.

The weight of it pressed down on her and Elizabeth fell to her knees in the soggy earth. Mary's despair wrapped around her. Every instinct in her wanted to comfort the child, to take her burden.

Slowly, Elizabeth reached out. "I'm here."

A great flash of lightning came, so bright and so close, Elizabeth had to shield her eyes. An enormous clap of thunder followed almost immediately. It was so powerful, so loud, Elizabeth could feel its rumble deep inside her.

When she opened her eyes again, Mary was gone. The loss of the connection was a shock. The feelings of anguish lifted, but left Elizabeth feeling lost. Her tears came unbidden and mixed with the rain. She slouched down, suddenly exhausted and the rain poured down upon her.

She didn't know how long she'd stayed that way. Her body ached when she moved again. She stood and read the small ornate headstones that Mary had stood near. The graves of children. Rose's lost children.

"Elizabeth!"

Poor Mary. So lost, so lonely.

"Elizabeth!"

She looked up then and saw Simon hurrying toward her. He'd hastily pulled on his pants and boots, but hadn't taken the time to button his shirt. He held an overcoat over his head as a makeshift umbrella. The panic on his face ebbed when she started toward him.

"Are you all right?" he asked as he pulled her into his arms.

"I'm fine," she said coming back to herself.

Simon searched her face and then lifted the overcoat to protect them both against the storm.

"You'll freeze to death," Simon said. The anxiety in his voice was edged with irritation, but she knew it was worry in disguise. "What the hell are you doing out here?"

"I'm sorry. I'm all right," Elizabeth said as she leaned into his side. Her teeth chattered traitorously.

As they emerged from the garden, the tall thin slave named Jacob appeared halfway across the lawn with a large umbrella. "All right, suh? You wants me to get someone?"

He held out the umbrella and Simon took it, giving him the sodden overcoat in exchange. "Thank you, Jacob," Simon said. "We're fine."

Jacob didn't seem to believe him, but nodded and followed them back to the house.

Simon asked Jacob not to speak of what he'd seen and the poor man looked relieved to pretend he hadn't seen a crazy woman running in the rain. She and Simon made their way quietly back up to their room. Simon closed the door and lit one of the oil lamps. Even in the dim light she could see his fear and concern.

"It was M-mary," Elizabeth said, fighting a shivering chill.

Simon nodded and looked around the room. He grabbed a quilt from the back of a chair and tossed it onto the bed.

"She was in Louisa's room," Elizabeth said, trying to recall what now felt like a dream.

Simon frowned and she hurried to add, "She's all right. I think Mary was playing with one of her dolls."

"Let's get this off you," Simon said as he touched the fabric of her sodden nightgown.

Elizabeth nodded and he pulled the cold, sopping wet shift over her head, leaving her naked and feeling a new chill. He grabbed the quilt from the bed and wrapped it around her shoulders.

"Then she led me outside."

"You should have woken me," Simon said sharply. Elizabeth pulled the quilt more tightly about her body.

Simon sighed. "I'm sorry." He pushed out another breath and closed his eyes for a moment to control his emotions. "I woke and you weren't there, and I feared—"

"It all happened so fast. I was afraid she'd be gone if I came to get you."

Simon nodded and then grabbed the towel that sat next to the basin and pitcher.

Elizabeth remembered how far she'd chased Mary into the garden and woods. "How did you find me?"

Simon draped the towel over Elizabeth's wet hair and rubbed her head quickly to dry it. "Jacob was downstairs and heard you leave through the back door."

Simon stopped tousling her hair and urged Elizabeth to sit on the edge of the bed. "She wanted me to follow her," Elizabeth said.

Simon knelt and rubbed life back into her cold feet with the towel.

"We ended up at the family cemetery. So many children," she said sadly. "That's where she belongs, Simon. I know it."

Simon looked up at her and nodded thoughtfully. He took her hands in his and rubbed warmth into them. "Yes, I think I sensed that as well, but couldn't put a name to it."

"Poor thing," Elizabeth said, remembering the feeling of sadness, of loss she'd felt in the girl's presence. And then she remembered something else. "She's fading, Simon."

"What do you mean fading?" He took the quilt off her shoulder and laid it on the bed. Then, he pulled back the covers.

Elizabeth crawled under the sheets. "Remember what Old Nan said? That time wasn't on our side and that the ghosts can't stay here forever, eventually they fade away and are trapped in the world in between? Mary's disappearing, Simon. Slowly, but it's happening."

Elizabeth pulled the blankets up to her chin and fought down another shiver. Simon nodded and then undressed. Naked, he got in bed and pulled her chilled body against his warmth. He wrapped his arms around her. His hands were large and warm and strong as they caressed her.

"We're running out of time," Elizabeth said, feeling the current of desperation that Mary had left with her surge anew.

Simon urged her to roll over and rubbed her arm before cupping her cool cheek in his warm palm. "We will help her," he said, sounding so sure, so confident.

"What if we can't?"

He moved closer, pressing their bodies together and kissed her. "We will," he said softly as he kissed again. "I promise."

Elizabeth let her fears and doubts melt away in the warmth of each kiss and the tenderness of each caress until all she felt was him.

ELIZABETH SETTLED INTO THEIR buggy and prepared herself for the long ride back to town. After breakfast, they'd agreed to return to Natchez to see what they could learn about the body found yesterday. They'd said their goodbyes to the Harpers, promising to see them again at Louisa's birthday party and started their two-hour journey back to their hotel.

Once they'd passed under the wrought iron gate and turned onto the main road, Simon looked back over his shoulder. "That was an interesting morning."

"Was it?" Elizabeth hadn't noticed anything out of the ordinary. Everyone seemed subdued, but after yesterday it would have been odd if they hadn't. "Breakfast seemed like the usual to me."

"After breakfast," Simon said. "I spent the morning thinking about what you'd seen last night with Mary. What that meant. Her being a Harper."

Elizabeth nodded. She'd thought of little else.

"That means she's either James's child or Eli's," Simon said.

"Or Rose's."

"Yes, or some combination." Simon leaned forward as he spoke. "If you're correct, and I think you are, about James and Rose's marriage not being the happiest, it's possible James had a child with another woman. Alice Stewart."

Elizabeth had considered that. "He seems so in love with Rose though."

"I've known several men whose love, even adoration, for their wives didn't preclude them from having affairs."

Maybe she was naïve on that score, but Elizabeth just couldn't see James cheating on Rose. "I have a hard time seeing either of them having an affair. Happy or not."

"Possibly," Simon said. "Which brings us to Elijah." He cast a wary glance at Elizabeth. "Putting aside my personal prejudice against the man, he is the most likely candidate to have fathered a child the family didn't or wouldn't claim. He is, after all, familiar with at least one of the local brothels."

"So are you," Elizabeth pointed out.

Simon made a sour face. "Don't let your prejudice *for* the man color your thinking, Elizabeth. It's a logical assumption that he might have been with Alice Stewart and Mary is his child."

She had to concede the point. Eli was the leading candidate. She just hated the idea that he would have a child and abandon her. He was so good with Louisa. But he'd hardly be the first man to do something like that. It was all too common for a man to have a child with another woman, even a slave, and disavow any responsibility.

"At least that's what I thought before breakfast," Simon said. "Now I'm not so sure." He leaned back in the buggy seat. "I happened upon a private moment between Rose and Eli."

"What?"

"Not that kind," Simon hastened to add. "They were just talking, but…Do you remember when I mentioned that I thought Eli had a secret?"

155

Elizabeth nodded.

"I'm fairly certain he's in love with his brother's wife."

"Hold the phone," Elizabeth said. She hadn't seen anything like that between them. "Eli and Rose?"

"I can't say how she feels, but I can with some certainty say how he feels."

Elizabeth shifted in her seat. "Did he say something?"

"No, not in so many words. It was the way he looked at her."

Elizabeth stared at Simon. Who was this man and what had he done with her husband? "A look?"

Simon glanced over at her and smiled, almost shyly. "Yes. He is secretly in love with Rose. He does his best to conceal it, but there have been a few unguarded moments and today when I came across them in the garden, I saw the way his expression changed, and I knew."

"How could you know?"

"It was mine for over a year. I loved you secretly," he confessed with a self-conscious smile. "I did everything in my power to keep anyone else from knowing, but I saw it in my own eyes, in my own reflection. And I saw that same pain and yearning in his today."

Could she possibly love this man more? Elizabeth slid closer. Simon put the reins into one hand and pulled her to his side with the other and kissed her temple.

They rode in silence for a few moments. "And if Mary is Eli and Rose's child, James could have found out and sent her away."

"But then what about Louisa?" Elizabeth said. "If Eli does love Rose and she doesn't or can't love him back because of James, we're back to Eli being the father with Alice Stewart as the mother."

Simon sighed. "I wish Mary could tell us more."

"We need a ghost telegraph or something."

"Maybe Old Nan can help us," Simon said.

Elizabeth hoped so. Time was running out.

Chapter Sixteen

Simon keyed open their hotel room door and stepped back for Elizabeth to precede him inside.

"Rut-roh," Elizabeth said softly.

Simon was about to ask her what that meant when he saw for himself. Their room had been ransacked. Furniture was overturned and their belongings scattered. Simon raised a hand asking Elizabeth to wait by the door. She made a face and he knew better than to argue the point. He carefully made his way toward the bedroom, Elizabeth's hand resting on his back as she followed. He grabbed two long heavy candlesticks and handed one to Elizabeth.

The door to the bedroom was open and he peered through the slit by the wall and hinges. He could only see a small section of the room though and had no choice but to continue forward, arm raised and ready to strike.

He pushed the door open with his foot and when no sound came from inside, he crossed the threshold. The room was empty. Whoever had been here was long gone. Thankfully, the watch and key were safe in his pocket, but the rest of their belongings looked to be destroyed.

Elizabeth put her candlestick down on the side table. "I wonder what they were looking for?"

"I don't know," Simon said, feeling the anger rise inside him. "To see who we are, why we're asking questions." He picked up one of Elizabeth's dresses from the floor, or what was left of it. It had been slashed to ribbons.

"Oh, I liked that one," she said with a frown as she took the shredded garment from him.

"Either way, they're trying to intimidate us," Simon said. "And it's making me rather cross."

Elizabeth looked as though she was going to say something about the pun, but thought better of it. It was just as well. He was in no mood for jokes at the moment. If whoever was behind this thought they could be put off by threats, they were sorely mistaken.

THEY'D SALVAGED WHAT THEY could and packed up the rest. After giving the hotel manager a dressing down for having let such a thing happen at his establishment, Simon instructed him to keep their trunk somewhere safe until other arrangements could be made.

He and Elizabeth stopped by dressmakers and haberdashers and everything in between to start the arduous process of repurchasing what they needed. Most shops had little on hand and had to special order items from New Orleans. Sending the order down river and waiting for the shipment could take weeks. It was time they didn't have. After two hours spent on that futility, the next step was finding a new, and hopefully, more secure place to stay. Unfortunately, the Mansion House Hotel was by far the best in town. If the security had been lax there, he shuddered to think what it would be like at the others.

Just as Simon was reaching a boiling point of frustration, fortune smiled on them in the form of Catherine Stanton. She was returning from her morning volunteering at the orphanage when they ran into her in town. Needing someone to trust and a little help, they confided in her. Mostly.

They were somewhat circumspect in providing the truth behind their curiosity about Mary, but that didn't seem to matter to Catherine. She saw their interest in the girl as a just cause and, if there was ever anyone Simon had met who was ready to mount a hobbyhorse and ride it into the ground in the name of a cause, it was Catherine Stanton. She was more than happy to offer them not just accommodation, but clothing.

In a whirlwind of activity, she began to take care of their needs. One of her brothers was just about Simon's size and would be, she assured them, happy to have offered the clothes. Elizabeth's situation was more difficult. Catherine was a half-foot taller and their shapes could not have been more dissimilar, but Catherine Stanton was not a woman to be put off by such minor impediments and managed to procure Elizabeth several dresses, one quite stunning that needed only minor alterations.

They were most obliged for her help with the clothing, but the place to stay was more complicated.

"Your offer is incredibly generous," Simon said, as one of the servants brought lemonade out onto the veranda of Cypress Hill. "But—"

"The Colonel won't mind," Catherine said with a dismissive wave. "The house is far too big for just the two of us. You can stay as long as you need."

"That's very kind," Elizabeth said, "but I think what Simon was going to say is that whoever broke into our hotel room could be violent. We don't know that they won't try something again. Maybe even worse."

Catherine's eyes sparkled at the challenge and she pushed back her chair. She dug around under the table, her petticoats fluffing up into the air. "Any man who tries to break into Cypress Hill uninvited will have a rather rude awakening," she said as she sat back up and brandished a large pistol she must have had concealed under her dress.

She waved it in the air as if she was rousing the troops at the charge of the Light Brigade. "I'd like to see them try!"

Abraham appeared almost out of nowhere and his hand shot out and grabbed the pistol. "Miss Catherine," he said with a frown as he took it from her. "What did the Colonel say about you and guns?"

She feigned ignorance.

"That it were like giving a banjo to a bear and half as much fun." Abraham made sure the gun wasn't cocked and tucked it into his waist.

"Really, you two are never going to forgive me for that, are you?" she said. "It was an accident. Most of his hair grew back."

ONCE THEY'D SETTLED IN at Cypress Hill, she and Simon had ventured over to the police station to see what they could learn about the body that had been unearthed. They scouted the small police station, waiting for the senior officers to go to dinner and leaving a young, green officer as the sole man on duty.

Simon walked into the station as if he owned it. He rang the bell on the desk with a sharp slap and waited impatiently for the duty clerk to come out of the backroom. Luckily for them, the man that emerged was little more than a teenager and not the barrel chested sergeant they'd seen at the house yesterday.

Elizabeth lingered by the bulletin board, looking at Mississippi's most wanted, giving Simon room to operate and ready to jump in with Plan B if Plan A failed. However, judging from the nervous and pimply face of the young officer, Simon would have this one well in hand.

The young officer's heavy wool uniform was so oversized the poor kid could have fit two of himself inside it. He tugged nervously on his jacket to make sure the buttons were all done properly and hurried to the desk.

"Ma'am," the boy said with a quick bow.

Elizabeth smiled at him and the boy smiled back, suddenly nervous. He pulled himself away from Elizabeth and back to Simon, who glared at him impatiently as if the man should have been able to divine his request from his mere presence. The young man swallowed hard, his Adam's apple bobbing in his throat like a Ping-Pong ball.

"Yes, sir?" he squeaked finally.

Simon tugged off his gloves with royal diffidence. "The report," he said simply.

"Sir?"

Simon sighed. "The coroner's report? The Jane Doe?"

The boy's head bobbled up and down, relieved to have some idea what was going on. "Right."

Simon narrowed his eyes. "Well?"

"Um, I—"

"I don't have all day, boy," Simon said as he slapped his gloves into one hand. "Are you familiar with the Harper family?"

The boy nodded.

"They are, as you would imagine, deeply upset by yesterday's events. Do you want me to tell them of how your impertinence added to their misery or should I deal directly with your sergeant?"

The boy quelled under the thought of either possibility. Elizabeth felt a little sorry for the kid. She'd seen confident college students reduced to puddles of gibbering insecurity for less by this imperious version of Professor Cross.

The boy gulped. "I'm sorry, sir."

"The report?"

The boy nodded quickly and hurriedly went through the top drawer of one of the large filing cabinets at the back of the room. He pulled out a piece of paper and handed it over to Simon.

Simon read it, his frown deepening. Elizabeth didn't like the looks of that. Deep frowning was never good. "This is the report in its entirety?"

"Yes, sir."

Simon put the paper down on the counter. "I see. You have been most helpful, Officer…?"

"Miller, sir."

Simon bowed and held out his arm for Elizabeth. She went to him and slipped her arm through his.

"Thank you, Miller," Simon said. "I'll be sure the Harpers know how helpful you've been."

Simon escorted Elizabeth out of the station and into the early night air.

"Well?" she asked, dying to know what the report said.

Simon looked anxiously behind and didn't answer until they'd put a little distance between themselves and the station. "The report was a farce."

Elizabeth shook her head in confusion. "What do you mean?"

"No cause of death determined, 'no injuries present'," Simon said with a sneer. "No inventory of clothing or personal items. No mention of the necklace I saw at all. The doctor didn't make any effort to identify the woman, or—"

"Already knew who she was," Elizabeth finished for him with a sinking feeling in her gut. "And didn't want anyone else to know."

Simon grimaced. "I'll give you two guesses as to the identity of the author of this fiction."

Elizabeth knew who it was before Simon had even finished asking. "Dr. Walker?"

Simon nodded. "The very one."

She wasn't shocked that there was a potential police cover-up. Not really. Sadly, very little of this was adding up in neat little columns. "Why would the police be in on it though?"

Simon led her over to a recessed doorway. "I'm not sure they are. They would have little reason to question the coroner's report. The body was beyond identification, if there was no physical evidence as the report indicated, there would be little they could do and little cause to pursue the case."

She knew this sort of thing happened all the time, throughout history, but it didn't make it any more palatable. "And no one wealthy has been reported missing, so she's just buried and forgotten?" Elizabeth asked.

"Tomorrow, as a matter of fact."

"That doesn't leave us much time."

Simon arched an eyebrow. "To do what?"

Elizabeth merely smiled.

Chapter Seventeen

Elizabeth pulled on her cap and looked in the mirror. A goofy-looking, and somewhat effeminate, boy looked back. She'd bound her chest with long strips of cloth to flatten her figure, but her face was too round and too soft. She swam inside her oversized clothes and generally looked like a dope. But she didn't care. She was finally free of that cursed corset and had never been so thrilled in all of her life to wear pants.

She'd settled on an old linen French blouse that hung out over her large brown wool trousers. The cuffs of the pants had to be rolled three times before she could keep from tripping on them. A piece of hemp rope tied tightly around the waist was the only thing that kept her trousers from falling around her ankles. It seemed that the Stanton boys were giants, even in their youth.

Her sack coat was made from rough and scratchy brown burlap. It almost looked like a small artist's frock with sloping shoulder and straight at the sides. It wasn't a good look. But, she reminded herself, this wasn't a fashion show; it was breaking and entering.

Initially, Simon had rejected the idea of breaking into the morgue, citing two reasons that were really rather reasonable. It was dangerous and it was a felony.

Elizabeth had tried to persuade him by pointing out that the danger was mitigated by the fact that in the middle of the night, the morgue would be deserted. Besides, it was a felony only if they got caught. If they let that woman be buried tomorrow, any clue as to who she might have been would be lost forever. That would be a far worse crime, and they couldn't let that happen. The woman deserved better than that. And, if their suspicions were right, knowing who the woman was would be the key to helping Mary. If Dr. Walker's report wasn't just laziness or incompetence, but a calculated cover-up, it was best they knew that too. Finding the necklace Simon had seen or some other identification was worth the risks.

Once again, though, they needed help. Elizabeth and her voluminous petticoats were hardly good breaking-in material. After some debate, they'd agreed to take Catherine Stanton further into their confidence. She already knew they were interested in what had become of Mary Stewart, but telling someone you were about to commit a crime was a whole different ball of wax.

Catherine had already heard the stories about the body's discovery and suspected the police would do little to solve the case. She was not only willing to help them uncover the truth, she was eager to. Any opportunity to help a downtrodden woman, she'd said, was one she couldn't ignore. If anything, Catherine was positively electrified by the idea. The only thing that had kept her from going along herself had been Abraham's promise to tag along after them. They knew he wasn't doing it for them, but to protect Catherine from herself, which *was* apparently a full-time job.

Elizabeth laughed as she heard Simon's voice in her head. Something about a pot and a kettle. She tugged on her jacket and refocused. She might have been an idealist, but she wasn't stupid. It was a risky plan. Despite a part of her being excited at the prospect of getting to do something and finally being free of her dang repressive clothes, she knew there were genuine risks involved.

She let out a breath and looked at herself in the mirror again when a knock at the door interrupted her thoughts.

"Come in," she said, knowing it was Simon.

He came into their room and closed the door. She could see his frown in the mirror as he walked up behind her. His dark wool suit and an old brown frock coat marked him as a man from the middle class, a low merchant. He held a short brimmed hat in one hand and tapped it against his thigh as he stared at their reflection. A surly man and his idiot son stared back.

Simon shook his head. "I'm not sure this is wise."

Elizabeth turned to face him. "Since when has that stopped us?"

"That is hardly a comfort."

At the appointed time, they snuck downstairs. While the Colonel had graciously allowed them to stay at Cypress Hill, they somehow doubted he'd condone their little late-night excursion. The stairs creaked under them with every step, but they managed to escape without being detected. They met Abraham by the back door and started their half-mile walk to the police station.

It was well after midnight when they turned the last corner. They'd crossed paths with barely a handful of men, most of whom were drunk or well on their way to being. A few solitary horses and draft carts trundled past, but in the darkness of the night, no one paid them any heed. There were no street lamps, so staying in the shadows was not difficult.

The police station was housed in a nondescript two-story brick building on the edge of town. They'd cased the area earlier in the day and discovered that the room that served as a morgue at the jail had its entrance at the back in a narrow alley between the station and a barbershop.

Simon instructed Abraham to remain at the mouth of the alley to warn them if anyone approached. For a moment, Elizabeth thought he might try to convince her to take the post instead, but if he'd considered it, he'd wisely kept the idea to himself.

Simon made his way as stealthily down the alley as he could. No matter how cautiously he stepped though, his footfalls resonated loudly in the echo chamber of the narrow alley. If they weren't careful, they were going to get caught before they even got started.

"All right?" he whispered once he was at her side.

Elizabeth nodded and knelt down in front of the door. The lock was simple enough, but not one she'd ever worked on before. Her "Uncle Tony" had taught her how to pick locks. He also taught her how to palm dice, mark cards and deal from the bottom of the deck. Growing up in the back of pool halls had its advantages. Now, she was ready to put some of that knowledge to use as she studied the keyhole and judged the striker. Old locks like these didn't have tumblers, so the usual picks wouldn't be any good; she needed something to work the lever inside the ratchet.

She patted her pockets and found two large hairpins. They were long, but the tips were wrong. She was just about to bend one into a crook when Simon tapped her shoulder.

"Just a sec," she said.

"Elizabeth," Simon said with another tap.

"What?" she said, turning impatiently.

A key dangled between his index finger and thumb. She stood. "You have the key"?"

"I have a key," he said and pulled out a handful of others. "Abraham culled these from various places at Cypress Hill and suggested we bring them."

Elizabeth scrunched up her face in disappointment.

Simon took a small key from his palm. "I'm sure we'll find something else for you to burgle before long," he said as he slid the key into the hole and turned. It moved freely, but was too small to catch the ratchet and move the bolt.

Elizabeth looked nervously down the alley and saw Abraham

leaning casually against the wall, his hat tipped forward over his eyes. It was *a ri*sk for him just being out seemingly alone at this time of night. There were some free blacks in Natchez at the time, but she somehow doubted their loitering presence would be anymore welcome than a slave's.

It took two more tries before Simon found the right sized key. The bolt slid back with an audible thunk that echoed loudly and unnervingly down the alley. Gently, he eased open the door. Elizabeth went in first, moving carefully into the darkness. The stench was immediate and overwhelming. It was a mixture of chemicals and rotting flesh and not one she would ever forget. She covered her nose and tried to see in the dark. But there were no windows and not a scrap of light entered the room once Simon closed the door. She heard his footsteps and then felt him as he bumped into her from behind.

"Sorry," he whispered.

She heard him strike a match and the small glow from it lit their corner of the room. He held the match in front of him until he found an oil lamp. He lit the wick and then put it on the desk in the corner.

The room wasn't very large, perhaps fifteen feet across with a tile floor. Shelves with various bottles and crates lined the wall opposite the desk. Filing cabinets were against the other, and a door to the jail rounded out the scene.

In the middle of the room sat a long narrow table. On top of it lay a body wrapped in a dirty white sheet. Mud and things Elizabeth didn't want to contemplate stained the lower half and seeped through the fabric like bruises at pressure points. The body had been bound with ropes about the ankles and midsection like some grotesque present.

"Check the files first," Simon said.

They rifled through the files as quickly and as quietly as they could. The only record they found was the paper Simon had seen earlier. There was no other trace of the case at all.

"Nothing," Elizabeth said and then cast a nervous glance at

Simon who nodded grimly and approached the body. The excitement from the start of the night wore off quickly and was replaced with a growing sense of dread.

His hands hovered over the sheet for a moment, fingers flexing, until he let out a breath and untucked the top edge of the sheet from its bindings. As soon as he unfolded the sheet, the stench in the room increased tenfold and Elizabeth felt the urge to wretch, but fought it down.

"I'll need the light," Simon said.

Elizabeth picked up the oil lamp and walked around to the other side of the body. She held the lamp over the woman's head, what was left of it. She'd seen some horrible things. King Kashian's death, a man shot, but she'd never seen anything like this. Her stomach lurched and she had to look away.

She could hear the sticky sound as the fabric was pulled away from something it had adhered to. Simon groaned and pushed out a quick breath. "I know I saw a necklace," he said.

Elizabeth couldn't leave him to face this alone and turned back to look. The woman's head was displaced, sitting just off center, her hollow eyes staring into nothingness. Her shoulder looked dislocated.

"Was she so…apart when you saw her?" Elizabeth asked.

"Some, but not like this."

Obviously, little care had been taken to preserve her or any evidence when they'd transported the body. There was no CSI: Natchez.

"Maybe it fell down there when they moved her," Elizabeth suggested waving her hand in the general direction of the woman's neck.

Simon nodded and took out his handkerchief. Slowly and carefully, Simon moved the woman's hair aside. "More light," he said.

Elizabeth walked around to the head of the table and held the lamp where Simon was focused. "There," he said in triumph.

Elizabeth leaned forward. She could barely make out the glint of something metal.

Simon quickly went to the desk and found a pencil. Then, like some twisted game of Operation, he reached down into the skeleton with it and hooked the end around the chain. Carefully, he lifted the chain up until it dangled and danced in the light.

"They must have missed it," Elizabeth said.

"Or didn't care enough to find it," Simon said. He wrapped it up in his handkerchief and stuffed it into his pocket. "Come on."

Elizabeth put the lamp back where Simon had found it while he rewrapped the body. Once he was finished and positioned at the door, she blew out the flame. He opened the door and after checking to make sure the coast was clear, they hurried out of the morgue and into the alley. The night seemed positively bright and cheery by comparison.

Abraham pushed off the wall and started down the alley toward them. Simon fumbled with the keys in his pocket to find one to relock the door. Just as he found the right key and locked the door, footsteps came from the street at the far end of the alley.

Abraham put his hand on Simon's arm to still his movements. Even in the dark, the silhouettes of two police officers were unmistakable. Elizabeth held her breath as the two men walked casually by arguing about whether Tom Hyer or Yankee Sullivan was the better fighter. They'd almost passed completely when one of them turned around to show Sullivan's jab when he froze in mid punch.

"You!" he called out. "What are you doin' down there?"

His partner followed his gaze and the two started down the alley toward them.

"Run," Abraham said in a hoarse whisper.

Both Simon and Elizabeth turned to him in a panic.

"Now," he said. "Run!"

Elizabeth didn't need to be told twice, except of course that she had been, and took off as fast as her feet would carry her. Sadly, that was not very fast. Between the oversized boots she wore and having skipped Pilates classes for the last year or three, she was painfully slow. She felt Simon pull up at her side and heard the clamor of other footsteps behind.

Suddenly, Abraham was with them, clearly scrubbing his speed to accommodate for theirs, or hers. "Left," he urged them in a coarse whisper.

When the alley dead-ended into the street, they took a sharp left and ran as fast as they could. Simon reached out *and grabbed ahold of Eliz*abeth's arm, trying to pull her along faster. The contact threw her off her stride and it was a miracle they didn't fall to the pavement in a tangle of limbs and regret.

She knew Simon and every hero in every movie nearly always grabbed onto the woman's arm or hand in a chivalrous, I'll not leave you behind! way, but all it really managed to do was turn running away into some three-legged race with arms.

Elizabeth had just managed to find a good rhythm again when Abraham gave them another instruction. All she could hear was "wall", but she saw Simon nod and trusted him to know what the heck that meant.

Almost seconds after their first sharp turn, Simon made another, this time, pulling her along with him. Out of the corner of her eye, Elizabeth could see Abraham turn the other way. But there wasn't time to ask any questions.

She and Simon slid to a halt in front of a six-foot tall granite wall. Elizabeth looked at him in a panic. Had he misunderstood? They were trapped!

Simon laced his hands together and turned to her. "Hurry!"

Elizabeth could hear the officers' footsteps, but didn't dare look back. Every second counted. She put her foot into the stirrup of Simon's hands. Bracing herself on his shoulder, he heaved and she felt herself fly up and over the wall like a human caber. She landed with a thud on the hard ground on the other side. Not exactly catlike, she barely had time to roll over and out of the way as Simon appeared at the top of the wall and vaulted down next to her.

She waited for Abraham to appear, but he didn't. She looked at Simon in a panic and he shook his head.

What the hell had happened?

They huddled up against the cold stone and listened. Elizabeth tried to control her rapid breathing. She was definitely signing up for a Zumba class when they got back. She could just make out the sound of footfalls echoing off into the distance. Simon waved for her to stay put and then slowly stood. Using the cover of one of the trees on their side of the wall, he peered cautiously over before kneeling down next to her. They waited in sil*ence crouched down in the bushes for a minute that* moved so slowly it virtually limped along as with a broken leg.

He took her hand and urged her to move quickly and quietly along the length of the wall. Elizabeth followed him and realized they'd jumped into someone's yard. She looked around in the darkness. Please, don't have dogs. Please, don't have dogs.

Either the family didn't or they were sound sleepers because Simon and Elizabeth managed to run the length of the yard undetected. When they arrived at the far end of the wall, Simon peeked over the edge again. "Clear," he whispered and laced his fingers together again.

This time, he merely lifted her up until she could clamber onto the top of the wall. He lifted himself up with annoying ease and flipped one leg over. He helped slow her descent to the other side as she slid down the wall to the street and then leapt down to join her.

"Where's Abraham?" Elizabeth asked as they tried to get their bearings.

"He led them off the other way."

Elizabeth felt a wave of guilt. He shouldn't have come in the first place. If they caught him, it would all be their fault. She shook her head; there would be time for recriminations later. Now, they had to get the heck out of here. She took quick measure of the streets. She recognized it. She'd come this way when she'd visited Dr. Walker's.

"This way," she said and they walked as quickly as they could away from the mess they'd made and back to Cypress Hill.

Catherine was waiting for them on the back porch when they arrived. She smiled with relief when she saw them, but it faded quickly. She hurried down the steps and peered out into the darkness of the back yard. "Where's Abraham?"

"We ran into a spot of trouble," Simon said in that uniquely British way of understating really bad things.

"We'd almost gotten away," Elizabeth said, "and then these two police officers showed up."

Catherine stepped forward, her face drawn and pale. "Did they catch him?"

"No," Simon said. "I don't think so. We ran and he led them away. Gave us a chance to escape."

Despite her worry, Catherine smiled. "That's Abraham."

"He was much faster than they were," Simon assured her. "I'm sure he lost them."

"I hope so. If they catch him…" she said and then let out a shaky breath. With an effort, she composed herself and ushered them back into the house. "You should change."

They agreed and made their way upstairs as quietly as they could.

Once inside their room, they set about shedding their disguises.

"Do you really think he made it?" Elizabeth asked.

Simon nodded, but the worry on his face was plain.

"If he gets caught, we'll come forward," Elizabeth said. "He won't take the fall for us."

Simon rolled their dirty clothes into a ball and set them aside. "Yes, but I fear it won't spare him."

"But if he's—"

"He's a slave, Elizabeth," Simon said and then sat down heavily on the bed. "If he's caught I doubt it will matter what we say."

Elizabeth felt like she'd been slapped. She'd been so stupid. How had she not realized that? She'd been so used to thinking of people as people that she still hadn't digested the notion that, here, that was not the case.

"We should never have let him come," Simon said, the weight of it all clear in his voice.

Elizabeth sat down next to him and took his hand in hers. "Maybe he got away?"

Simon nodded slowly. He patted her hand and stood, then bundled up their dirty clothes. "Maybe."

Once they'd changed back into their usual clothes and cleaned up a little, Simon and Elizabeth went back downstairs. They found Catherine sitting in the second parlor at the back of the house. She'd lit a single oil lamp and was sitting on the settee near the large bay window at the back of the house. She turned away from her vigil when they entered.

"I'm sure he'll be along shortly," Catherine said, forcing a smile to her face.

Elizabeth sat down opposite her. "I'm sure."

Simon remained standing in a posture Elizabeth had come to recognize as "still pacing"—feet shoulder width apart, hands clasped behind his back and a far off look in his eyes. He was replaying it all in his head, just as she was. Self-reproach and worry mixing in equal parts.

Simon might prefer silence's company to mindless chatter, but Elizabeth did not. She couldn't stand the "what ifs" that lurked in the quiet. "How long have you known Abraham?" she asked.

Catherine smiled again, this one genuine and fond. "Nearly all of my life. We practically grew up together." Her smile faded a bit. "As much as two in our positions can. We were very close until I went away to school."

Catherine turned away from the window and settled into the sofa. "I'm the youngest and only girl. When my mother died, my father sent me away to finishing school." Her eyes held a hint of laughter and a little pain. "Apparently, I was unfinished. I think I still am."

"I'm not sure any of us are ever fully cooked," Elizabeth said.

Catherine laughed lightly. "You're right about that. I resisted my father's efforts to refine me and I found myself shuttled from one school to another. I finally ended up with my mother's sister in Connecticut where I attended Miss Porter's. One day, I heard Mrs. Elizabeth Cady Stanton, no relation I'm afraid, give a speech."

Elizabeth knew only a handful of names, she thought shamefully, of the women who had fought in the early days for women's suffrage, but Elizabeth Cady Stanton was one.

"I had friends who'd spoken of the Women's Rights movement," Catherine said, "but despite my bluster I was still a good Southern girl at heart. I might be able to argue with my father about Euripides or what silver to use at supper, but… I will admit I was afraid of him. But then, Mrs. Stanton said something I will never forget, 'The greatest protection any woman can have is courage.' And so I found myself some."

Elizabeth smiled. "And you went to Seneca Falls?"

"I did and then returned home to drive my father crazy."

Suddenly, Simon moved and stepped toward the window. "Thank God," he said.

Catherine spun around and then practically ran to the back door. Elizabeth and Simon weren't far behind. Catherine pulled the door open just as Abraham was about to reach for the handle and threw herself into his arms.

Abraham's face was slick with sweat and covered with confusion. He held his arms out, not daring to return the bear hug Catherine was giving him. Finally, she released him. "Thank heaven. Are you all right?"

"I'm fine," he said and looked to Simon and Elizabeth with questioning eyes.

"We are as well," Simon said. "Thanks to you."

"Good, now I don't—"

The sound of a throat clearing from the stairway stopped the rest of the words. They all turned to find the Colonel, wrapped in a robe and deep displeasure. "What," he said, lingering over the word, "is going on here?"

Elizabeth did her best not to look guilty and was sure she did a poor job of it. The Colonel's eyes shifted from one of them to the next, pausing at each and silently demanding an answer.

"We thought we heard something, papa," Catherine said quickly. "Someone in the yard. Abraham chased them away."

The Colonel's eyes shifted from his daughter to Abraham and then back again. His usual sour disposition masked any hint of whether he believed them or not. He cast a quick accusing glare at Simon and then Elizabeth that clearly said, this is your fault, but he merely grunted and let them squirm under the pressure for a moment before saying, "I see."

"You best go to bed now, Abraham," the Colonel continued.

"Yassuh."

"I will speak with the rest of you in the morning," the Colonel said before turning and starting back upstairs. "Do not wake me again."

CHAPTER EIGHTEEN

The following morning over breakfast, Simon and Elizabeth did their best to dissuade Catherine from becoming further embroiled in their mission. After last night's near disaster, the last thing Simon wanted was someone else to worry about, but Catherine Stanton was not the sort to stop her flag carrying because of a hurricane force wind.

"I wonder what they're hiding," Catherine said as she buttered her toast.

"Maybe it was an honest oversight?" Elizabeth said with a quick glance to Simon.

"I think that's likely," Simon agreed, although he and Elizabeth believed quite the opposite.

Catherine chewed her bite of toast ferociously as she thought. "Maybe we should go to see Dr. Walker? Confront him."

"Are you ill?" the Colonel said as he joined them in the dining room.

"No, papa." Catherine took another bite of toast and, thankfully, had enough sense not to explain further.

"Good," the Colonel said as he sat down at the end of the table.

"If you are, you're not to see that charlatan. Dr. Parish or Smith, anyone else."

The Colonel opened his newspaper as one of the servants came in with a fresh cup of tea and put it in front of him.

"Really?" Elizabeth said and looked to Simon for an encouraging nod. "I saw him the other day and he seemed quite nice."

The Colonel snorted and unfolded his newspaper. "To women with more in their purses than in their heads, perhaps."

Simon arched an eyebrow in disapproval and the Colonel amended, although a little reluctantly, "Present company excluded, of course."

He lifted his newspaper and Elizabeth stuck out her tongue at him.

Catherine choked on her tea.

The Colonel put down his paper and frowned at her. "Are you sure you're not ill?"

Catherine shook her head and dabbed at her mouth with her napkin.

"I don't know," Elizabeth said. "He volunteers at the orphanage and I understand he's the one who examined the body of that poor woman they found the other day, for the police."

The Colonel harrumphed. "Walker's only charitable cause is himself. The man is a degenerate and a gambler. Losing money he can ill afford," the Colonel said with repulsion. "He makes an appearance to impress the town widows and loosen their pocketbooks."

"At least he makes an appearance," Catherine said not so quietly.

The Colonel glared at her. She'd told Elizabeth that she'd tried again and again to get her father to volunteer there. The boys there would make perfect little soldiers, she'd said. Besides, he was always looking for someone to boss around and the boys would be far more willing victims than she was. Somehow, that hadn't won him over.

The Colonel didn't rise to Catherine's bait. "I am far too busy for such things. As to the other business, Walker helping the police," he said, "I find that highly unlikely."

"No, it's true papa."

The Colonel seemed about to reply when his frown deepened. "And just what is your interest in the matter?"

Catherine shrugged. "Idle curiosity."

Her father pursed his lips. He knew that there was nothing remotely idle about his daughter. "Stay out of other people's business, Catherine."

He fixed her with a pointed glare and she offered an innocent smile in return. He humphed again and went back to reading his paper. Catherine wiggled her eyebrows over her cup of tea and Elizabeth stifled a giggle.

Between the two of them, Simon was doomed.

SIMON TRIED TO BE more discreet than he had the last time he'd traveled down Water Street to Smiley's Saloon. To his knowledge, Elijah Harper had not gossiped about his previous sojourn, but he doubted he'd be so lucky should he be seen a second time.

Simon pushed open the swinging doors and stepped inside. The lower floor was nearly empty with just a few people, all too tired or still too drunk to care about anything. Two saloon girls, including Genevieve lingered at the end of the bar.

"Back again?" Genevieve said with a smile.

"I just need a few minutes," he said.

The brunette with smeared lipstick next to her laughed. "You and every other man."

Simon nodded toward a table in the corner. "I only have a few questions."

"If you need help, honey," the brunette said as she swayed precariously close, "I'm your girl."

Genevieve pushed her friend away. "Go, dry up, Sal."

Sal frowned and pouted but slid down the bar away from them.

Genevieve motioned to the corner table. Out of habit, Simon held out her chair. She looked at him as if he'd grown a second head, then laughed and sat down, shaking her head.

Simon pulled up his own chair and placed a ten-dollar bill on the table. "Just a few questions." He pulled his handkerchief from his jacket pocket and unfolded it. "Do you recognize this?"

Genevieve leaned forward and picked up the necklace to examine it. Her expression shifted from bored to interested and then quickly to worry. "Where'd you get this?"

"Do you know who it belongs to?"

She shrugged. "It's Alice's. She never took it off. How'd you get it?"

"You're sure?"

"Said it was her mother's or something, from Scotland or Ireland or someplace."

Simon nodded thoughtfully and put the necklace back into his handkerchief. "Thank you."

"Why do you care? What's she to you?"

Simon put the folded handkerchief back into his pocket. "Someone who needs help."

Genevieve slid the ten-dollar bill toward her and stuffed it into her bosom. "Ain't we all?"

Elizabeth took a few moments to study the girls as they changed their bed linens. While Simon was otherwise occupied, Elizabeth had decided to tag along with Catherine to the orphanage. She'd helped in the kitchen until the cook had practically kicked her out. Catherine was busy teaching the boy's morning class, leaving Elizabeth to her own devices, and so she sought out the girl's dormitory.

The children fluffed and wrestled with their sheets as they made their beds. One girl, bigger than the others sat and watched a little one do the work, until Elizabeth's watchful eye forced her to help.

Most of the others tended to their own small beds, except for one little girl at the end of the hall. She still had her nightgown on and sat perched on the edge of a bed watching as another girl worked.

At first Elizabeth thought it was another bullying situation, but she soon realized it was anything but. The girl in the nightgown coughed and shivered and the other put a blanket around her shoulders before getting back to finishing making the bed. She smoothed down the sheets and then folded back the covers. The littler one slid in between the sheets and curled up. Poor little bug.

The other girl handed her something, a doll maybe, and then tucked her in. This was the one Elizabeth would want to talk to—the little mother. She was hardly ten years old, but Elizabeth could tell she was the one who looked out for the little ones. If anyone had taken the time to get to know Mary, it would have been her.

Elizabeth walked down the corridor between the beds.

"Is she all right?" Elizabeth asked.

The girl looked up at her in surprise and back down at her charge with such compassion it made Elizabeth's heart tighten. "She'll be fine," she said as she petted the little girl's head. "Won't you, Mellie?"

Mellie nodded and curled up tighter, hugging her doll beneath the covers.

The other girl turned and started work on what Elizabeth assumed was her own bed.

"What's your name?" Elizabeth asked.

"Alison. And you're Miss Elizabeth," she said. "I remember from when you come before."

"That's right," Elizabeth said. "Do you think we could talk? Just you and me?"

Alison looked at her shyly and then nodded. "I have to finish this first."

Elizabeth picked up one end of the sheet and pulled it taut. "We'll have it done in a jiff."

Once they'd finished making the bed and Alison had checked

on Mellie one last time, she led Elizabeth outside to a bench under a shady oak. A tiny gray and brown sparrow pecked at the ground looking for seeds.

Alison smoothed out her threadbare calico dress, and sat primly and politely waiting for Elizabeth to begin.

"I was hoping you could tell me a little something about Mary Stewart," Elizabeth said. "Were you friends with her?"

Alison thought about the question quite seriously, her little brow furrowing as she considered her answer. "She weren't here very long, but we was friends a little."

"Did she ever talk to you about her mother or father?"

"Not at first. She didn't talk much to nobody, but when I started taking care of her—"

"When she got sick?"

Alison nodded. "She used to tell me about them then, but it was just the fever talking. It does that," she added with a sad, knowing look.

Elizabeth gave her a sympathetic smile. "What did she say? Do you remember?"

Alison bit her lip and squinted to try to remember. "She said her momma and daddy lived in a big house, like a king and queen. Course I knew her momma up and left her. Everybody did. Some kids used to tease her about it. Her momma bein' a whore and all."

Elizabeth swallowed her shock at the casual way the girl had said it. But then, perhaps here, sadly, it wasn't all that an uncommon a thing for a single mother to be. "That upset her?"

Alison shook her head. "Mary'd just say that weren't her momma anyway so they could say what they wanted, didn't mean nothing to her."

Elizabeth felt a tingle. "She said that the woman who took care of her wasn't her mother? That Alice Stewart wasn't her mother?"

Alison shrugged. "That's what she said."

Elizabeth tried to stop her mind from racing. What could that mean? "She said her parents lived in a big house?"

"She thought they was gonna come for her. Said her daddy told her he would." Alison smiled up at her, sadly. "They never come."

Elizabeth clasped her hands to keep her from taking the girl into her arms and comforting her. What could she say? Don't worry little orphan girl, someone will come for you? She knew it wasn't true. It wasn't true for any of them.

Alison sighed and Elizabeth's heart couldn't take much more of this. She heard Simon's voice in the back of her head. *We cannot save them all.* Understanding the reality of her limitations didn't help her aching heart.

"Dr. Walker and me took care of her," Alison said proudly. "He said I was his best nurse."

"I'm sure you were."

"He gave me her medicine and I made sure she took it every day with hot tea," Alison said. "One for her and one for her baby."

Elizabeth's brows arched in question.

"You know how little ones is. She wouldn't take nothin' unless her doll took it too."

"Ah, I see. I'm sure you took very good care of her."

"She was always sickly, even before she come, Dr. Walker said. And sometimes, he said, there ain't nothin' nobody can do for the real sick ones. Sometimes a child isn't meant for this world."

Those words felt like a physical blow. Poor Mary. Elizabeth forced a sad smile. Alison smiled back thoughtfully and then leaned back into the bench. They sat quietly together watching the little sparrow hop around in the grass, until it had its fill and flew up into the branches of the oak and landed in a small round nest.

They watched the mother bird care for her chicks until Mrs. Nolan called them back inside.

Simon and Elizabeth met for lunch at a small restaurant in town and shared what they'd learned that morning. Simon wasn't quite sure what to make of Elizabeth's talk with the girl from the orphanage. Had Mary really known who her parents were or weren't, or was it just her imagination painting castles in the clouds?

Armed with the evidence that Alice Stewart was indeed the dead woman and concerned about Elizabeth's description of Mary the night before last at River Run, they decided to go see Old Nan again. The old woman had been vague the first time. Why couldn't psychics be straightforward, Simon thought irritably. Why must everything be masked in a riddle like they were the bloody Sphinx?

Abraham was kind enough to get them another audience with the elderly woman that afternoon. As they climbed the steps of her small cabin again, Simon was determined to get some actual answers this time.

Old Nan sat as she had before in her rocking chair, but this time she was talking to a small boy in tattered clothes. "You be sad now," she said. "But it won't always be dat way."

The boy nodded, but his lower lip trembled as he fought back tears.

"You listen to Old Nan," she said kindly, but firmly. "She know best."

Abraham shifted his feet nervously and tugged on his fingers. Simon noticed him looking around the room anxiously and then staring at Nan.

"Now, you run 'long," Nan said. "Tomorrow be better. Hmm?"

The boy chewed his lip and then noticed Elizabeth and Simon for the first time. He glanced back at Nan who nodded and he turned and ran for the door, and right through it. Simon had suspected the boy might be a spirit, but seeing him run through solid wood still caught him off guard. He could see that Elizabeth felt much the same way. The same could not be said of Abraham, however. His eyes never left Nan, his expression unchanged, and Simon suddenly realized Abraham hadn't seen the boy, that he *couldn't* see the boy.

Nan leaned back in her rocking chair.

"Will he be all right?" Elizabeth asked.

Nan smiled and started rocking. "He be gone by sundown. Sometime dey just need a kind word to set 'em on dere way."

Abraham swallowed and looked nervously between the two women. "Maybe I should just wait outside?"

He looked to Simon for permission and once he got it wasted no time leaving the small cottage.

Once the door was closed, Nan studied Simon and Elizabeth again, just as she had the first time. Her milky white eyes danced over them, seeing without seeing, and an odd smile came over her wrinkled face. "You is peculiar. Part of you is here and part of you later."

While Simon found her second sight fascinating, it was somewhat discomfiting when it was turned his way. Despite that, he couldn't help but wonder if she could be sensing some sort of temporal wash from the watch? Simon had experienced it when the watch had first come into his possession, but it was nothing like this. As interesting as that theory was, he refocused. He was resolute about getting actual answers about Mary this time.

"Yes, well," Simon said, "be that as it may, we're concerned about Mary. Mary Stewart, you remember?"

"I remember."

Simon waited, but that was apparently all the woman had to say. He turned to Elizabeth silently entreating her to help.

"I saw her again," Elizabeth said. "The night before last, and she was starting to fade. Like you said she might."

Nan hummed and kept rocking.

"We were hoping," Simon said, feeling his impatience grow, "that you might be able to tell us more. Help us, help her. Has she come to see you? Has she told you anything that might help?"

Nan smiled. "She chose you."

"Why?" Elizabeth asked, casting a quick glance at Simon. "Why us?"

"Why do any of us choose another?" Nan said. "We all has holes inside dat need fillin'. Dat child need you as much as you need her."

"I don't understand," Simon said.

"Your burden," she said as she continued to rock back and forth slowly, rhythmically.

She'd said that the last time as well, but Simon still had no idea what it meant.

Nan nodded. "She help you heal your pain. Your loss."

Elizabeth cast a nervous and curious glance at Simon. "What loss?"

Nan smiled sadly. "Your child."

Simon shook his head in confusion. "We don't have any children," he said and then looked quickly at Elizabeth. "We haven't had any children yet."

Nan stopped rocking and cocked her head to the side. "You is peculiar."

Elizabeth looked at Simon in concern. "What do you mean, the loss of our child?" she said, stepping forward and kneeling at the old woman's feet.

Nan leaned forward, her sightless eyes seeing something in Elizabeth's face. She reached out and Elizabeth took her hand. Nan looked off into the distance and covered Elizabeth's hand with both of her own.

Simon's sense of foreboding grew with every moment that slipped past in the quiet of the little shack. He stood there watching them, watching the old woman seek out answers only she could see.

Finally, Nan shook her head and released Elizabeth. "Most peculiar. Only de ones dat have lost a child can see de children."

Simon helped Elizabeth stand, and squeezed her hand tightly in his. He remembered Isaac that afternoon at River Run when he'd thought Simon had been talking to the flowers, and just a minute ago, Abraham—it made sense now. "Some people can't see them."

Nan nodded.

"But we haven't lost a child," Elizabeth said and then added with a nervous laugh, "I'm pretty sure I'd remember that."

Despite her laughter, Simon could see and feel the tension in her body. He shared it.

"Perhaps it has not yet come to pass," Nan said.

"Wait," Elizabeth said. "Are you saying we will have a child and then…"

Under other circumstances, it would have been easy to disregard such a prognostication. In his experience, most clairvoyants were misguided souls at best and frauds at worst. But Old Nan was neither of those. He had seen her confer with dead. He'd witnessed her powers.

But he could not, would not, accept her words. Simon shook his head. "No. There's some other explanation. You're mistaken."

Nan leaned back in her chair. "It is your burden."

"No," Simon said, more firmly. This could not be.

"I see what I see," Nan said sadly.

Simon felt anger and denial bubble up inside him.

Elizabeth moved closer and gripped his arm. "Simon?"

He controlled himself and turned to her. She looked so pained. "No one can see the future," he said trying to reassure her, and himself.

"I am sorry for your loss," Nan said.

Simon spun toward her. He didn't want her misplaced condolences or sympathy. This would not be. He was ready to lash out at her when Elizabeth spoke. Her voice was barely a whisper.

"What happens?"

Nan smiled at her sadly. "Oh, child. I wished I could say."

"You mean you can't or you won't," Simon bit out.

Elizabeth laid a hand on his arm.

Nan turned her white eyes full of pity to him. "I see things here," she said, laying a fragile hand over her heart. "And there," she pointing

187

a long, slender finger toward Simon's chest. "Your heart tell me it's so. I feel it in you."

Elizabeth squeezed his arm tightly and he looked down into her eyes, already wet with coming tears. Simon shook his head. He would not accept that. "Impossible."

Nan brought her hand back down and laid it on the arm of her chair.

"And Mary?" Simon said. "Can you help us help her?"

Old Nan began rocking again. "She chose you."

Simon pushed out a heavy breath. The air in the little cabin felt thick in his lungs.

"Thank you for your time," he said with a slight bow of his head.

Elizabeth started to say something, but managed only a weak smile of thanks for the old woman.

Simon barely remembered walking out of the little cottage. Gripping Elizabeth's hand tightly in his, he waved off Abraham as he started to stand up from his spot beneath a shade tree and come toward them. "A moment, please," Simon said. "Give us a moment."

Simon's breath came in short staccato bursts as he tried to rein in his anger and stop the fear that clawed away at the edges of his heart. He felt Elizabeth's hand grip his arm and saw the terror in her eyes. He stopped walking and held her upper arms.

Leaning down so he could see her eye to eye he said, "She's wrong."

Elizabeth shook head, tears filling her eyes. "What if she isn't? She sees things, Simon. What if she really saw—"

"The future?" Simon finished for her, pushing down his own growing sense of panic. "No."

"It's possible though, isn't it?"

Simon shook his head, trying to convince himself as much as Elizabeth. "Our future is not yet written. What she saw, whatever she thinks she saw, she's mistaken."

"What if she isn't, Simon? I can do a lot of things, but I don't know if I could bare—"

Simon cupped her cheeks gently in his hands. "Elizabeth." Her tear-filled eyes, wide with worry, met his.

He swept away a tear. "Nothing is fixed in place, not today, not tomorrow, not even yesterday. The fact that we're here, doing what we're doing, changing things, proves that."

"There are some things even we can't change, Simon. You know that."

"I know two things. That I love you," he said, caressing her cheek. "And that whatever comes, I will find a way to protect our family. *We* will find a way."

Elizabeth nodded, but he could still see the shadows of doubt in her eyes. She sniffled and pushed out a breath. "It's what we do, right?"

Simon pulled her into his arms. "It's what we do."

Chapter Nineteen

Simon listened to the sound of Elizabeth's breathing as she slept. He'd always found it comforting, the slow, steady rhythm and the knowledge that she was safe by his side.

A half an hour ago, she'd finally fallen asleep, but rest still eluded him. They'd both been unsettled by the meeting with Old Nan, quiet through dinner, struggling to put aside what might be and deal with what was.

When they'd retired to their rooms and the lights had been put out, they talked again, finding hope and strength in each other. If Simon had learned anything in the last year and a half of his life, it was that whatever you expected to happen, seldom did. And, much to his amazement, what did happen was usually quite wonderful.

Elizabeth groaned softly in her sleep. A small frown creased her forehead.

"It's all right," he whispered and the worry lines melted away. He leaned over and kissed her temple and a sleepy smile came to her lips.

If only every fear were so easily assuaged.

Simon lay back down, folded his arms behind his head and stared up into the darkness. He had spent the better part of a lifetime worrying about what had been and fearing what had yet to come. Now that he had a life worth living, he'd sworn he would never go back to the way it was before, to never waste today worrying about tomorrow. Be prepared, he'd told himself, but be present.

There was no way to know if what Old Nan had prophesied would come to be until it had come to be. He would not spend his life living in fear. He would not let Elizabeth live her life that way either. They would face whatever came together and together there was nothing they could not do. It should have been an absurd thought. It was childish and fanciful. And yet, for a man of no faith, he had faith in this. He had faith in her, in himself, in what they were together.

Prophecies be damned.

He pushed out a heavy breath. They had work to do *here. Now.* There was a child who needed them. Now. And he'd made a promise to her. One he would not break, although he did not know how to keep it.

He lowered his arms and Elizabeth rolled toward him. He slipped his arm around her and pulled her to his chest. She rested her head on his shoulder and he closed his eyes.

They would find a way, he thought. That was what they did.

Elizabeth held Louisa's birthday present in her lap and tried not to think about yesterday. She'd spent the morning reminding herself, with an assist from Simon, that psychics were notoriously inaccurate. In fact, they'd met only a handful that were ever right. The odds of Old Nan's prediction, if it could even be called that, being accurate, were negligible.

Of course, even the possibility that she might be right weighed like a bad burrito in the pit of Elizabeth's stomach. Simon had been right about something else as well, though. Worrying about what was yet to be was pointless. They could do nothing to alter the future, but they could do something here and now. Mary Stewart needed them, and letting her down was unthinkable.

A wheel of their buggy dipped into a rut made by the recent storms and the entire thing lurched and bounced until Simon steered them clear of it.

"Sorry," Simon said.

Elizabeth gripped the arm railing. "How far do you think we are?"

Simon looked around at the nondescript woods and shook his head. "Not far, but Genevieve's description was somewhat vague."

The woman had given Simon a rough description of the house Alice and Mary Stewart had lived in. It was a small cottage down a shady lane near a split oak. Genevieve had said she thought it was about four or five miles out of town and just off the main road, but she'd never actually been there herself.

They traveled another half-mile or so before they came upon a man and his small wagon stopped by the side of the road. Judging from the rough shape his horse and clothes were in, it looked like the man might be a tenant farmer or a day laborer who worked for one of the so-called yeoman farmers. Both classes of poor whites in the South lived on the rung just above free blacks and slaves.

The man bent over next to his horse and coaxed it to give him his leg. He pried dirt and debris free from the horseshoe with a short knife. He looked up as their buggy drew along side and tipped his hat. Elizabeth smiled back at him as Simon eased the buggy to a stop.

"Good day," Simon said.

The man let the horse's leg drop and then rubbed the lower calf before standing again. "Suh. Ma'am," he said, taking off his hat and clutching it to his chest. He squinted up at them through the bright morning sun.

"We were wondering," Simon said. "Do you know of a small cottage nearby? A woman and her child used to live there. Alice Stewart?"

The man scratched his neck and nodded. "Yassuh." He pointed up the road. "About hundred yards up thataway."

"Thank you."

Elizabeth settled back in her seat as Simon lifted the reins to give them a flick.

"But, uh, it ain't there no more," he said. "They tored it down last week."

They both turned back to the man. "Who did?" Simon asked.

The man frowned. "Owners. I s'pose."

She could feel Simon's impatience as he looked beseechingly to the heavens.

"Do you know who they are?" Elizabeth asked.

The man smiled up at her and then ducked his head shyly, apparently not used to speaking to a wealthy woman. "That's Harper land, ma'am."

"James Harper of River Run?" Simon asked.

He nodded. "Yassuh. All the way back to that creek y'all just passed," he said with a stab of his thumb back down the road.

"Do you work for them? The Harpers?"

"Naw, suh. I work for the Millers just over yonder. They's neighbors to the Harpers."

"I see," Simon said. He tipped his hat and the man bowed in response. "Thank you very much."

"Yassuh. Ma'am," the man said, bobbing his head and bowing as Simon shook the reins to their buggy and they pulled away.

"Well," Elizabeth said. "That was interesting, wasn't it?"

"It was indeed," Simon said. "So the Harpers were Alice's landlord."

"And more?"

Simon sighed. "It's hard to imagine otherwise at this point, isn't it? If Mary is a Harper, either James or Eli has to be her father. They wouldn't be the first man to set up a mistress in a secluded hideaway."

Elizabeth wrinkled her nose. He'd told her about the hole he'd seen in Alice's skull. "Having an affair is one thing, but killing her is another."

"It could have been an accident," Simon said.

"Yeah, but you don't accidentally bury someone."

"No," he conceded with a wry smile. "The grave was shallow, hastily dug. Perhaps whoever killed her, panicked. If he'd taken the time to do the job properly, we'd be none the wiser."

Elizabeth studied the terrain as they traveled on to River Run. "I'm kind of turned around. We're not that far from where they found her, are we?"

"No," Simon said. "Not far at all, I think." He nodded toward the woods to their left. "That small hollow. We drove the fox that way and then doubled back. That was just before I found you and that snake-charmer."

Simon glowered at the memory and Elizabeth giggled. He turned his glare on her. "Should our positions have been reversed, I doubt you would find it quite so amusing."

He definitely had a point there. Mostly. "You're right. Imagine though if I had to sneak into a brothel to interview a handsome gigolo. Twice."

Simon snorted.

"Anyway," Elizabeth said. "I just have trouble picturing Eli doing any of this."

"He's not unfamiliar with prostitutes," Simon pointed out with a small measure of smugness.

Elizabeth rolled her eyes. "I know, but having a child with one and setting her up in a love-nest when he's already in love with Rose? It just doesn't fit."

"Perhaps it wasn't quite so romantic," he said. "But more of a practical nature."

"I don't know. Eli's handsome," Elizabeth said and ignored his derisive snort. "And wealthy and fun to be with. For some of us, it just feels off."

Simon frowned and hmm'd out loud.

"What?" Elizabeth asked.

"Well," he said, a little reluctantly. "We've assumed Alice was the wronged party."

Elizabeth shrugged. "Well, she is the dead party, so—"

"Yes, but what if it wasn't a love-nest or anything of the sort. There are women who seek out wealthy men…Become involved and then use a pregnancy to…"

"Blackmail them?"

"Yes," Simon said.

"You sound familiar with this," Elizabeth said, squinting at him, but unable to hide her smile. "Anything you'd like to tell me?"

She'd been joking, but Simon was stinking rich and honorable. He'd make a heck of a target for any gold-digger.

"Not personally," he said with a smile. "But there were friends at school."

Elizabeth watched the scenery roll by and said, thinking aloud, "So maybe one of them had an affair with Alice, and whether it was their own sense of responsibility for the child or her leveraging the situation, she got set up in a nice little house in the country."

"Until something changed," Simon said. "A month ago, something changed. Something drastic enough to cost her her life."

"And possibly Mary's," Elizabeth added. "Everyone's said she was a sickly child. But don't you wonder? If her mother was murdered…"

"Yes," he said with a dark look in his eyes. "And if that's the case, God help them."

Elizabeth felt the same way. If Mary had been murdered, she and Simon would turn over heaven and earth for justice. If only they knew where to start.

THE PARTY WAS IN full swing by the time Simon and Elizabeth arrived. A dozen or so children, wearing their finest dresses and suits, played on the back lawn at River Run. Elizabeth could see two boys playing hoop and stick, which involved rolling a large wooden hoop and chasing after it, using the stick to keep it rolling. An Xbox, it was not. But, judging from the peals of joyful laughter, it hardly mattered. A group of girls watched primly from the sidelines, missing all the fun, as the boys raced from one end of the manicured lawn to the other.

Long tables had been elaborately set up with fine silver and porcelain for the coming lunch. Slaves hurried back and forth from the kitchen to make sure everything was perfect for the meal. Adults either lingered on the veranda or under a large white tent that provided additional shade. They chatted and drank, admiring the extravagant table overflowing with already opened presents.

Rose pulled herself away from a few guests and ascended the back steps to Simon and Elizabeth on the veranda. "I'm so glad you could come," she said with a genuine and warm smile. "Louisa!"

Her daughter dutifully hurried over to them and curtseyed. Simon gave her a gentlemanly bow in return.

"Thank you so much for coming to my party," she said and looked to her mother for approval.

Rose smiled.

"This is for you," Elizabeth said as she held out their gift. "Happy birthday."

"Happy birthday," Simon said.

Louisa took the box and looked to her mother again for confirmation. Rose nodded and Louisa set it down and carefully unwrapped the brightly colored paper.

"Cross," James said as he appeared at the bottom of the stairs. "Miss Elizabeth."

He joined them on the veranda and shook Simon's hand.

Louisa put the wrapping paper aside and opened the long flat mahogany box to reveal a set of pearl handled combs and brushes. She smiled up at her mother and held one up for her to see. "Oh, they're so beautiful! Look momma, like yours!"

Rose leaned down to admire them. "They're lovely," she said, smiling her thanks to Simon and Elizabeth.

"Look daddy!"

James scooped her up into his arms. "Very pretty. For a very pretty girl."

Louisa giggled and toyed with the bristles of one of the brushes.

She was a pretty girl and her hair was lovely. It had been the reason they'd thought of the brushes in the first place. Enviable, gentle auburn curls framed her heart-shaped face.

As Elizabeth took in the handsome family—mother, father and daughter—at the same time, her throat went dry. She knew now what had been nagging at the back of her mind since the races: Louisa's heart-shaped face. She had a widow's peak, but neither James nor Rose did. To anyone else it would have meant nothing, but to Elizabeth it was a three-alarm job.

Everything else seemed to fade into the background as Elizabeth digested the truth. Louisa was not their biological child. She couldn't be.

Elizabeth came back to herself as James said something that made Louisa giggle.

"It's perfect," Louisa said.

Elizabeth struggled to catch up.

"Already?" James said with a mock frown. "Even before your big present? Perhaps you don't need it after all."

"What is it?" Louisa said, bouncing in his arms.

"Come and see," he said as he carried her down the stairs.

Elizabeth wanted to drag Simon off and tell him, but Rose turned to her and smiled, somewhat ashamed. "He spoils her so. Well," she said as she looped her arm through Elizabeth's, "shall we go see what he's done?"

"Yes," Elizabeth said, still stunned by the revelation. "What has he done?"

Chapter Twenty

Simon watched as the children and the parents cooed over Louisa's "big present". As James covered Louisa's eyes one of the grooms led out a stunning white pony. The child squealed with joy in an octave only little girls and castrati could achieve, and then ran back and forth between her father and her new horse. The other children were duly impressed and wasted no time on working on their parents for the next gift opportunity.

James lifted Louisa up onto the elaborate saddle on the pony's back and walked her past her guests like the queen leaving Buckingham Palace. It reminded Simon of parties he'd been forced to attend as a child. Those were usually displays of wealth meant to impress adults and had little to do with the child's happiness. At least, in this case, the girl was clearly ecstatic.

"Just like Bonnie Blue," Elizabeth said as she came to his side.

Simon frowned down at her. She'd promised no *Gone With the Wind* references. He was actually amazed she'd lasted this long.

She slipped her arm through his and nodded toward the far side of the garden. "Walk with me?"

Always happy to be alone with her, he gladly complied. They

walked away from the crowd and Elizabeth steered him to a semi-secluded spot out of earshot of the others.

"The picture of a happy family, aren't they?" she said as they turned back to watch James lead Louisa past Rose.

"Something is out of focus?" Simon asked.

"Photoshopped. It's going to sound crazy, but in 8th grade I was obsessed with Marilyn Monroe."

"Of course you were."

Elizabeth's eyes flashed with annoyance. "Anyway, I wanted a widow's peak. I thought they were the most glamorous thing ever. I tried to train my hair, I even tweezed once, like Marilyn," she admitted. Simon winced. "But you can't make it happen," she added. "It's either in your genes or it isn't."

Simon waited patiently for the point.

Exasperated that he was apparently too dull to see it, she sighed and nodded toward Louisa. "Genetics."

He followed her gaze and the light suddenly dawned. "Louisa has a widow's peak."

Elizabeth nodded. "But neither Rose nor James does. Basic high school science. It's impossible for Louisa to be their child."

All this time he'd been so fixated on Mary, and with good reason, it had never occurred to him that Louisa could play a part in this. "Rose had an affair as well?" he wondered out loud.

"Hard to believe," Elizabeth said. "But what other explanation could there be?"

"I don't know," Simon said, trying to process the possibilities. He turned to catch a glimpse of Louisa when something familiar caught his eye. "Mary."

Mary stood hunched in the bushes watching the children through parted branches, watching the party that should have been hers. Perhaps it really was hers. Mrs. Nolan at the orphanage had said that Mary had died a week before her eighth birthday. It could hardly be a coincidence that Louisa had met that mark today.

Mary must have sensed them looking at her, because she turned away from the party and toward them. Elizabeth had been right; she was fading, but it was far worse than he'd imagined. She looked so sad, so small, so frail.

Mary took a step toward them, and with her closeness he felt the same wave of despair he had before, and with a new sense of helplessness. With each step her image became more translucent, almost transparent. She must have felt it, felt herself draining away, because her expression shifted from surprise to fear. She ran toward them. Instinctively, Simon started toward her. Only steps before they could touch, she vanished.

Simon felt the surge of panic and pushed it down. It was too soon, wasn't it? They had to have more time.

"Simon?" Elizabeth breathed, her anxiety echoing his own.

He looked to Elizabeth and back to the empty spot where Mary had just been. "We are running out of time."

He had to *do* something. They'd stood back and watched long enough, he decided. It was time to act. Searching the party, he found James standing by the veranda talking with Dr. Walker, and another man. He started toward them.

Elizabeth trailed behind. "What are you going to do?"

Simon stopped and turned back to her. "I think it's time I had a little chat with James Harper."

Elizabeth looked surprised. "What are you going to say? Nice party. By the way, had any affairs lately?"

Simon frowned. He honestly didn't know what he was going to say, but it was time something was said. If they were to save Mary from an eternity "in between" as Old Nan had put it, they'd have to do more than attend children's parties.

"If Mary is a Harper," Simon said, "James or Elijah is her father. She won't find peace in death until they admit their part in her life."

He turned to Elizabeth. "We've no reason to believe they're going to suddenly see the light and claim her as their own. Can we really afford to wait any longer before we confront them?"

Elizabeth's brow furrowed. "No." She looked back to where Mary had been a few minutes ago. "I just hope we haven't waited too long."

Simon set his jaw and nodded. He walked over to James and forced a smile to his lips. "I'm sorry to interrupt, but would it be possible to speak with you and your brother privately for a moment?"

James excused himself and they gathered Eli from a flock of women and went into James' study.

James sat on the corner of his desk. "If this is about the investment opportunity, it's not too late—"

Eli leaned against the bookcase, prepared to be bored.

"No," Simon said impatiently. "It's not about that."

James spread his arms as if to say go ahead.

Simon looked at one brother and then the other. "This is about a personal matter."

"If this is about my seeing your wife naked—" Eli said.

"Eli!" James said in shock.

Simon clenched his jaw. "No, this is about a child."

James stood, tense and concerned. He glanced at the window. "Louisa?"

"Mary Stewart."

Eli shrugged. "Who's that?"

James leaned against his desk, arms crossed over his chest and worked hard to make his expression appear neutral, even disinterested.

"Alice Stewart's daughter," Simon said, looking both men in the eye. "Perhaps that helps."

"I don't see what any of this has to do with us," James said as he toyed with a paperweight on his desk.

"No?" Simon said as he took a step closer. "Are there so many bodies buried on your property that you lose track?"

James dropped the paperweight, his voice rising. "Now, see here—"

"That woman was never identified," Eli said, raising a finger to emphasize his point.

"Not officially," Simon said, turning his attention back to Eli.

"Thanks to a little influence wielded by a powerful family? A family friend conveniently installed as temporary coroner and overlooking evidence? Ignoring her injuries, ignoring her murder." Simon saw them both blanch at that. "A poor woman like that. A prostitute. No one would ask questions."

"I don't like what you're implying," James said.

Eli stepped forward. "I don't understand."

"Then let me be clear," Simon said, his fury growing. "Alice Stewart was a tenant on River Run."

"We have several tenants," Eli said.

"And do you father all their children?" Simon demanded. He could feel his blood pressure rising.

James stood and his eyes flashed with anger. "That's quite enough."

"No, it's hardly enough," Simon said, as he took another step closer to the brothers. "If you are man enough to create a child, you damn well better be man enough claim her as your own."

Eli looked honestly confused. "Would one of you tell me what the hell this is all about?"

"I think you need to leave this house," James said.

Simon was barely able to control his anger now. He would give anything, do anything, to protect his own child. The idea that one of these men had discarded theirs made him sick. "One of you had an affair with Alice Stewart. Mary was your child. If there is a shred of decency inside you, you will do what you know is right."

James strode forward until they were nearly nose to nose. Simon stood in front of James, ready to fight.

Eli stepped between them. "I think you'd better go, Cross. Now."

Simon's eyes shifted to Eli briefly. James looked about ready to hit him, and even though a part of Simon would have relished a physical confrontation, it would not be the best course. Not yet.

Simon nodded to Eli and took a step back. "You may be able to bury their bodies," he said. "But you cannot bury the truth with them."

CHAPTER TWENTY-ONE

E LIZABETH TRIED TO FIND something kind or at least interesting to say about Millard Fillmore. After all, he was the President. Somehow she doubted she could share her honest views on the Compromise of 1850 or the Fugitive Slave Act with the wives of the Old South. Sadly, that was about all she knew, too. It would have been so much easier if the women had fit her vision of them as sweet, retiring, gossipy flowers. But they were not. Oh, they gossiped enough, but the most popular topics of conversation weren't puffery, but politics. Politics meant talk in the defense of slavery, the demonization of abolition and the threat of secession. There weren't poles long enough to touch those subjects.

She smiled at something Mrs. Goode said and wondered how Simon was getting on. At least he could meet the issues head-on. Although, she didn't envy him his task.

From across the veranda, Rose caught her eye and smiled sympathetically. If only she knew that her world was going to change, she might not be so kind right now. And that troubled Elizabeth. Rose was kind. Genuinely kind. Elizabeth considered herself a good judge of character. Rose was honest and good. No matter the circumstances it was nearly impossible to imagine her having a part in any of this, or having an affair of her own. And yet, Elizabeth thought as Louisa came to her mother's side, she must have.

It just didn't make any sense. When Rose had told Elizabeth about Louisa's birth, how difficult it was, how the doctor had thought they both might die, there was not a hint of dishonesty about it. Not a trace of guilt about having another man's child. She must truly believe that Louisa was theirs, but how could she forget the whole sleeping with the other man part. That was usually hard to forget.

Rose pulled Louisa into her lap and the girl leaned back against her chest.

What else could it be? Elizabeth tried to let go of her conclusions and look at the evidence with a fresh perspective. Sherlock Holmes, and he knew his stuff, fictional or not, said that one should approach a problem with a blank mind. Don't twist facts to suit theories, let the theories fit the facts.

While the ladies discussed whether "that doughface Franklin Pierce could actually win", Elizabeth settled in for a little silent sleuthing. First, she had to clear her mind. She pushed out a long slow breath and had just started to fall into the zone when she caught sight of Simon coming toward her. He looked agitated. Holmes would have to wait.

"We should go," he said.

Simon hastily made excuses for their abrupt departure, promising to see them all again at the Colonel's gala ball tomorrow night. In a tense silence they waited for the buggy to be brought around to the front of the house. Whatever had happened inside had left Simon wound up tighter than a tick.

They traveled nearly a quarter mile of the way down the road toward town before he calmed himself sufficiently to tell her about the conversation. Elizabeth listened raptly. Simon certainly hadn't pulled any punches.

"I wish I'd done a better job of it," he said.

"I don't know how you could. It's not exactly an easy conversation to have."

Simon nodded and let out a deep breath. "Frankly, I wish you'd been there. I was so angry that I'm not sure I can judge their reactions properly. I let my emotions get the better of me."

Elizabeth squeezed his arm. "I don't blame you."

"Reason, if I could have managed it, would have been a far superior tool."

Elizabeth could feel the tension in the corded muscles of his arm. "We can try again tomorrow."

Simon sighed again. "I don't know. Whoever is at fault here has gone to great lengths to cover up their misdeeds. I don't think they'll give in so easily."

"We'll just keep trying until they do," Elizabeth said.

"And hope we're not too late."

They rode in silence for a while after that, each lost in their own thoughts. The afternoon sun began to fade and long shadows stretched out across the road. The horse's hooves and the wooden buggy wheels beat out a steady rhythm on the hard dirt road as one mile rolled into the next. They were about twenty minutes outside of town when two men on horseback rode out from the woods and stopped in front of them. Elizabeth instinctively tensed. The sun was directly behind them, leaving only dark, intimidating silhouettes.

Simon pulled the reins back to stop the buggy. "Can I help you?" he said, as he casually shifted the reins to one hand and reached for the gun in his pocket with the other.

Elizabeth heard the hammer of the man's gun cock before she saw it. Her heart stuttered at the sound and then dropped as she saw the taller of the two point a long barreled gun at Simon's chest. "I wouldn't do that, friend," he warned as he walked his horse a little closer. "Take your hand out real slow."

Simon paused for a moment, his jaw muscle tightening, before following the instructions.

"Now, you're gonna keep your hands up," the man said. "Y'understand?"

"If this is a robbery," Simon said. "Take what you will and leave us."

The thin man laughed and nodded his head to his partner. "Gonna be fun, right?"

The other man snickered. Elizabeth felt sick. She'd seen that look on men's faces before and it always ended badly.

"Now, shut up and do what I say or I shoot your wife right between her pretty eyes." The long gun barrel of the man's dragoon shifted to Elizabeth.

Simon glanced at her, angry and helpless, and raised his hands. Elizabeth met his eyes with her bravest, most resolute face, silently pleading with Simon to have heart.

"Take his gun."

The other man, who wasn't as tall, but was much more muscular, slid off his horse and walked over to them. He fished into Simon's pocket and pulled out his gun. He admired it for a moment before stuffing it into the back of his waistband.

"I think we could use a little privacy," the tall man said and indicated a small clearing off the road. "Over there. Don't try nothin'."

Simon ground his teeth, but did as he was told and drove their carriage into the small clearing. Privacy was not good. If they were robbers, they would have wanted to get what they came for and get away as quickly as possible. Moving off the road meant they had other plans. Elizabeth swallowed hard and tried not to let her imagination get ahead of her. She had to keep a clear head and deal with what was happening, not what might happen. She pushed out a quick, short breath and braced herself for what was to come.

"That's far enough," the leader said. "Now git out." He waved the muzzle of his gun.

Simon looked over at Elizabeth. His expression was pained and angry and a dozen other things. In that instant, his eyes said everything from, *Get away if you can* to *I'm sorry* and, above all else, *I love you*. He squeezed her hand, for what she realized might be the last time. She had trouble letting go.

"Hurry up!"

Simon gave her hand another squeeze, his eyes still pleading with her, before he slowly climbed out of the carriage.

"Both of you."

Simon's head snapped up and Elizabeth saw the alarm in his eyes. "Just leave her—"

"Shut up!" The leader nodded toward his partner who came to Elizabeth's side of the carriage and grabbed her around the waist.

Elizabeth slapped at his hands. "I can do it myself."

He ignored her and lifted her out of the buggy. Once she'd found her feet, Elizabeth tried to go to Simon's side, but the big ape held onto her arms. She felt angry tears prick at her eyes, but she would not give them the satisfaction.

"Now," the tall one said as he slid out of his saddle. "We can git down to business."

He approached Simon, eyeing him up and down. "You two been pokin' yer nose in where you were told it don't belong." He wrinkled up his face and tilted back his hat. "That's just rude."

His partner laughed and Elizabeth could smell the liquor on his breath. And something else. The smell of rotten fish. Was this the same man who'd threatened her at the horse race? She'd bet all she had that it was.

"This is what we like to call," the tall man said, "your final warning."

Simon stood stock still, his eyes following the man as he walked casually back and forth in front of him.

"Now, if it was up to me, I'd just kill ya." The words sent a cold shiver through her, but there was a glimmer of hope, too. Maybe they would survive this.

The man holding Elizabeth laughed again and her hope dimmed

a little. God, she hated that sound. It was cruel. The laugh of a man who enjoyed other people's pain.

"But as it is, I'm just here to make sure you learn your lesson this time. You understand?"

Simon's hands flexed at his sides. "Yes, I understand."

The man smirked at his friend. "I don't think he means it."

The tall man tucked his gun into the back of his belt. He took a step forward and spit into one hand before rubbing them together. Before Simon had a chance to react, the man punched him hard across the jaw. Elizabeth cried out, surprised by the sudden violence.

Simon stumbled backwards, but kept his feet.

The tall man laughed with appreciation. "Even better," he said and held out his hands palms up and curled his fingers, urging Simon forward. "Come on!"

Simon didn't need a second invitation. He shed his coat and stepped forward, fists raised and ready. The other man smiled. Elizabeth looked around their little clearing for something, anything she might be able to use to help him, but the man holding her, as if sensing her thoughts, tightened his grip on her arms.

Simon and the other man circled each other, each sizing up his opponent. The man threw a wild right that Simon was just able to duck under. He countered with a short jab that connected with the man's jaw in a sharp crack.

Elizabeth hoped it had been enough to stun him, and that Simon could get the upper hand. But the man shook his head, recovered quickly and lunged forward again. He wound up his right again, but it was a feint. Simon realized it too late and couldn't stop his counter punch in time. He'd stepped right into the man's short left, his head snapped back with the power of the blow. Simon staggered back and blinked to clear his head. Blood trickled down his chin.

"Simon!" Elizabeth cried.

The man holding her shook her and laughed. He leaned down and whispered in her ear. "Fun's just gettin' started." His hands rubbed up and down her arms as he pulled her back against his body. Elizabeth shuddered and fought down her growing sense of panic.

Simon wiped the blood from his mouth and suddenly charged. He lowered his shoulder and drove it right into the other man's chest. They tumbled to the ground. Simon rolled on top of the other man and hit him twice before he was bucked off. They both scrambled back to their feet.

The gun had fallen out of the man's waistband and lay in the grass between them. He saw Simon eyeing it and smirked through the blood that poured out of his broken nose. Hope flared in Elizabeth's chest until he pulled a long Bowie knife from a sheath and waved the blade in the air. "Try for it," he said.

This was bad. The man flipped the knife expertly in his hand. Very, very bad.

Simon crouched and tried to lunge for the gun. The knife caught him on the arm and he cried out in pain as it sliced through his skin. Blood blossomed on his shirt sleeve.

"Simon!" Elizabeth cried out.

He turned to look at her and was nearly cut again, barely dodging the man's attack. Elizabeth silently cursed herself. Simon couldn't afford any distractions. She struggled against the iron hands that held her, but kept silent.

Simon grabbed his arm before quickly releasing it. His breath came in short, pained bursts as he tried to avoid another strike. The other man wasted no time now. He might not have been the best with the punch, but he could handle a knife. He made a lunging swipe with the long blade and it cut Simon's shirt just below the ribs.

Elizabeth gasped. There was only a little blood, but it was just a matter of time now. She knew she had to do something, but she wasn't sure what. This was all just a sick game to them. No matter what Simon did, he could not win this fight.

The man's breath behind her was hot on her neck and cheek as he pulled her flush against him again. Elizabeth fought down the urge to wretch and closed her eyes as he whispered horrible things in her ear. Suddenly, he jerked her around to face him.

"Can't let my friend have all the fun, now can I?" he said with a leer that made her feel like she'd already been violated.

His breath was hot and fetid. She felt repulsed and angry and frightened. His kiss was rough and disgusting. She tried to turn her head away, to twist out of his arms, but his fingers dug into the already bruised flesh and would not let her go.

Once he'd had his fill of that kiss, he held her away from his body for a moment to admire his prize. Elizabeth squirmed, but her arms were still trapped at her sides. Then, in a flash of understanding, she realized that her legs were free. Eighteenth century ladies might not be taught self-defense, but modern women were. As he started to pull her closer, she brought her knee up into his groin with all the force she could muster.

He gasped in pain, frozen in place for a moment and then released her. Reflex made him double over and reach for his shrinking manhood. As he fell to his knees, Elizabeth grabbed the gun from his waistband and stepped away from him. Her hands trembled with fear and adrenaline, but she willed them to be steady.

"Enough!" she cried as she pointed the gun at the man with the knife.

Both he and Simon stopped their fight and turned to her.

Her breathing was short and quick, as she took a step closer. "That's enough."

The man behind her grunted and she spun back toward him as he lunged at her. She fired. It sounded like a miniature cannon. There was no sharp crack or pop, but a deafening boom. A large puff of smoke and sparks shot out of the barrel. The gun kicked hard in her hand and she nearly lost hold of it, but she'd held on for dear life.

The man cried out as the bullet tore through his arm. He clutched at his arm and staggered back. Ignoring the fact that she'd just shot a man, she quickly turned back around just in time to see the man with the knife raise it again, ready to strike.

She pulled back the hammer on the gun with her free hand and leveled it at his chest. "Drop it."

He held onto his knife and she could see behind his smile, he was calculating his chances.

"Consider this your final warning," she said.

The man's smile finally fell and he let his knife drop to the ground. She waved him away from it. Simon hurried over and picked up the other gun and the discarded knife. He repositioned himself and pointed his gun at the man she'd left in a puddle by the carriage.

"Are you all right?" he asked, still trying to catch his breath. His eyes darted over her, looking for injuries and then shifted to the man on the ground.

She nodded. "How badly are you hurt?" His face was covered with a sheen of sweat and streaks of blood and dirt.

"I'll be fine," he said, but his right sleeve was already drenched in blood.

They herded the men together and Elizabeth kept a gun on them as he went to one of their horses and removed a coil of rope. Elizabeth kept a wary eye on their prisoners as Simon cut a few lengths and then forced one of them to bind the hands of the other behind his back. He made quick work of the second. Next, he used a third length of rope to tie one man's ankle to the other like a chain gang.

Once they were secure, Elizabeth asked for the knife.

Simon frowned, but gave it to her.

She lifted up her skirt and cut a long strip of material from one of her petticoats. "For your arm."

Simon looked down at it briefly and frowned. He didn't argue.

Even in the dying light, Elizabeth could see the cut was long and deep. She needed something to clean it with. She rummaged through the saddlebags on the back of the horses and found a small bottle of whisky.

She tore away the bottom of Simon's sleeve and held the bottle over the open wound. The cut was long and deep, the flesh slightly flayed to the sides. It was awful. She shook herself out of it. This was going to sting like nobody's business, but they had to do something to help fight off infection. She held up the bottle, and looked at him with sympathy.

"I know," Simon said. He steeled himself and clenched his jaw, then nodded. "Go ahead."

He hissed in pain, but held his arm steady as she poured what was left of the bottle over the cut, saving only a small amount. Then, she bound his arm as best as she could, and quickly inspected the cut by his ribs. Thank God it wasn't too deep and the bleeding had already stopped. She splashed it with the last bit of alcohol, wincing in sympathy as Simon's breath caught, his stomach muscles tightening.

"I'm sorry," she said, and finished binding his wounds.

Simon's injuries tended to, she tore off another strip of cloth and wrapped it tightly around the injured man's arm. She was far from gentle with him as she had been with Simon, but she still didn't want him to bleed to death.

Simon tied one of their horses to the back of the buggy.

"Do you think you can manage the buggy on your own?" he asked her.

She had no idea. "Absolutely."

Simon nodded and mounted the other horse. He waved his gun at their prisoners. "Get up."

Slowly and awkwardly, the men did as they were told, glaring at Simon as they did.

He brought his horse a step closer. "You can walk or I can put a bullet in you and drag you back to town."

Reluctantly, the men started forward with Simon riding behind them. Elizabeth climbed up into the carriage and put the gun on the seat next to her. She'd been paying more attention than she'd thought and drove the buggy along behind them without much trouble.

It took a half an hour for their little parade to reach town, and she could see Simon's shoulders beginning to slump forward. Townspeople stepped out of the way and whispered as Simon drove his prisoners down the middle of the street. A few men on horseback and young boys on foot followed behind, curious and wanting to get in on the action if anything happened.

Finally, they arrived at the police station. Young Officer Miller snapped to attention as they marched their prisoners inside. The barrel chested sergeant's eyes flashed with recognition at both men. Apparently, this wasn't their first visit to the Natchez jail.

Elizabeth gave the officers a quick sketch of the attack. Highwaymen who'd chosen the wrong people to rob and try to murder. Simon added some details, his voice betraying his pain and exhaustion. She could see how tired he was and could hardly blame him. Also, there was no telling just how much blood he'd lost. She told the officers where to find them and helped Simon back to the buggy. He didn't argue when Elizabeth took the reins. He just leaned back in the seat in silence.

When they arrived at Cypress Hill, she helped Simon into the back parlor.

"Good heavens!" Catherine exclaimed when she saw him. She sprang from her reading chair, leaving her book behind, forgotten. "What happened? Papa!"

The Colonel appeared in the doorway and Elizabeth gave them the short version and sent Abraham to fetch a doctor, anyone but Dr. Walker. The Colonel told him to find Dr. Parish and Abraham raced out into the night.

"Let's take him upstairs," the Colonel said. The calm in the storm. For once, she welcomed his authoritative stoicism. "Abraham will be back shortly. Best get him comfortable."

Simon was able to stand and started toward the stairs without assistance, but it was clear he was near the point of total exhaustion.

Elizabeth put her hand around his waist to help him, but the Colonel interceded.

"You look about ready to fall down yourself," he said and took Simon's arm and placed it over his shoulder. Without another word, he helped Simon make his way upstairs to their room.

Once there, he eased Simon down onto the bed and then retreated to the doorway as Elizabeth and Catherine came in.

The Colonel lingered in the open doorway as Elizabeth sat down next to Simon.

"I'll be back shortly," the Colonel said.

Elizabeth glanced over her shoulder, offering a quick thanks. Her focus was fully on Simon as she began to unbutton his vest and shirt. She carefully helped him out of them and set them aside. Red blotches on his ribs marked where bruises would be tomorrow. The thin cut on his side just above his waist wasn't too bad, but it would need to be cleaned.

Right on cue, Catherine appeared with clean cloths and a basin of water.

"Can you bring some whisky?" Elizabeth asked. "And another basin. An empty one?"

Catherine nodded and disappeared again.

"How are you doing?" Elizabeth asked Simon.

"Tired, but all right."

He looked tired, but not quite all right. This was far worse than anything he'd suffered before. This had not been a bar fight that left him with a few bruises. This had been a fight for his life, for their lives.

Simon's face was drawn and pinched. Elizabeth carefully probed his ribs. He grunted quietly when she touched a few tender spots, but nothing too bad.

"I don't think anything's broken," she said. "Can you lie down?"

"I'm not an invalid," he said with his customary crankiness.

It was good to hear, but despite his protests, he moved slowly and painfully as he sat down on the bed. She piled up pillows against the headboard and urged him to lean back.

She'd just pulled off his boots when Catherine returned with the whisky, basin and a glass. "Anything else I can do?"

Elizabeth shook her head. "Just bring up the doctor when he arrives."

Catherine nodded and hurried back downstairs. Elizabeth closed their bedroom door and noticed how filthy her hands were. They were covered with Simon's blood and dirt. She quickly washed her hands and wiped her face before she opened their trunk. She rummaged around inside until she found the small pillbox at the bottom. Inside were several baby blue-colored pills, doxycycline. She removed one and hid the pillbox back in their trunk.

"I'm glad you thought to bring these," Elizabeth said as she poured him a small glass of water. "God only knows what was on that knife."

Simon grunted in agreement and took the antibiotic. He'd insisted they take Malaria pills before they left and bring these just in case. Thank God he had.

Elizabeth took the empty glass from his hand and poured in some whisky.

"I probably shouldn't," he said. "Not with the antibiotics."

Elizabeth nodded and then looked at the half-full glass. She shrugged and downed the glass in one swig. It burned as it went down and she fought a cough and squinted in discomfort.

Simon grimaced and held his side. "Don't make me laugh."

Dr. Parish arrived a few minutes later. He was what a country doctor should be. He was tall, slightly stooped over, but kind and gentle. He unwrapped Simon's arm and said reassuring things as he did. Simon hardly cared, but Elizabeth was grateful.

The cut was long, about four inches, and deep, but the bleeding had almost stopped so that meant no artery had been cut. Simon had lost a fair amount of blood, but not enough to be worrying.

The doctor dug into his medical bag and took out a suture kit.

The kit was little more than a few large and slightly curved needles and some thick silk thread.

Elizabeth cast a sympathetic look at Simon. "About that drink?"

He looked at the whisky bottle and back to the large needles. "Maybe just one."

Elizabeth poured him a shot and he threw it back.

The doctor started to thread one of his needles when Elizabeth stopped him. "I know this will sound silly," she said, "but would you mind soaking those in the whisky for a few minutes?"

She poured half the bottle of whisky into the empty basin Catherine had brought.

"What on earth for?"

"It's good for the insides and for the outside," she said, holding out the basin. The doctor frowned. "Please?"

He clearly thought she was insane, but saw no harm in humoring her. Of course, he knew nothing about germs or the importance of disinfecting. Louis Pasteur's discoveries were still a decade away. And it would be another twenty before doctors would even begin to sterilize their instruments. How on earth anyone had survived to see the other side of the century was a miracle.

Elizabeth doused Simon's arm again with more alcohol, ignoring the doctor's arched eyebrows. Simon remained ridiculously stoic, although she knew it must have hurt like the devil.

How Simon managed not to cry out when the doctor stitched up his arm, Elizabeth would never know. He'd turned down the offer of laudanum and just gritted his teeth as the huge hooked needle pierced his skin over and over as the doctor sewed his arm closed.

Elizabeth watched it all with horror. Finally, the doctor tied off the thread and was finished. Despite the bulky thread, he'd actually done a fine job of closing the wound. There would no doubt be a scar, but they'd learned to live with those.

Just as the doctor was wrapping the wound, the Colonel returned. "How's our patient?"

"He should be fine," the doctor said. "Keep the dressing clean and come see me in a few days, sooner if you have increased pain or swelling."

"Thank you," Simon said.

Catherine offered to show the doctor out, as the Colonel lingered in the doorway. "I went to the police station." He noticed Elizabeth's questioning expression. "You are guests in my city, in my house. This is unacceptable."

His scowl deepened. "Dr. Walker was there, like a bad penny that man. But competent enough, I suppose for their needs. Those two men, they've…let's just say this is not their first brush with the law." He cleared his throat. "You can be assured they will not bother you again."

Elizabeth wasn't quite sure what he'd done, but she couldn't argue with the outcome. "Thank you."

"If you think you'll be up to it, I'll send Cassie up with food later," he said.

"That would be very kind," Elizabeth said.

He nodded curtly before closing the door behind him.

Elizabeth turned to Simon, one eyebrow raised. "The Colonel does have a heart after all."

Simon grunted. "I'm not sure I'll have any appetite."

"I will."

Simon smiled and took her hand. "You were magnificent. But how did you escape? I didn't see."

Elizabeth let out a breath and shook her head. She didn't have the energy to tell him all the dirty details just now. Besides, it would just upset him and he needed rest more than anything else right now. "I'll tell you later."

Simon nodded and closed his eyes.

"Why don't you try to get some rest?"

He opened his eyes and nodded again. She started to stand, but he tugged her hand. "Stay with me."

She nodded and moved some of the pillows so he could slide down the bed and lie down fully. Once he was settled, she lay down next to him. His uninjured arm curled around her shoulders and pulled her against his side.

He turned his head and kissed her temple. "Your hair smells like fish," he said drowsily.

Elizabeth laughed tiredly, and then rested her head on his shoulder, putting her hand on his chest. "Later," she said.

It was only minutes before his breathing slowed and sleep took him. Elizabeth was not far behind.

A few hours later, Simon groaned. Elizabeth awoke instantly and sat up.

Simon's eyes opened and he blinked against the light. He saw the concern in her eyes. "I'm fine," he said. "Just bumped my arm."

He held it out for her to see. The bandage was still clean, no blood. He flexed his fingers. "It's all right, just sore."

Elizabeth let out a breath. "Good."

She noticed that a tray of food had been left on the table by the door. "Are you hungry? Do you think you can eat something?"

"A little."

Elizabeth rearranged the pillows. Simon sat up and then leaned back against the headboard. The tray had bread and cheese and some cold meat. A small tureen of soup had gone cold, but it was better than nothing. She ladled a cup of soup and handed it to him.

Simon took a sip and then another. His color was good. In some places, bilious even.

"You're going to have a heck of a bruise there," she said touching his jaw.

"All things considered…" he said, as he put down his cup of soup.

"Ain't that the truth," Elizabeth said.

Simon shifted his position and groaned. "I think that fight filled my quota for this trip." He settled back down and narrowed his eyes at her. "You're not hurt, are you? Being brave and pretending you aren't for my sake?"

Elizabeth laughed. "No. Really." She held out her arms to show him. "See?"

Simon appeared appeased and took a bite of cheese. He chewed slowly, his jaw clearly already sore. "There's something I'm not clear about. How did you get the gun?"

Elizabeth shrugged. "The man holding me became…distracted, and I just used it to my advantage." It wasn't an outright lie and she hoped he was too tired to delve too deeply into the details.

Simon frowned; obviously not ready to let her off the hook so easily. "Distracted?"

She knew he would wind himself up over it if she told him the whole truth of it. "I'm fine. No scars, emotional or otherwise. Heck, I'd do a lot worse to save our bacon if I had to."

Simon tilted his head back and looked at the ceiling. She probably shouldn't have said that.

She took his hand. "I'm fine; you're mostly fine. I'd say, Simon and Elizabeth for the win!"

Simon hmm'd and she knew that was the best she was going to get under the circumstances. She let go of his hand and he picked up his cup again.

"At least we won't have to worry about those two anymore. I've had enough of fish face for a lifetime." Simon looked at her questioningly. "He was the man at the racetrack who sent the first warning."

Simon put down his cup and closed his eyes as the pieces seemed to fall into place. "Of course! I knew I'd seen his face before."

"You saw him there?"

"Talking with Dr. Walker."

"That's something I don't quite get," Elizabeth said. "Walker seems to be involved, but why?"

Simon sighed thoughtfully. "Blackmail?" he suggested. "Perhaps he knew about James or Eli's affair and child, and has been covering it up for a price?"

Elizabeth nodded and remembered what the Colonel had said about the doctor's penchant for losing high stakes wagers. "Pay off his gambling debts. That makes sense, but I feel like there's something else."

Simon had stopped picking at the tray of food. "Finished?"

He nodded and she put the tray back on the side table and began to undress. "There was something I was thinking about at the party," she said, "before we were kicked out."

Simon snorted.

Elizabeth stepped out of her dress and unhooked her corset. "Eight years ago, there were two children born on the same day. Or close to it at least. One to a rich family, and the other to a poor one."

"Very *Prince and the Pauper*."

Elizabeth took off her petticoats and then climbed back onto the bed. She sat Indian-style facing Simon.

"Exactly. But they're not twins. No one would confuse one for the other."

Simon frowned. "No."

"What if," Elizabeth said, leaning forward. Something was starting to gel. "Rose said that everyone feared Louisa would be born too sickly to live, but by some miracle she was healthy. Perfect."

"But Mary was sickly, wasn't she?" Simon said.

"Yes. What if it wasn't a miracle at all? What if someone switched them? Biologically, we think Mary's a Harper, and that Louisa isn't."

Simon shook his head. "Why? Why would someone send their own child away and take in another?"

Elizabeth frowned. There was something floating in her mind just beyond her reach. "I don't know, but the doctor was there for both births, and I wouldn't put anything past him."

Simon agreed and rested his head back against the pillows. Clearly, he was exhausted, too exhausted for this.

"Let's talk more about it tomorrow," she said. "We could both use a good night's sleep."

"Agreed."

Elizabeth got off the bed and walked over to the nightstand with a fresh basin of water.

"Are you going to sleep over there?" he asked, straining his neck to watch her.

She picked up a washcloth. "Just going to clean up a bit first. I smell like fish." Simon's eyebrows drew together in genuine confusion and concern. "I could give you a sponge bath," she added.

He smiled, but just barely. "Tomorrow. I'd like to have enough energy to enjoy it properly."

Elizabeth laughed and helped him settle into bed. By the time she'd finished cleaning up he was fast asleep. She watched him for a few minutes before rolling onto her back and staring up into the night. Somewhere in it, there was an answer. If only she could see in the dark.

Chapter Twenty-Two

T HE LAST THING ON earth Simon wanted to do was attend the Veterans' Spring Gala, and yet, here he was, forcing a smile to his face and making small talk with Mrs. Goode and Mrs. Cobb. His head hurt, his jaw ached and his arm throbbed. But he had little choice. This might well be their last chance to talk to the Harpers, if they even decided to arrive. He and Elizabeth had to convince them to do the right thing. He would not fail Mary.

"It's a wonderful cause," Elizabeth said, pulling Simon back to the present. "Isn't it, Simon?"

"Yes," he said, unsure of just what she was talking about.

Mrs. Goode stared at him expectantly. He looked back confused until he noticed the ream of raffle tickets in her hands.

Simon reached for his wallet, but winced.

Elizabeth laughed and patted his chest. "Ah!" She reached inside his jacket and took out his wallet.

Mrs. Goode's eyebrows arched in surprise and with no small measure of pleasure at the size of the bills Elizabeth pulled out.

"One of a wife's many pleasures," Elizabeth said as she put his wallet back. "Spending her husband's money."

"Yes," Mrs. Goode said. "Here you are." She held out a fan of raffle tickets.

Elizabeth took them and carelessly stuffed them into her small purse.

Mrs. Goode smiled and then stepped forward conspiratorially. "I heard what happened yesterday. Attacked by Indians!"

"I'm sorry?" Elizabeth said.

"What have you to be sorry for," the woman said and she shuddered. "Good heavens, I can't imagine. I would have fainted dead away."

"I heard they were Sioux," Mrs. Cobb added.

"Six of them!" Mrs. Goode said.

"Six Sioux?" Elizabeth said, barely fighting her smile.

"And a herd of buffalo," Catherine said, appearing at their side and winking at Elizabeth. "I think my father was looking for the two of you," she added with a rather wide-eyed and obvious *get out of here while you can* look.

"Of course. You'll excuse us," Elizabeth said, and without waiting for an answer, looped her arm through Simon's left arm and started around the perimeter of the room.

The large town hall had been turned into a ballroom for the gala. Small tables and chairs lined the walls leaving the center free for dancing. A small orchestra filled the stage and played painfully jaunty quadrilles and more elegant waltzes.

All of Natchez's elite were in attendance to benefit the city's war veterans. Everyone from old men who'd fought in the War of 1812 to young ones yet to see battle mixed and mingled and filled up ladies' dance cards. Not surprisingly, Elizabeth was a rather hot commodity.

Men, young and old, lingered by the Colonel hoping for an introduction. Married or not, it didn't seem to matter. Any beautiful woman, and especially one new in town, was a much sought-after prize. Elizabeth's dance card had filled within ten minutes of their arrival. Simon had been lucky to get two spots for himself. Although, his damn arm was throbbing badly in time with the beat of the music, dancing was the last thing on his mind.

They reached the far side of the room, safe from Mrs. Goode's incessant gossip. Elizabeth gestured to the refreshment table where a crystal bowl held some undefined punch.

"Would you like some?" Simon asked, indicating the drinks.

Elizabeth nodded and held out one of the cups so he didn't have to use his right arm. He ladled some into her cup.

She took a sip and they both turned back to look through the crowd.

"They'll come," Elizabeth said, sounding much more sure than she was.

Another half-hour passed without a sign of the Harpers and Simon grew worried, and impatient. He'd already had to explain twice that they were not attacked by Sioux nor set upon by river pirates. The truth, or at least the version they were willing to share, wasn't apparently as exciting as the fictions that spread around the ballroom like wildfire. He was just about to lose his already shortened temper with a man who insisted he'd "seen the whole thing" when he saw the Harpers enter the room.

Simon took Elizabeth's arm. "You'll pardon us," he said and led Elizabeth a few paces away from the group.

Across the room, Eli grinned like an idiot at Mrs. Cobb and Mrs. Goode while James appeared more taciturn than usual, his scowl bending only slightly when Rose touched his arm. After having dutifully bought their share of raffle tickets, they started across the ballroom.

Elizabeth's smile brightened when she saw them. "Hello!"

Rose began to smile in greeting, but James took her elbow and angled her away. He gave Elizabeth a curt nod and glared at Simon as he led his wife in another direction. Rose looked over her shoulder briefly before turning back and disappearing into the crowd with her husband.

"Hello," Eli said to Elizabeth. He glanced at Simon mistrustfully, but nodded, before following his brother.

Simon sighed. "That does not bode well."

Elizabeth put her hand on Simon's good arm. "Let me see if I can find a moment alone with Rose. If I can get her without James, I think she wants to talk about what happened."

It was a sensible approach. Perhaps that's what they should have done in the first place. Nothing to be done for it now. "Good."

A tall, young man in a smart West Point dress uniform appeared in front of them. "Sir," he said with a bow before turning to Elizabeth and holding out his hand. "I believe this is my dance, Mrs. Cross."

"Mister Pierce isn't it?" she said.

His grin broadened with delight. "Yes!"

Elizabeth handed Simon her empty cup and took Mr. Pierce's hand and let him lead her out onto the floor. Under different circumstances, Simon might have been slightly annoyed by it all. Men had hovered around her all night, like bees to a flower, grinning like fools. But, as Elizabeth had reminded him, in ten years time, their smart, clean uniforms and dreams of heroic deeds in battle would be met with the harsh reality of the Civil War. At least one in four would die. For those that lived, their homes and their very way of life would never be the same again. It was a sobering thought. As he looked around the room, he saw men, really boys barely out of short pants, playing soldier and not knowing what was to come.

There was nothing he or Elizabeth could do to change that. They could, however, change one small thing here, and give a child peace.

Just the thought of it made his chest tighten and he instinctively sought out Elizabeth on the dance floor. In her exquisite, yellow silk evening gown, she was not hard to find. She laughed and smiled. Even though it was meant for another man, he felt renewed again.

"Lovely."

Simon's jaw clenched. He knew the voice before he turned. "Walker."

Dr. Walker admired Elizabeth for too long a moment before turning and facing Simon. "Beautiful and a good shot. A rare combination."

Simon glared down at him, but held his tongue.

The doctor arched his eyebrows and smiled before glancing to the dance floor. "I wouldn't worry. I doubt there will be any charges filed."

"Charges?" Simon said.

Dr. Walker shrugged. "A man did die."

"Die? What are you talking about?"

The doctor smiled and then forced a false sincerity to it. "The man your wife shot succumbed to his wounds in the night."

Simon knew that was impossible. He'd seen the man's arm for himself. It wasn't pretty, but it was not a mortal wound. Even if it had become infected, it was highly improbable that the infection could have caused his death so quickly.

"Perhaps I'm losing my touch," the doctor said with a sigh. "The police usually bring in Dr. Parish for such things, but he was…" the doctor continued with a glance toward Simon's injured arm, "otherwise occupied and so they requested my humble services."

"And a man in your care died from a flesh wound to the arm," Simon said, not bothering to hide his disbelief and disgust.

"Pyemia," the doctor said. "Blood poisoning. I've never seen such a virulent case before."

Simon knew exactly what had happened. His blood might have been poisoned, but it had nothing to do with his wound. The man was a loose end, one that could have implicated Walker. A loose end that needed to be cut and the doctor had found an opportunity to do just that.

"Went straight to his heart. But then," Dr. Walker said with another glance to Elizabeth, "that is where a man is most vulnerable, is it not?"

Simon clenched his jaw and his hands tightened into fists at his side. He could feel the muscles in his forearm pull the skin taut straining his stitches. The pain was strangely welcome. It kept him grounded. It kept him from tearing Walker's head off.

"Dr. Walker!" a portly man said as he appeared at their side. "Pardon me," he added nervously seeing Simon's eyes flash with anger. He quickly added a bow. "My wife has been having some discomfort…"

"Of course," Dr. Walker said with a smug grin Simon dreamt of wiping off his face. "You'll excuse me, Mr. Cross." The doctor bowed once more before following the portly man off into the crowd.

Simon looked after them both and then, sour taste in his mouth, turned to find Elizabeth. With any luck she'd managed to duck out on a few of her dances and convince Rose to speak with her.

ELIZABETH NEEDED TO CATCH her breath. The dance lessons Simon had given her before they'd traveled here had paid off. However, dancing in the comfort of their living room and dancing here in a hot, crowded ballroom with a corset squeezing the life out of her was a different matter. She headed back for the punchbowl, hoping someone had finally spiked it, when she saw Rose talking with several other women. James was nowhere to be seen.

Elizabeth walked up to them and fanned herself with her dance card. "Quite an evening," she said.

The other women greeted her politely. Rose, however, shot a nervous glance over her shoulder before forcing a small smile.

"I do hope it's nothing serious," Mrs. Pitchford said to Rose continuing whatever conversation Elizabeth had interrupted.

"No, she's fine," Rose said.

"Her Louisa's not feeling well," Mrs. Turnbull added for Elizabeth's benefit.

"She just overdid it a bit at the party yesterday, is all," Rose said, showing no sign of downplaying her daughter's state. "The doctor is coming by tomorrow to check on her, but I'm sure she's fine really."

"I'm glad to hear it," Elizabeth said.

Rose looked over her shoulder again. Clearly, she'd been instructed not to talk to Elizabeth but was too polite to ignore her completely.

Mrs. Pitchford started a story about her son's recurring bilious fever and Elizabeth stepped closer to Rose and whispered, "I'd like to speak with you, if I could. About yesterday."

Rose shook her head and turned to walk away.

Elizabeth reached out and touched her arm. "Please?"

Rose shot another look toward the corner of the room where Elizabeth could now see James. He had his back to them and, after a moment's hesitation, Rose nodded to Elizabeth and then toward a side door.

They escaped the heat of the ballroom only to find the evening air thick and cloying. It was a clear night, but the air was still and humid. They walked out into the side garden. Rose looked back anxiously at the door. The muffled sound of music coming from inside the building could just be heard in the distance.

"James will not be pleased if he finds me speaking with you," Rose said.

"I know," Elizabeth admitted. "And, yet you're here anyway."

Rose shifted uncomfortably.

"You're curious," Elizabeth guessed.

"No," Rose lied. She was a terrible liar. "I thought you were going to apologize for your husband's behavior. I thought it polite to give you the opportunity."

"I am sorry," Elizabeth said. And she was, but there was something far greater at stake here. "For the pain it's caused you. If we could have done this without that, we would have."

Rose's eyes flared with irritation. "And just *what* are you doing?"

"Finding the truth."

Elizabeth could see the anger and injury in her eyes, but there was something else there as well. Doubt. "I cannot imagine why you would want to hurt my family," Rose said as she started to turn away.

"Don't you want to know the truth?" Elizabeth asked. A silence hung in the air and Rose took another step away. Elizabeth nearly started after her, but held back. "About the girl in the garden."

Rose stopped.

"I know you saw her," Elizabeth said. "I've seen her too. A lost spirit."

Rose kept her back turned. "I don't know what you mean."

"Aren't there enough lies already?" When Rose still wouldn't turn, Elizabeth took a step closer. "Her name is Mary. And she needs your help."

Rose turned and Elizabeth could see her eyes glistening in the moonlight. She felt it. She felt something.

"Mary," Elizabeth said then stopped to swallow down the lump that was forming in her throat. "Mary belongs at River Run."

Rose shook her head, but it was a weak attempt to deny something she seemed to have sensed herself.

"Elijah told me what your husband said. That was cruel and unjust. James is a good man."

Elizabeth nodded. "I believe you," Elizabeth said. "I believe he is. That you are both good people. The kind who would never knowingly hurt a child."

"Of course not!"

"Or deny aid to one in need. I don't know who fathered Mary," Elizabeth continued. Rose's eyes flashed with anger and warning, but

229

Elizabeth pushed on. "But I do know that she is lost and afraid, and we're running out of time to help her."

Rose closed her eyes for a moment and then opened them, and shook her head in defeat. "What can we possibly do to help a dead child? She is beyond our comfort now."

"Do you believe in an afterlife?" Elizabeth asked, already knowing the answer. "Would you deny that to Mary? She's caught in between our world and the next and if she cannot find peace here, she will not find it anywhere. Ever."

Rose let out a shuddering breath and then squared her shoulders. "My husband did not have an affair."

"Maybe she's Eli's?"

Rose sighed and shook her head. "Elijah had an accident when he was younger. He cannot father children."

Elizabeth's heart sank. Elizabeth suddenly realized why Rose's father had insisted she marry James and not Eli—heirs. If Eli couldn't be the father, that left only James. "I'm sorry."

Rose shook her head again. "No, there is some mistake. I am sorry for the child. Truly I am, but there is nothing I can do."

Elizabeth felt hope slipping further away. "Rose, please? I know it's hard to accept—"

Rose clasped her hands in front of her. "You are mistaken." Her newfound resolve shook for a moment before she regained it. "And I would appreciate it if you would leave my family alone."

Elizabeth was desperate for something, anything to change her mind, but Rose couldn't or wouldn't see the truth. "What if she's your child? Your flesh and blood?"

"I have one child—"

"And what if it's Mary?" Elizabeth said, pressing on, "and not Louisa—"

"You think I don't know my own child?" Rose said, growing angry now.

"Please," Elizabeth said. "If you'll just hear me out."

"I think I've heard quite enough. Good night, Mrs. Cross." And with that Rose walked back to the town hall, leaving Elizabeth alone in the garden.

ELIZABETH STOOD AT THE open window of their upstairs bedroom hoping it might offer a cooling breeze. Hours ago, she'd traded her nightgown for the thin cotton of her chemise. If modesty hadn't forced her to wear something, she would have happily stood outside under the moon, naked, arms out, waiting for a wind to come up off the river. As it was, she stood by their window, looking out at the garden below. Through the darkness all she could see were vague shapes, blankets of flowers devoid of color and trees with long thin arms reaching out for things she could not see.

Sleep had been impossible. She'd tried for a few hours, before giving up and coming to stare at the night. In each shadow she tried to see Mary, hoped for one more glimpse. But all she saw was the dark. It might be too late, she thought. *They* might be too late. It was a sickening feeling, to know they might have failed her, that a poor innocent child would be condemned because they hadn't acted soon enough, because they hadn't done…something.

She let out a sigh and looked up at the man in the moon. He was as inscrutable as ever, keeping counsel to himself.

The bed creaked and she heard Simon's footsteps as he came up behind her. His fingers swept her hair away from her shoulder and he bent down and dropped a kiss on her bare skin. She could feel the heat coming off his body. He always ran hot.

Despite the heat of the night, she gently leaned back into his bare chest. He'd long given up on his nightshirt and settled for sleeping in a pair of drawers and she could feel the warmth of his skin.

He put his left arm around her waist and pulled her back against his body. As they'd undressed that night after the ball, she'd seen just how badly he'd been injured in the fight the night before. Dark purple bruises bloomed on his chest and arms. She changed the dressing on his forearm, trying not to let her pain at the sight of the wound show.

He'd done all of this for her, for Mary, and what did they have to show for it? Dr. Walker was as cocky and free to threaten them as ever. The Harpers wouldn't speak to them. And Mary was nowhere to be seen.

It all felt on the verge of hopeless.

Elizabeth laid her head back against Simon's chest. He kissed the top of her head and tightened his grip around her waist. She closed her eyes and listened to the sound of his heart beating. Strong. Steady. Sure.

But tonight there were no promises spoken. No assurances given. No faith reaffirmed. Tonight, there was only the quiet and the darkness and the knowledge that she was not alone.

Chapter Twenty-Three

THE FOLLOWING DAY WAS an exercise in patience, which Elizabeth failed. Repeatedly. Like a hummingbird trapped in a cage, she fussed around Cypress Hill until even the servants asked her to stop.

Even Simon had sought refuge from her restlessness. In the afternoon, he'd taken a short walk to the rear of the property to the bluffs above the river. The view of the mighty river, powerful and relentless was both beautiful and humbling.

In his mind, he went over everything again. Everything they'd done so far, everything they'd seen, looking for an answer. Something they'd forgotten, some stone unturned. But there was nothing. They were at the mercy of others. That would have been maddening enough, if he hadn't also been haunted by Old Nan's vision of their future.

If he could not save this child, would he be able to save his own?

Just as he started to fall into that particular well of despair, he heard Elizabeth call out for him.

"Simon!" She hurried toward him waving a piece of paper in the air.

He ran toward her. "What is it? What's wrong?"

"A note from Catherine at the orphanage. One of the children wants to speak with me."

"Whatever about?" Simon asked as they started back toward the house.

"I'm not sure," Elizabeth said. "But I have a feeling it has to do with Mary."

THE GIRL'S DORMITORY WAS nearly empty when they arrived. Most of the children were outside playing, enjoying the last remnants of a beautiful Spring day. Only two girls remained inside. One lay curled up in a bed at the far end of the room and the other sat nearby watching her.

"Alison?" Elizabeth said.

The girl turned toward her. With one last look at Mellie in the nearby bed, she came down the long aisle to meet them. Alison's small face was creased with worry. Poor little thing, Elizabeth thought. She'd taken so much onto her shoulders.

Alison looked anxiously at Catherine and then to Elizabeth.

"Hello," Elizabeth said.

The girl chewed her lower lip and looked nervously up at Simon.

"This is my husband," Elizabeth said. "You can trust him."

Alison looked up at him and then nodded. Her forehead wrinkled in concern. "I don't want to get anyone in trouble."

"It'll be all right," Elizabeth said. "Tells us what's wrong."

Alison looked over at the little girl in bed. "I know she didn't mean to steal it," she said and then turned back and quickly added, "she a good girl."

Elizabeth knelt down and took her by the shoulders. "I'm sure she is. No one will be punished. I promise you."

Alison looked to Catherine for confirmation. "It's all right."

Alison nodded again and then took Elizabeth's hand and led them over to the sick little girl's bed. Behind them Elizabeth heard Simon ask, "Melanie?"

"Getting worse by the day, I'm afraid," Catherine said quietly.

Elizabeth's heart sank. Hadn't there been enough death here already?

Alison took them to Melanie's bedside and then carefully pulled down the covers, just enough to reveal a doll clutched in Melanie's arms. Elizabeth gasped softly. It was Jammy. Or a doll that looked exactly like Louisa's Jamaican doll, the one James had brought back just for her.

"I wanted to tell you before," Alison said, "but I didn't want Mellie to get into trouble."

The pieces started to fit together. James hadn't just brought back a doll for Louisa, but one for Mary as well.

"That was Mary's doll," Elizabeth said.

Alison nodded and worried her bottom lip. "I knew it was wrong, but Mellie loved it so much."

Simon knelt down next to Melanie's bed and gently brushed her hair away from the child's face. She had sores around her mouth and judging from the sheen of sweat a high fever as well.

"What's wrong with her?" Simon asked.

"Doctor says it's Malaria," Catherine said.

Simon frowned and turned back to the child. He gently lifted her hand from its hold on the doll and briefly examined her hands. She whimpered and he caressed her cheek to sooth her. After a moment, she rolled over, away from the doll. Simon picked it up and stood.

Elizabeth pulled the covers back up over Melanie and touched her *hair. Poor little thing.*

Simon examined the doll and Elizabeth could feel something shift inside him. His body tensed almost imperceptibly, but she knew him too well to miss it. His jaw muscle clenched and unclenched as he then looked down at Alison. He nodded for them all to step away from Melanie's bed so they could speak without waking her.

Once they were far enough away, Simon knelt down in front of Alison. "You told Elizabeth that you helped Dr. Walker give Mary her medicine?"

Alison looked nervously to Elizabeth. "It's all right," she reassured the girl. "Tell him the truth."

Alison nodded.

"You said that you used to give one spoonful of medicine to Mary and another to the doll?"

Alison nodded again.

"Do you have any of the medicine left?"

Alison went over to a small set of drawers to retrieve it. As she did, Elizabeth leaned closer to Simon. "What's going on?"

Simon's eyes slid toward Alison and he shook his head in a not in front of the child expression.

Elizabeth looked at the doll's face trying to see what Simon had seen. The cloth around the mouth had been stained, probably from the medicine the girl's had given it. But what had upset him so much?

Alison returned with a large green bottle and handed it to Simon. It was labeled "Quinine", which would make sense for Malaria. Simon held out the doll for Elizabeth to take as he examined the bottle.

"And Doctor Walker told you to make sure this was given with hot tea? Always something hot?"

"Yes," Alison said.

"You haven't been giving this to Melanie, have you?"

"No," she said quickly. "Dr. Parish doesn't let me help. Did I do something wrong?"

"No," Simon said with a smile. "You did very well, Alison. We're very grateful to you. Catherine, perhaps you can take Alison out with the other children?"

Catherine frowned, but put her hand on Alison's shoulder.

Elizabeth knelt down in front her before they left. "Thank you." She kissed the little's girl cheek and then watched as Catherine began to lead her from the room.

"And would you send for Dr. Parish?" Simon asked Catherine. "Quickly."

Catherine glanced at Melanie and then nodded her understanding.

Elizabeth waited until the door had shut behind them. Simon took out the bottle's stopper and peered inside. A sinking and sickening feeling welled inside her stomach. "You don't think that's Quinine, do you?"

"No," Simon said. "Judging from Melanie's condition, the mouth sores and what look to be the beginning of Mee's lines on her fingernails, I'd say it's arsenic."

"Arsenic?" Dear God. Had Dr. Walker poisoned Mary?

"Dr. Parish will have to perform tests, but," he said with a glower toward Melanie's bed. "The symptoms of malaria and arsenic poisoning are remarkably similar—vomiting, diarrhea, chills, fever. But those lesions are not."

Elizabeth had thought the doctor was evil, but this was a whole new level. Murdering a child. It was so horrible, she couldn't quite process it.

"Are you sure?"

Simon nodded. "Fairly certain, yes. I remember reading several books about it—the Medicis, the Borjas and others. There were even rumors Napoleon was poisoned with arsenic."

Simon touched the inside of the open bottle and then brought his finger to his mouth.

Elizabeth gasped and nearly reached out to stop him. "Simon!"

He pulled out his handkerchief and spit into it. "Definitely not quinine. That has a strong bitter taste."

"So you taste the poison?" And she was the reckless one.

"That much won't harm me."

Elizabeth stuffed her heart back into her chest and realized he was right.

"This is probably cut with chalk," Simon said, "to make sure the poisoning didn't act too quickly, draw attention. It needed to mimic malaria."

"And Melanie," Elizabeth reasoned aloud. "She's not taking the same medicine, but she didn't need to, did she?"

Simon pointed to the doll's stained face. "Every time they gave that doll a dose of the medicine, the arsenic soaked into the fabric."

Elizabeth nodded.

"And you don't have to ingest it to suffer the effects," Simon continued. "It can be inhaled or absorbed through the skin."

Elizabeth looked down at the doll in her hand. "So the doll was slowly poisoning her."

"Yes. Hopefully, we're not too late to help her."

"Why would the doctor poison Mary?"

Simon took the doll from her. "I don't know. But we're damn well going to find out."

Chapter Twenty-Four

Dr. Parish arrived just a few minutes later. He'd been skeptical of their premise at first, but had to admit that the medicine in the bottle marked quinine was not quinine. Thankfully, he was familiar with the Marsh test to identify arsenic and promised to run it after he'd seen to Melanie. They could only hope they hadn't made their discovery too late.

Elizabeth gripped the doll in her hands as they made the long drive to River Run. She ran over everything in her head asking again and again; what could the doctor possibly have gained from killing Mary? And was she the only one?

It was dark by the time they arrived. Rose and James' carriage had pulled up to the front of house before them. James was just helping Rose step out of it when Simon pulled their buggy up along side. He quickly got out and helped Elizabeth jump down.

James waved his groom to remove the carriage and glared at Simon. Rose looked at Elizabeth briefly, then ducked her head.

"You're not welcome here," James said as he took Rose's arm and they started up the front steps. "The Crosses will not be staying," he informed the servant who opened the front door for them.

"We will be staying," Simon said as he took the doll from Elizabeth's hand and stood at the bottom of the steps. "Until you tell us the truth about Mary."

James blanched. "Where did you get that?"

Rose looked confused and Elizabeth felt a pang of pity for her. No matter what happened that night, her life would change.

"Louisa has one just like this, doesn't she?" Simon asked Rose as he took one step and then another.

"James?" Rose said nervously.

James glared down at Simon, who met his anger with fury of his own. "This is none of your affair," James said and started to lead Rose inside the open front door.

"She was murdered," Elizabeth said. Rose and James froze midstep. James turned back, his expression a mixture of confusion and wariness. Elizabeth walked up the stairs to stand next to Simon.

"What are they talking about, James?" Rose asked.

James looked down at the doll. "Murdered? That's not possible."

His eyes were filled with denial, but Elizabeth could sense a sliver of something more. "Perhaps we should continue this inside?"

James came back to himself and noticed the retinue of servants standing nearby. "Yes," he said.

He led them into the front parlor and then turned to Rose. "It might be best, if you waited upstairs."

Rose looked to Elizabeth and then back to her husband. "No."

James had fully expected her to acquiesce and was unprepared for her response. He spluttered for a moment before clearing his throat, but she didn't let him protest.

"I want to hear what they have to say."

He looked ready to argue, but clamped his jaw shut and nodded. He gave one of the servants instructions for them not to be disturbed and closed the large double doors. He gestured for Rose to take a seat and then turned to face Simon. He paced across the room and put his hands on his hips. "I really don't see how any of this is your business, Cross."

Simon turned the doll over in his hands and Elizabeth could see him rein in his emotions. He stared down at the doll for a long moment before lifting his eyes to James. She could feel the anger radiating off him. "The welfare of a child is everyone's business."

James rolled his shoulders. "The girl is dead, what difference can it make now?"

"And the fact that she was murdered...?" Elizabeth asked.

James spun around. "You say that, but what proof have you? She was ill. She...she died of the ague."

Rose stood and walked over to Simon. She took the doll from him. "This girl," Rose said. "Mary Stewart. Who was she to you, James?"

Her husband shook his head. "It's not what you think."

"How can I know what to think when you won't talk to me," Rose said. "Please, James, I want to know the truth. I deserve at least that, don't I?"

James' jaw worked, but his eyes softened before he turned away. "Yes," he said, his voice hoarse with emotion. He strode to the window and looked out for a moment. "I did it for you," he said before turning around and facing Rose again. "You have to know that. All of it was for you."

Rose held the doll in her hands and sat down. Her voice was deceptively calm. "All of what, James?"

He cleared his throat and paced to the far side of the room. He glared at Simon, weighing the possibility that he might be able to kick him out and have this conversation in private. Simon stood in the middle of the room; feet shoulder width apart, and folded his arms over his chest. He was immovable.

James seemed to realize this finally and turned his focus to Rose. His temporary discomfiture at Simon's presence was shed and he resumed his usual commanding air, although it was unnatural and forced. "I knew it would destroy you to lose another child. When Dr. Walker told me the chances of our baby dying, I had to do something. I couldn't go through that again. Let you go through that again."

He waited for Rose to agree, and when she merely stared at him, struggling to maintain her own control, his façade faltered briefly before he found his mask again. "Your labor was…difficult. I thought I might lose you, too, that day."

Rose held unnaturally still for a moment before she spoke. "What do you mean 'too'"? Her voice trembled with the horror of dawning realization.

"I was told our baby would die before the week was over. I tried to spare you that. To give you a healthy child to love," James said. "To have a life with."

"What are you saying, James?" Rose asked breathlessly, her face pale.

James shook his head, trying to find a foothold, but every bit of reason he tried to reach for crumbled beneath him.

"Mary was your child," Elizabeth said softly. "Yours and Rose's."

James blinked at her. It was as if he'd realized what he'd done for the first time. "We thought she would die."

Rose gasped quietly and covered her mouth with her hands. Elizabeth wanted to comfort her, but what could she do?

"But she didn't," Simon said. "She lived, lived as Mary Stewart."

James nodded, his jaw slack, his breath coming faster as the harsh truth of what he'd done finally came to him. "When I found out she'd lived, I tried to look after her. I made sure she didn't want for anything," he said, his composure crumbling. He looked pleadingly at his wife. "I swear."

Rose's voice trembled as she looked at him with shock and horror. "You gave away our child."

James tried to speak, tried to find some words, but there were none to be found. His eyes glistened with tears and darted around the room looking for something to keep him from falling apart.

"Is…Louisa Alice Stewart's child?" Simon asked.

James nodded and blinked back tears.

"Oh, my God," Rose said and Elizabeth went to kneel at her side. "How could you do such a thing? Our baby."

"You gave Alice money, gave them both a home on River Run?" Simon prompted him.

"Yes," James said numbly.

Elizabeth nearly asked Simon to stop, but she knew the truth of it all had to come out.

"Until a month ago," Simon said.

James nodded and wiped at his face. "I was there to check on Mary," he said, as if hoping to please Rose. But his wife wouldn't even look at him now. "Alice wanted more money, threatened to tell everyone the truth. It would ruin us. It would be the end of everything we'd worked so hard for." He shook his head as the memory of that night played in his head. "We argued."

He looked at Simon, imploring him to understand. "It was an accident. I would never…She fell and hit her head."

"Dear God," Rose said as she stood. "That woman they found. You killed her?"

"It was an accident," James said as he came to stand in front of her. He tried to take her hands in his but she pulled them away and looked at him with disgust. She walked across the room and kept her back to him.

"You panicked?" Simon said.

James stared at his wife's back and spoke emotionlessly now. "Dr. Walker helped me bury her and he took Mary to the orphanage."

"Was Mary there that night?" Simon asked. "Could she have overheard your argument with Alice? What you said to the doctor afterward?" Simon asked.

243

James frowned and stood in a daze.

Simon grabbed his arms. "Could she have heard you that night?"

The sudden movement pulled James from his haze and he thought about what Simon asked. Finally, he nodded. "Yes, but…."

Simon *looke*d to Elizabeth and they shared their grief and anger in that moment. They both knew what had happened.

"Mary told the other children that her father lived in a big house," Elizabeth said.

"The doctor *mu*st have found out that she'd heard everything," Simon said. "He had to keep her from revealing the truth or the house of cards you two built would fall apart."

James shook his head, trying to deny everything. "No, he wouldn't."

"He poisoned her," Simon said, taking a step toward James. "He made it look like malaria, but he poisoned that child to keep her quiet."

Rose gasped and covered her mouth with both her hands. "Oh, dear God."

"No," James said again.

Simon took another step. Elizabeth saw his hands tighten into fists. "To protect you and your lies."

"Simon—"

"Stop," Rose said. Simon turned to her; they all turned to her. Tears shone in her eyes. Her shock had given way to something much more powerful, fury.

"That child," she said, "was my daughter." She took a step toward James and then stopped. She lifted a hand, it trembled in what Elizabeth knew was both pain and rage. She pointed an accusing finger at James. "And you stole her from me."

"Rose?" James said, pleading.

"I thought you'd had an affair," Rose said, "I wish you had. I could forgive that in time. But this…"

"Please?"

Rose shook her head and walked to the door. She put her hand on the handle and kept her back to them all. "I am going upstairs to see my daughter. When I come back down, I want you out of this house. Do you understand?"

"Rose, please."

She ignored his pleas and pulled open the doors. She called for a servant. "Mr. Elijah should be home soon. When he comes in, tell him to come to me upstairs."

The girl nodded.

"And do not, under any circumstances," Rose continued, "Let Dr. Walker in this house."

"But, ma'am, Dr. Walker already here."

"What?" James said as he came to the door.

The girl looked up the stairs. "He with Miss Louisa when you come in. I tried to tell you—"

James pushed past the girl and took the stairs two at a time. Simon ran after him, Rose and Elizabeth not far behind.

Louisa's door at the end of the landing was already open and James and Simon burst into the room.

"What's this?" Dr. Walker said as he stood calmly on the far side of the room, one hand resting on Louisa's shoulder, the other behind her. Elizabeth's heart raced in her chest.

Rose moved into the room and reached out for her daughter. "Come here, darling."

Simon must have pulled his gun out of his pocket as they'd run up the stairs. He pointed it at the doctor and pulled back the hammer. "Let the girl go."

Louisa started to move, but Dr. Walker tightened his grip and kept her in place. The doctor eyed him and the others warily. "I don't think I will." He showed his other hand now and pointed the gun it held at the girl's side. "Drop your gun," he told Simon.

"Momma," Louisa said, trembling.

"It's all right honey," Rose said, forcing a tremulous smile and trying to keep her voice calm. "It'll be all right."

Simon eased the hammer forward, uncocking the gun and lowered his arm. He tossed it to the floor between them.

"Please, doctor," Rose said, but the man shook his head.

"I had hoped it would not come to this," he said and then looked at Simon and Elizabeth with cold fury. "But my hand has been forced, it seems."

"Let her go," James said.

"And you'll let me go, is that it?" the doctor said with a smirk.

"Yes," James said. He waved his hand toward the doorway where Simon stood blocking his path. "They can't prove anything. I… I won't say anything. Just let my girl go."

The doctor waved the gun toward the doorway. "Get back," he said. "All of you."

They had little choice but to do as he said and backed into the hallway.

The doctor kept Louisa close, his gun ready to fire. The girl whimpered and tears came. Rose's voice broke as she assured her over and over that it would be all right. Elizabeth reached for Simon's hand as the doctor forced them to walk down to the far end of the landing near the room where Simon and Elizabeth had stayed.

He stood at the top of the landing and glanced down the grand stairs where servants had started to gather. "Get outta here!" he yelled at them.

A few scattered, and the others looked to Rose or James for guidance. "Go," James said, his eyes wild. "Now!"

Finally, the downstairs was cleared and the doctor stood at the top of the stairs, Louisa clutched tightly in front of him. "If you follow us, I will kill her."

Elizabeth had been poised to follow him, but she knew he would do as he threatened. What was one more dead body to him now?

Slowly, he started down the stairs, keeping the girl close, too close for anyone to do anything without risking her life.

"Please," Rose said again. "Don't take her." She stepped forward, compelled by a mother's love to save her child.

James grabbed her arm, trying to hold her back, but she struggled against him.

The doctor glared at her and then looked at James with disdain. "I always knew you could not control your wife." He raised his gun and leveled it at Rose for a brief second before shifting it to the side and firing.

In a bright flash, the oil lamp on the wall exploded. Shards of glass flew toward them and fiery oil splashed in all directions. Someone screamed.

Simon spun around and shielded Elizabeth with his body.

"Rose!"

Elizabeth felt Simon release her and she turned with him toward Rose. It took a moment for what she saw to register. James, his sleeve alight with flame, tore off his coat and tried to beat down the flames that licked up Rose's skirts. The horror of it froze Elizabeth in place for a split-second. Simon ripped off his own coat and they tried to smother the quickly growing flames. Rose cried out and covered her face.

Elizabeth ran into the bedroom and found a pitcher. She ran back out onto the landing and the scene was out of a horror film. The oil had spilled down the wall and across the floor. Flames had already spread across the landing to the stairs and were licking up the walls and curtains, and curling toward the ceiling.

Simon and James had managed to keep the fire on Rose's dress from growing. Elizabeth threw the pitcher of water on her and they were able to tamp out the remaining flames.

"Are you hurt?" James asked.

Rose shook her head. She turned to look at the stairs where the doctor had made his escape, but they were unreachable. A set of curtains caught fire then and went up in flames with an audible *whomp*. The hallway was quickly engulfed in fire and smoke.

"In here," Simon said, gesturing to the doorway to what had been their bedroom.

The four of them hurried inside the bedroom and Simon closed the door behind them.

"The gallery," James said as he ran to the large French doors that let to the upstairs balcony. "We can reach the back stairs through the other guest room."

He pulled the doors open and they ran out onto the upper gallery.

"What's happened?" Eli called from below as he jumped off his horse.

"Fire! Get help!" James cried as he ran down the long gallery.

"Rose!" Eli called.

The rest of them ran the length of the gallery, Eli mirroring them on the ground.

Behind him, slaves had already started a bucket brigade that stretched around the house.

At the end of the gallery, Rose leaned over the landing and called down to Eli. "Hurry, Eli!"

James threw open the doors to the guest bedroom and they rushed inside. He reached for the bedroom door, but Simon grabbed his arm and stopped him.

"What are you doing?" James demanded.

Simon shoved him aside and put his hand on the door and immediately pulled it back and shook it. "The fire is on the other side of this door. You open it and we're all dead."

"Is there another way out?" Elizabeth asked Rose.

"No."

Simon looked around the room and then strode to the bed. He yanked off the quilt and pulled at it, testing its strength. "We have to jump."

Elizabeth ran back out onto the gallery. It had to be over 15 feet to the ground. "Eli, get six strong men. Now!"

He looked at her in confusion for a moment before nodding and rushing over to one of the slaves who nodded and ran off.

Simon came out of the room, followed by Rose and James. He threw the quilt down to the men gathering below. "Keep it as taut as you can."

Rose's eyes were wild with worry, but not in fear for herself. Elizabeth knew all she could think of was Louisa.

"Rose, you go first," Elizabeth said, grabbing her arm and pulling her to the railing.

Rose looked at her in confusion and then down at the men who'd stretched the quilt into a makeshift net. She shook her head.

The wooden door to the guest room cracked loudly behind them.

"You can do it," Elizabeth said as she knelt down and helped gather Rose's skirts, what was left of them, as Simon took her other arm.

"Hurry!" James said, his voice on the verge of panic.

Flames were already crawling across the guest room floor.

"It'll be all right," Eli called up, as he gripped his end of the quilt even more tightly.

Rose nodded, and Simon and Elizabeth helped her over the railing. She held onto the edge and slowly turned to face the outside.

"Come on!" Eli urged her.

Rose closed her eyes and jumped. She flew through the air, her skirts billowing out as she fell. The men shifted a little to adjust, but they caught her. They lowered one edge of the quilt and she crawled off. When she was clear, the men then pulled the quilt taut again and looked up, ready for the next person.

"Elizabeth," Simon said and he picked her up and held her until she got her footing on the small outside ledge. Elizabeth glanced anxiously down. It looked a lot farther than fifteen feet from the other side of the railing. She didn't have time to panic though and stepped forward, turning onto her back as she fell. The landing wasn't exactly pillow soft, but she was unhurt and scrambled out of the way.

James was next and then Simon. Once they were all down, Eli grabbed Rose by the arms. "Are you hurt?"

Rose shook her head and tugged at his sleeves. "He's got Louisa!"

Chapter Twenty-Five

Simon helped Rose quickly fill Elijah in on what had happened. Rose was, understandably, near hysteria and James not much better. He stared up at River Run, struck numb by what he saw. Flames rolled out of two of the upstairs windows like angry red fingers clawing their way onto the roof.

Eli called for his horse. The slave who'd taken the reins for him tried to bring the horse closer, but the fire made it rear and pull away. It was all the man could do to keep hold of it.

"Where did he go?" Eli said.

Rose just shook her head and Eli took her into his arms.

Eli grabbed a man by his shirtsleeve as he ran to help fight the fire. "Samuel! Go to the Millers' and get help. Send others to the Parks' and the Browns'. Get the Millers' hounds out. We need to find Miss Louisa. You understand?" Samuel nodded and Eli shoved the man away. "Go on! Hurry!"

Simon looked around at the growing chaos. The doctor might be mad, but he was no fool, he'd find the fastest method of escape.

"The stables," Simon said, as he took hold of Elizabeth's hand and started toward the outbuildings. "He must have had a carriage."

They ran for the stables, Rose, Eli and James not far behind. The movement seemed to jolt James from his stupor.

Grooms were leading nervous horses out of the stables and into the far corral to protect them from the encroaching fire. Even though the house and the fire were nearly fifty yards apart, fire could travel in an instant.

A distressed looking groom ran toward James. "I tried to stop him, suh, but he had a gun!"

"What happened?" James demanded.

"The doctor, he come with Miss Louisa, and take the Cross buggy." The groom waved a hand down the long drive to the main road. "They went down that way, suh."

James gripped the man's shoulders. "Horses. We need horses."

"Four," Simon said.

James looked at him in confusion. "Four?"

Rose stepped forward. "I am coming, James."

A loud clap of thunder echoed in the distance, the sound of a mother's fury.

At least James knew enough not to waste time arguing that point, Simon thought, and James shoved the groom away with orders to saddle four horses and get two men to help.

"I'll be back," Eli said to Rose and he ran off. Simon turned and watched him run back to the main house.

Dozens and dozens of slaves had formed a long bucket brigade from the well to the house.

"Where's the cart?" James yelled and as if to answer a low, flatbed cart with a long seesaw-like lever on top appeared out of the darkness. Two men pulled it toward the house, leaving a tail of hose behind them that Simon could see led to the large water cistern.

Three more men came over to help. One attached a second hose to a large spigot and the others grabbed onto the poles extending from the arms of the lever and began to pump. The men pushed the lever down to their waists then up above their heads as the other side pushed down. They seesawed up and down and took a few agonizing moments before they'd built up enough pressure. Finally, water came out of the hose and the man holding the free-end ran inside the house.

Another clap of thunder came and then a lightning strike not too far away.

"Mister James!" the groom who he'd sent to fetch the horses called. He led two horses and another man two more.

Simon helped Elizabeth up into her saddle as James helped Rose before they mounted their own horses. Eli ran toward them carrying several guns. He handed James a large musket and Simon a handgun, keeping a shotgun for himself. The handgun was an older cap and ball. Simon checked the cylinder. It was loaded with fresh powder caps and lead balls. He made sure the hammer was in the safety position and shoved it in his waistband before looking over at Elizabeth.

Her horse pranced nervously, but she seemed to have control of it.

"I'm all right," she said.

Eli mounted his horse and three slaves rode up on saddleless horses and joined their party. "We help find Miss Louisa."

James nodded and the eight of them took off at a gallop down the long drive to the main road, Eli in the lead. At the end of the drive Eli pulled up. Their horses pranced anxiously in place waiting for commands. The doctor could have gone either way.

"We should split up," Elizabeth said, as her horse turned in a circle, looking down one long stretch of dark road and then the other.

Simon didn't like that idea, but they had little choice. A light rain began to fall. Simon looked south and then north trying to gauge which direction the doctor would go. To town or away from it?

Thunder rumbled overhead and then a flash of lightning illuminated the night. In the distance, at the top of a small rise to the north, Simon could just make out a figure in the road. The second flash of lightning came and he saw that it was Mary. Her white gown appeared in the night and then disappeared again just as quickly.

"This way," Simon said and spurred his horse toward the north. The others followed without question.

They rode as quickly as they dared in the darkness and the rain.

They'd barely gone a mile when Simon saw something by the side of the road. As he got closer, he could make out the shape. It was their buggy, stuck in a ditch. The horse struggled in place, one wheel buried in a deep rut.

Simon and James leapt off their horses, and ran to the carriage. Simon grabbed James' arm and forced him to stop, silently urging caution. If the doctor was there, he was still armed. Slowly, they approached one on each side, guns at the ready.

"Empty!" James said and pounded his fist against the railing.

There were thick woods on either side of the road.

"There!" Rose suddenly cried.

Simon turned and saw the brief flash of a white dress in the woods to the west.

Rose struggled to dismount, her skirts catching on the saddle horn. Eli was by her side in an instant and with the help of one of the slaves disentangled her.

Elizabeth had taken more care with her skirts and slid off her saddle easily into Simon's waiting arms.

"This way," Rose said as she led their search party across the road and toward the thick woods.

The rain was coming down much harder now and the natural gully on the far side of the road was already filled with water rapidly flowing downhill. They waded through it and plunged into the woods beyond.

James reached out to help Rose pick her way through the heavy underbrush, but she pulled her arm away from him and struggled on her own until Eli came to her aid. Simon reached out to do the same for Elizabeth, but she wasn't at his side. He turned back and saw her lifting her dress hem up and fighting with her petticoats. She glanced up at him.

"Help me get these things off," she said. "They weigh a ton."

Simon hurried back to her and knelt in the mud. She lifted her dress skirt up and he unfastened her petticoats. They were muddy and sodden. Each had easily already soaked up gallons of water. It would have been impossible to slog through the woods with the added encumbrance.

He held her steady as she stepped out of them and, once free, they made quick work of catching up with the others.

"Take off your skirts," Elizabeth said.

"What?" James asked, but Rose was already nodding and Elizabeth helped her shed the under layers until all that was left was the burnt remnants of her dress skirt.

The thick undergrowth soon gave way to a dense forest. Even the occasional flash of lightning did little to light the way and they had to travel carefully, slowly. Footing was treacherous. Fallen branches and thick roots covered the ground in front of them.

"Where is he going?" Eli wondered aloud. "I can see leaving the road, but…"

"The river," James said, as he tried to catch his breath. "He's heading for the river."

"Birch's landing," Eli said. "There are boats and rafts to be had. If he gets on the river…"

He didn't need to finish the thought. Simon and Elizabeth exchanged knowing glances. They all knew what that would mean. He would be long gone and Louisa would never be seen again.

James stopped and grabbed one of the slaves. "Go back to the horses and ride up around to the landing."

The man nodded and ran back in the direction they'd just come from. The rest of them pressed on.

Minute after agonizing minute they picked their way through the woods. The sound of dogs barking in the distance told Simon word had reached the Millers' and their hounds were out. But in this rain, any scent they might have been able to find would be well washed away by now.

They fought through the dense woods until finally Simon could make out an opening ahead. A flash of lightning came and he could see a stretch of tall grass through the empty space between the trees. It would be a welcome change. They were making slow progress through the thick woods and might be able to make up some time on open ground.

They'd just reached the small clearing when a shot rang out.

Simon pulled Elizabeth to the ground and covered her body with his. Another shot came. Then a scream.

Simon lifted himself up onto his elbows and cradled Elizabeth's head in his hands. "Are you all right?"

She nodded and he rolled off her as a few feet away Rose called out. "James!"

Simon and Elizabeth crawled toward them, staying low enough to be hidden by the tall grass.

"Rose, are you hurt?" Eli asked. She shook her head, but her eyes never left James lying next to her.

Eli scrambled next to his brother and looked over his shoulder as Simon and Elizabeth approached. "James has been hit."

James groaned as he lay on his back and reached up to grab his shoulder. Blood seeped through his fingers as he clutched his wound.

"We're too exposed here," Simon said. He indicated the woods they'd just left. "Help him back behind those trees."

The remaining slaves and Eli half carried James back into the woods. They helped him to sit leaning against the trunk on the far side of one of the large oak trees.

Judging from the amount of blood he was losing, it was a very serious wound. His pallor was already starting to gray.

Simon took out his handkerchief and handed it to Rose. "We need to stop the bleeding."

She took it and then looked at her husband. Myriad expressions played across her face—worry, fear, loathing.

James winced. "Rose," he said as he reached up to cover her hand.

She shook her head and looked away. She handed Eli the handkerchief and moved away from them. Confused, Eli took it and pressed it onto his brother's shoulder. He looked up at Simon.

"We have to keep moving," Simon said, ignoring the unspoken question. "And he needs medical attention."

Eli looked down at his brother and Simon could tell he knew the truth of it.

Simon edged toward the tree closest to the field and kept one eye out for movement from the doctor. He pulled the gun from his waistband and looked at it in disgust. It was caked with mud. It would be a miracle if the damn thing still worked, but it was all he had and he kept it ready.

Elizabeth went to Rose and put a comforting arm around her shoulders. She whispered something Simon couldn't hear, but Rose nodded.

"Cuffy," Eli called out to one of the slaves who knelt nearby. "Take Mister James to the Millers'. Ask them to do what they can for him."

Cuffy nodded and came over to them.

James grabbed his brother's sleeve. "Please."

"We'll find her," Eli said.

Cuffy helped James to stand and put his uninjured arm over his shoulder. James implored Rose again, but she looked away, refusing to even look at him as Cuffy helped him back into the forest.

"You should go with him," Eli said to her. "It's too dangerous here."

Rose lifted her head. "Mr. Cross is right. We have to keep moving."

"Rose, please?" Eli said. "We will find her and bring her back to you."

"I am her mother," Rose said simply and then joined Simon at the edge of the field.

Simon peered around the edge of the tree. He couldn't see anything on the far side of the grass. If the doctor was there, he was well hidden. Odds were, he was long gone and headed toward the river.

The trees circled the little field to the south. They could stay at the edge of the forest and have enough cover to keep after him. Eli came to his side and held out James' musket. Simon glared at it. The damn thing must weigh ten pounds and was nearly as tall as Elizabeth.

"I have a gun," Simon said, showing him his handgun. "Give it to Jacob."

Eli looked over at the tall house slave and hesitated. It took Simon a moment to realize that it was probably rather unusual for a master to give a slave a gun. He didn't have time to coddle Eli's fear of a slave uprising.

"For heaven's sake, man," Simon said. "Give it to him."

Eli hesitated once more, but only briefly before he shoved the gun toward him. "Jacob."

Jacob took the gun. "Suh."

"We'll circle around," Simon said. "All right?" he asked and sought out Elizabeth.

She gave him an encouraging nod and he held out his hand. "Stay close."

She took it and came to his side. "Not a problem."

Their circular path had probably put them farther behind the doctor, but he could not have been making good time with a child. Simon could only hope they reached Louisa before the doctor decided she was more trouble than she was worth.

On the far side of the meadow, the dense forest opened a little. Simon's eyes had adjusted to the night and he could see much further ahead now. But what he didn't see was the only thing he'd hoped to see. There was no sign of the doctor or Louisa.

"Which way is that landing?" he asked.

"Birch's?" Eli said. He looked around and nodded. "That way."

"That way be de swamp," Jacob said, looking nervous.

"What of it?" Eli said, as he helped Rose continue on.

Jacob shook his head. Simon was confused by his sudden change. Jacob had been a stalwart so far.

"Osay's swamp?" Elizabeth asked.

Jacob nodded, his frightened eyes never leaving the horizon. Simon remembered the legend Abraham had told them of the slave who led a rebellion and drowned his people to escape, but there wasn't time for superstitions now.

"Come on," Simon said, and he and Elizabeth hurried as best they could to catch up and overtake Eli and Rose.

"Lord protect me," Jacob said behind them as he whispered a prayer.

They continued through the woods, the ground getting soggier and muddier beneath their feet, slowing them down even further. Every step was an effort now, and with each one Simon's feet would sink deeper into the mud.

Suddenly, Elizabeth laid her hand on his arm. "Shhh."

She waved her hands for the others to stop. "Quiet."

They all froze where they were and listened. Simon didn't hear anything at first, but clearly Elizabeth did. Her eyes widened and a second later, Simon heard it too. It was faint, carried from somewhere in the distance. But the sound was unmistakable—a child crying.

Rose covered her mouth with her hands. "Louisa," she whispered.

It was difficult to tell exactly what direction the sound was coming from. The rain falling on the leaves and pelting the muddy earth was white noise. Simon could just make out an occasional sob and his heart raced faster.

Elizabeth closed her eyes and turned her head to listen. After a moment, she opened them again. "This way."

Simon stayed at Elizabeth's side, his gun drawn. Rose and Eli were right behind them with Jacob bringing up the rear.

They had to stop once more to listen, but this time the sound was clear. The girl couldn't be far now. They all scanned the darkness. Simon didn't see anything, but Rose did.

"Louisa!" she suddenly cried out and ran forward, stumbling as she went. Eli hurried to her side. Simon and Jacob raised their guns and scanned for any sign of the doctor. Rose got to her feet and her daughter turned and saw her.

The girl had been huddled on the edge of the swamp. She was filthy and soaked to the bone, but unhurt, and ran to her mother's arms.

"Thank God," Simon said.

Rose fell to her knees and hugged Louisa, wrapping both arms protectively around her. "Oh, baby," she said. "Are you hurt? Did he hurt you?"

Louisa cried and buried her head in her mother's chest. Eli knelt down and ran his hands over the girl. "She's all right, I think."

Rose kissed her daughter's tear stained cheeks. "You're safe now."

Simon only wished that were true. As long as the doctor was out there, none of them were safe. He looked back into the wilderness, searching for some sign of the doctor, when he noticed Elizabeth walk to the water's edge.

"Simon, look."

He joined her and followed her gaze. The pool of water had a mossy green layer that covered the top of it like a blanket. The canopy of trees above had kept it mostly undisturbed from the falling rain, but there was a clear path cut through it now. The blanket of algae had been split down the middle and a trail of dark water marked where the doctor had waded into the water and deeper into the swamp.

Simon knew she would bristle at the suggestion, but they'd pressed their luck with every step so far. He unhooked his watch chain from his vest button and then reached into his vest pocket.

He held the watch and key out to Elizabeth. "You should stay here with Rose."

Elizabeth stared down at the watch and then glared up at him. "And let you have all the fun?"

She was trying to make light of it, but he heard the tension in her voice.

"Elizabeth—"

"Jacob can stay with her."

"I stay," Jacob offered quickly, casting uneasy glances at the swamp. "I be glad to stay."

Simon ground his teeth.

"It's settled then," Elizabeth said as she took the watch and key from his hand and walked over to Jacob. "Keep an eye on these for us?"

Jacob nodded and reached for the watch.

"Just don't...open it," Elizabeth cautioned him wisely before handing it over.

Jacob took the watch and key, and carefully slipped them into his pants pocket.

"There," Elizabeth said as she strode back in front of Simon.

He knew it was no use arguing with her, but he did anyway. "Elizabeth, you can't." She was about to protest when he added, "Not in that."

She frowned down at her dress and then looked back up at him with narrowed eyes. She began unbuttoning her dress. "Fine."

"For God's sake," Simon said and he put his gun away and knelt in front of her. He gripped the edge of her skirt and started to rip it off. Her dress had been badly torn by the thorns and sharp branches they'd already journeyed through and it was easily removed. He tossed her skirt to the side and stood.

Her chemise and drawers were already soaked and dark with mud, but if she noticed, she didn't care. She turned back to Eli. "Are you coming?"

Eli turned to Rose.

"Be careful," Rose said, still clinging to Louisa.

Eli nodded and then came to Simon's side.

Simon took out his gun and waded into the murky water. He held his gun up to keep it dry and turned back as Elizabeth followed and then Eli, his shotgun held over his head.

Thankfully, the water never got above his waist. If it were much higher, Elizabeth would be swimming instead of walking. Although, walking might have been a generous characterization. With each step, their feet sank into the soft bottom. But that was hardly the worst of it. Fallen branches, snags and submerged logs and rocks made each step treacherous. God only knew what sort of snakes and creatures called this place home. They stumbled their way through the water following the narrowing path left in the doctor's wake.

Simon heard a gasp and turned in time to see Elizabeth nearly disappear under the water. Simon tried to grab her, but he was too far away. Eli was closer and grabbed her arm, helping her right herself.

She swept her hair from her face and spit out the fetid water that had gotten into her mouth. "I'm all right," she said and they pushed on.

Eli frowned and shook his head. In his haste to help Elizabeth he'd let his shotgun dip into the water. Long green slime hung off the barrel. He looked at Simon in apology. They both knew the gun was likely useless now. That left them with only Simon's pistol.

It was exhausting work, pushing through the heavy water, having to yank each foot up out of the mud as the mire sucked it down. Simon's legs burned with the effort. Worse yet, the trail they were following was disappearing. The swath the doctor had cut through the algae was reforming, the two sides rejoining. Just as it was nearly completely impossible to see, they reached a bank.

Simon managed to get himself halfway up it before turning back and helping Elizabeth climb the short, but steep slope that led to what passed for dry land in a swamp. Once she was safely up, Simon followed, Eli close behind.

The rain had mercifully stopped, but it was of little comfort now. It was good to be out of the water, but it also meant the end of the trail they'd followed. They tried to find some sign to follow, some path, but it was no use.

They stood helpless until the clouds above parted, and a pale haze of light from the moon shone down through a break in the trees. Simon could hear the river in the distance. Birch's landing couldn't be far.

"There!" Eli said. Simon turned and saw a dark figure in the distance, no more than twenty yards away. Eli ran forward and raised his shotgun. Simon heard the hammer fall, but there was no spark, no fire. With a frustrated grunt, Eli tossed the gun aside.

They hurried after him. Simon could just make out the doctor as he weaved his way between the trees. The doctor stumbled, swore and regained his footing. They were close now. The doctor turned back and saw them. He made a sharp turn and waded into another pool of water.

Simon raised his gun and called out, "That's far enough!"

The doctor stopped. His back heaved with the effort of his flight. His gun dangled from his right hand as he stood in water up to his thighs.

Elizabeth moved between Simon and Eli. They stood on the shore of the little island as the doctor slowly turned around.

"Drop your gun!" Simon said and pulled back the hammer on his pistol.

The doctor ignored him and continued his slow turn.

Simon squeezed the trigger.

Nothing.

The doctor laughed and raised his gun as he faced them. "You've got to keep your powder dry," he said.

He trained his gun on Elizabeth. Simon could tell that the doctor knew what he was thinking, that he was calculating the odds of the doctor's gun working after what they'd been through. "Is it worth her life to find out?" he asked.

Simon's silence was answer enough. The doctor smiled. "Good. You just stay right where you are and old Doc Walker is going down the river."

The doctor took a step backward and shook his head.

Simon was about to say something, but stopped when he heard something he couldn't quite identify. In his periphery he could tell that the others had clearly heard it too, including Doctor Walker.

It started out as a whisper that floated all around them. It grew in intensity as voice after voice joined it until it was a chorus of voices whispering in the dark.

"The water will take you home."

They all turned, trying to see where the voices were coming from, but they were coming from everywhere. Simon reached for Elizabeth's hand and gripped it firmly in his.

"The water will take you home."

Doctor Walker took another stumbling step, up to his waist now. He glanced back at them, frightened, but determined. And then, suddenly, a hand shot up out of the water and grabbed his arm. He struggled against it, but the grip was as iron as the manacle around its black wrist.

The hand squeezed his arm until it trembled and the gun fell into the water.

Another hand reached out from the murky water, and then another.

"Help me!" the doctor cried, but none of them could or would come to his aid.

All Simon could do was watch in awe and terror and disbelief, as more hands with iron shackles and thick black chains reached up out of the water and grabbed at the doctor. They clutched at his clothing and gripped his arms and legs. And pulled.

He began to sink down into the mud, the water coming up to his chest now. He gasped and his eyes shot wide open, the whites caught in the now bright moonlight. "Help me."

Simon watched as the hands dragged him down into the water. The whispering voices surged as they took him completely under. As the surface of the water stilled, the voices faded.

A final burst of bubbles disturbed the water and then all was still and silent.

Chapter Twenty-Six

Elizabeth's everything hurt. She was cold and tired and muddy. She was also fairly certain there were leeches involved, but she didn't want to think about that. She shivered at the memory of the doctor's last call for help. Despite his, what she could only describe as evil, it was still shocking to have watched him die. It was justice and she was glad for that, but it wouldn't help Mary. Not now.

They found Jacob, Louisa and Rose exactly where they'd left them. Jacob lifted the musket and waved it in their general direction as they approached. "Who dere?"

"Easy there. It's us," Eli said as they came out of the woods.

Thankfully, they'd managed to find a path back that didn't involve wading through the swamp again. The adrenaline of the chase was wearing off and the exertion from the day started to take its toll.

Jacob came to Simon and handed him the watch and key. "I didn't touch it."

"Thank you, Jacob."

Elizabeth leaned into Simon's side and he wrapped an arm around her and she laid her hand on it. He gave a slight groan and she pulled her hand away. His bandaged arm was filthy, and she could see red seeping through the dirty gauze.

She stepped away and held up his arm. "Oh, Simon." He hadn't said a word about it. Who knows when he'd torn his stitches?

"It's all right," he said and pulled her back to his side.

For a moment, they watched as Rose and Eli embraced, then awkwardly separated.

"It's over," Eli assured her. "He won't bother you again."

Rose smiled and knelt down in front of Louisa. She pulled her daughter to her and there in the darkness, just behind the child, was Mary. She was barely visible now, just the faintest image of who she'd once been.

Rose saw her and her eyes widened and then spilled over with tears. She held Louisa in her arms, but she spoke to both of her children. "It's time to take you home."

Rose reached out to Mary, who raised her ghostly hand.

"My darling child."

Their fingers touched and Mary glowed brightly for the briefest moment.

Mary turned her head and looked at Simon and Elizabeth and smiled.

And then, she was gone.

Elizabeth drew in a sharp breath and felt Simon's arm tighten around her shoulder. She didn't bother to wipe away the tears that rolled down her cheeks.

Rose gasped and hugged Louisa tightly with both arms.

"Are you all right?" Eli asked in confusion.

Rose stood and took Louisa's hand. She looked at Elizabeth and then back to Eli. "We will be," she said. "We will be."

When they arrived back at River Run, the fire had been put out. Between the hard work of the slaves, the neighbors and the heaven's rains, most of the house had been spared. The damage had been limited to the upper floor. It would take time to rebuild, but it would be whole again.

They'd all cleaned up as best they could and spent the night at the Millers'. By then, Doctor Parish had come to see to James. His injuries were serious, but he would live. Where and how, would be up to Rose. Elizabeth knew what she'd do with James if he'd been her husband, but he wasn't and his fate was not up to her.

Simon's arm was cleaned and re-stitched. It was even more painful to watch than the first time and Elizabeth's stomach roiled at the sight, although, the shots of swamp juice she'd swallowed the night before might have had something to do with it.

The following morning, Simon and Elizabeth went back into town to give the Harpers a chance to recover. They were welcomed back to Cypress Hill and spent the day taking antibiotics and convalescing.

The next morning, it was time to say goodbye.

"I hope you'll come back to see us sometime," Catherine said as they stood out front waiting for her carriage to be brought around.

"I'd like to," Elizabeth said, very much meaning it, but knowing it wouldn't happen.

"Think of all the trouble we could get into," Catherine said to her with a wink.

Simon looked to the heavens. "God help us."

Catherine frowned as her carriage pulled up. "Are you sure you have to go? Where am I going to find a new cohort?"

"I'm afraid, I'll have to do," the Colonel said as he came out of the house and instructed Abraham to put a box into the back of the carriage.

He shook Simon's hand. "God speed." He turned to Elizabeth and narrowed his eyes before bowing, a slight smile cracking his stern face. "Miss Elizabeth."

Elizabeth stifled a laugh and curtsied. "Colonel."

"Thank you, for everything," Simon said to both of them, but his eyes lingered on Catherine. She nodded and smiled in return.

"We should be going, Cat," the Colonel said as he opened the carriage door. "Those boys at the orphanage won't learn discipline if we set a bad example by being late."

Catherine pulled Elizabeth into a hug before turning and climbing into the carriage. The Colonel followed her in and closed the door. Elizabeth waved as they drove away.

Abraham appeared beside them. "Your trunks are ready whenever you are, suh."

"Thank you," Simon said, and then held out his hand.

Abraham looked at it unsure for a moment and then took it.

"Thank you, Abraham," Simon said as he gave it a firm shake. "For everything."

Abraham nodded, clearly moved by the sentiment. "Thank you, suh."

THEY MADE THE DRIVE up to River Run for the last time. Construction had already begun on the damaged portions of the house to bring it back to its Antebellum majesty.

Elizabeth tried to take everything in. She wanted to commit the scene to memory because she knew she and the world would never see the likes of it again.

Jacob led them through the house and out onto the back veranda. "Miss Rose is in the garden."

They walked down the back steps and into the garden, but Rose was nowhere to be found. They ventured a little deeper into the yard. Simon nodded toward a figure off in the distance.

Rose was standing over a freshly dug grave in the family cemetery.

"We've come to say goodbye," Elizabeth said.

Rose looked up sadly, but smiled. Her eyes fell back to the ground.

"We had her brought home yesterday afternoon," she said. "They're carving a stone for her. With her true name."

Elizabeth slipped her hand into Simon's and looked down at the small grave. She felt a tightness in her throat and a melancholy only lifted by the knowledge that Mary was finally home.

She cleared her throat. "The flowers are beautiful."

"I came to put these flowers here," Rose said, holding out a bouquet of roses, "and found these already here." A small patch of deep blue forget-me-nots blossomed in the dark soil.

Beside her, she heard Simon let out a soft breath. It was a sigh of release. Elizabeth nodded to herself. Mary was at peace.

Rose laid the flowers on the grave and gestured for them to follow her back to the house. As they did, Eli appeared leading Louisa around on her pony. The girl laughed and Elizabeth smiled.

"She seems to be doing well," Simon said.

Rose looked out at her daughter and Eli and something in her eyes lightened. "She is. Children are inspiringly resilient, aren't they?"

They climbed the stairs to the veranda and looked out over the estate for a quiet moment before Elizabeth said, "I'm sorry it all came to this."

Rose took a deep breath as she looked out at her daughter and Eli. "Life is a crucible. We are either broken by it or our bonds strengthened." She turned to them. "James will be taking a long trip to facilitate his recovery. Elijah will see to things while he's gone."

Rose watched them for a minute before turning back and resuming her role as the perfect Southern lady. "Where are my manners? Would you like some refreshments?"

"No, thank you," Simon said. "We should be going."

"It's time we moved on," Elizabeth said.

Rose smiled and reached for her hand. She squeezed it once and her eyes filled with fresh tears. "Godspeed."

She smiled one last time then walked over to join Eli and Louisa.

Elizabeth and Simon stood on the porch, arms around each other's waists, and watched the remnants of a family try to rebuild anew.

After a minute, Simon held out his hand. "Ready?"

She knew he meant ready to leave, but suddenly it felt like more than that. They weren't just leaving the past; they were stepping into their future, one that, until this trip, Elizabeth had never worried over. Old Nan's prophecy echoed in her mind. *It is your burden.*

Elizabeth sighed. Rose was right. Life was a crucible, and it either broke you or made you stronger. And she and Simon were always stronger together.

She took his hand. "Ready."

Whatever fate had in store for them, they would face it and overcome it. Together.

THE END

NOTE TO THE READERS

Thank you for reading THURSDAY'S CHILD; I truly hope you enjoyed reading it as much as I enjoyed writing it. I know we really put Simon and Elizabeth through the ringer in that one, but have faith. They will find a way to meet whatever challenge comes their way. Don't miss the next book coming later this year and Jack will be back!

If you enjoyed this book, please consider posting a short review.

Thanks again for reading!

Have an idea for a time and/or location you'd like to see Simon & Elizabeth (or Jack) visit? Drop me a line or come on by Facebook and let me know. I have quite a few ideas for future adventures, but would love to hear from you!

Sign up for the new releases newsletter!
Visit: http://moniquemartin.weebly.com

ABOUT THE AUTHOR

ONIQUE WAS BORN IN Houston, Texas, but her family soon moved to Southern California. She grew up on both coasts, living in Connecticut and California. She currently resides in Southern California with her naughty Siamese cat, Monkey.

She's currently working on an adaptation of one of her screenplays, several short stories and novels and the next book in the Out of Time series.

For news and information about Monique and upcoming releases, please visit: http://moniquemartin.weebly.com/

www.ingramcontent.com/pod-product-compliance
Lightning Source LLC
Chambersburg PA
CBHW031704170626
46808CB00005B/1601